Early reader reviews

'This thought-provoking novel is full of unexpected psychological layers and twists and turns'

'A fantastic read that had me gripped ... I read it in one suspenseful sitting'

'A very well-written book which has you hooked from the start... A great read'

'This was one of those books where the suspense just kept building'

'...kept up the tension and suspense throughout'

'I couldn't put it down, cannot recommend it highly enough'

MY SISTER IS MISSING

JULIA BARRETT

RedDoor

Published by RedDoor
www.reddoorpublishing.com

ISBN 978-1-910453-67-4

This is a work of fiction. Names, characters, businesses, places, events, locales, and incidents are either the products of the author's imagination or used in a fictitious manner. Any resemblance to actual persons, living or dead, or actual events is purely coincidental.

A CIP catalogue record for this book is available from the British Library

Cover design: Clare Connie Shepherd
www.clareconnieshepherd.com

Typesetting: Tutis Innovative E-Solutions Pte. Ltd

Printed and bound in Denmark by Nørhaven

For Brendan

Part One

10th Jan 2017

Some secrets are easy to keep. Others require more ingenuity to conceal. An affair turns two people into liars bound inextricably in a carefully woven web of deceit. Signs can be hidden, precautions can be taken, but sometimes they fail and result in a body of evidence. Something tangible, something alive.

I gaze at her searching eyes. Their almond shape is unlike mine. Will you notice, husband? Will you manage to convince yourself that you can see your features in hers? A genetic mix of my code and yours? Or will you see what I see? His eyes, his nose, with my mouth and chin.

The women in the beds opposite me feed or cuddle close their new, precious bundles. All look calm and content. A perfect image of a second chance. A new life. A fresh start.

How could I have done this to you? To us? I don't deserve you. I'm not the wife you think I am.

Missing Day One

Jess

Jess opened one eye. The room tilted. Only slightly, but enough to remind her how much alcohol she'd consumed last night. The stale taste of Prosecco made her reach for the glass of water she'd placed on her bedside chest of drawers. Her hand sent make-up flying and her mobile clattering to the floor.

Head throbbing, she hauled herself upright. The events of last night seeped into her brain. The launch of the new research facility had gone well; lots of press interest and a great piece to camera, but after the business end of the event the press office drifted on to Redemption Bar in Shoreditch. The details of the evening from there on blurred into a haze of laughter with colleagues and a fuzzy image of her staggering out of a cab and home to bed.

Forcing herself out of bed she peeked through a slice of window where the curtains failed in their job. Outside, the drab patch of grass which claimed to be a garden was shrouded in mist and the low winter sunlight confirmed that she was probably going to be late for work.

Her pace quickened as she began her morning routine. Showered, dressed, kettle on, she had just enough time to catch the news while eating breakfast before heading into the office. She turned the TV on and began with Sky.

She always made sure that she got a flavour of the news before arriving at work. It helped her keep on top of her game. A game which she knew she was good at too; the University had received significant media coverage since she'd started running the PR team.

Cranking the volume up, she watched the ticker to see if there was anything she could link to a current research project, or whether the launch event was being featured this morning. Nothing yet. It was a big event, and a slow news day, surely someone would want to run the story?

Switching to BBC Breakfast, she brewed her coffee and chased the low-sugar, low-taste cereal around her bowl. Her head pulsated and her scalp seemed to tighten. The cereal made her feel queasy and she quickly scraped the mushy flakes into the bin. Leaning against the kitchen counter and breathing deeply in order to quell the nausea, she stared out of the small window behind the stainless steel sink.

Her gaze was drawn to the flats that reared up from behind the garden wall by the repetitive movement of an arm slowly raising its hand to a mouth, and now and again flicking ash away from the cigarette's end.

As always, the woman from the flat opposite was stood at the top of the fire escape having a smoke. Clad in a white dressing gown, tinged grey either by the wintery haze or the mixing of white washing with colours, she blew clouds of smoke up into the dull sky.

Jess inhaled deeply. She longed for a cigarette to take the edge off the anxiety that was exacerbated every time she had a hangover. Her neighbour twisted her foot over the cigarette and retreated inside. Jess shivered at the thought of being outside wearing only pyjamas and a dressing gown. The mist looked cold, the sort of mist in which you feel the different air pockets' temperature rise and fall as you move through it.

The local newscaster's upbeat voice drew her attention away from the drab yard. From the kitchen she could see into the lounge, and on screen the stunning glass building of the university came into view. The camera panned across, highlighting its scope and architectural prowess, before coming to rest on the presenter and the familiar face of the vice-principal for health.

She moved closer to the TV and listened as the words she'd been writing, mulling over for months, fell out of the presenter's mouth, hitting her ears like music: 'award-winning architecture and centre of leading-edge medical research.' The vice-principal began to talk about the great potential that these world-class facilities offered the researchers and more importantly, how their research could save lives.

'Local to national,' Jess whispered and crossed her fingers.

Scurrying into the bedroom to retrieve her phone, she expected to see the usual excited texts from colleagues filling the screen. She scooped up her phone. Several missed calls were listed. All from Adam. A cold breeze prickled her neck. Before dialling her brother-in-law she double-checked the windows were closed. They were. Locked tight.

Adam never calls. Ever.

She touched his name to call him back. *Maybe there's been an accident?* Her mind always leapt to the worst-case scenario. It was a reflex action, ingrained into her psyche, as natural as draining the first coffee of the day.

On the end of the line, a small strained voice explained that Steph didn't come home last night. She'd left her mobile and taken Natalie god knows where with hardly any clothes, and could Jess come over and help him talk to the police?

His words washed over her. She felt like her ears were detached from her brain and a puzzled scowl gripped her brow.

'Yes, course I'll come over, but are you sure the police need to be involved? I mean if she's not taken her mobile, she can't call you and... I'm sure she's probably on her way home now.'

As she spoke she realised that not having her mobile wouldn't stop her sister from getting in touch. She had a memory for numbers, unlike Jess who never felt it necessary to commit any to memory. Perhaps he was right to call the police. A swirling sensation gripped her guts and made her sink down onto the bed.

'OK. Sit tight. I'll see you soon.'

Jess stared at her phone and began to rehearse her reason for not coming into work today. She knew today would be busy, her deputy could handle it, but for her own reputation it wouldn't be ideal. She'd have to ham up the concern. She touched dial and waited for the nasal Mancunian tones of her boss to hit her ears. Instead it went to voicemail. *Shit, I can't leave him a message.* She scrolled back through her contacts and winced as she dialled his personal number. She didn't like using it; it was kept for emergencies.

His booming voice answered. Instead of hearing the usual irritation lodged in his voice, he reassured her it was OK and the right thing to do, but to be available whenever her deputy needed her.

This was a rare moment of empathy on his part. His normal reaction to anyone having a non-work crisis was to belittle them, or make them feel they were being incredibly disloyal. Coupled with his tendency to shout and then drop his voice to a whisper, his simmering menace reminded Jess of her primary school head teacher who had the same vocal range when delivering a good telling-off. Jess felt relieved she wasn't on the receiving end of one of his well-publicised rants. Yet.

Dashing to the door and fumbling for her keys in the depths of her handbag, she managed to double-lock it despite the key fighting against the lock. She paused in the doorway. Driving rain and a bitter wind lashed the street. She desperately wanted to return to bed, to nurse her pounding headache, but Adam needed her and more importantly, her sister Steph needed her. She forced herself to meet the rain and dash towards the tube station.

Leytonstone station with its Hitchcock mosaics and smell of stale urine mixed with chips and lager was Jess's usual point of departure each morning. Today the smell made her heave.

Usually she'd walk at speed, heels clipping the pavement, weaving in and out of commuters in the underpass, determined to get ahead of the crowd, but now she drifted in a daze. Her feet seemed to be fighting against an invisible tide of treacle.

My sister is missing? There's going to be a perfectly reasonable explanation for why she didn't come home last night. But it did strike her as odd.

Why would she not call Adam or take her mobile? Why would she go off and stay somewhere else for the night with her newborn baby? Maybe her and Adam had a rare argument? Even Mr Perfect must be finding the return to work and the sleepless nights a challenge.

Jess paused her negative thoughts about her brother-in-law as a missing person's report began to form in her mind. A TV appeal. She shuddered at the notion of people picking over their lives, that voyeuristic tendency, the Facebook gazing. The hidden secrets. *Not that Steph has any. No, it's a misunderstanding, a miscommunication between husband and wife,* she told herself firmly, before swiping her Oyster card and making her way through the barriers.

The thundering noise of the tube up above made her catch her breath and pause before running up the steps. At this time of day the majority of passengers were getting on the west-bound train, not heading east, away from the city. A few people stepped into the carriage as she did.

The journey to Epping takes place overground, providing her with a view rather than cloaking her mind with darkness. Daylight to help push aside her fears and the anxious thoughts that she battled daily.

Her gaze retreated from the gardens and the Victorian properties that fell away from the train tracks, and she became aware of a man sat opposite her, staring at her. Greasy black hair was plastered to his forehead and specks of dandruff littered his side-parting. She caught his eye for a moment before he delicately moved his away to appraise her body. He lingered at her chest, her thighs, and then looked at her shoes. She watched him. He didn't flinch in his blatant leer and his eyes remained transfixed on her feet.

She folded her arms to cover her flat chest, and crossed her legs. His eyes followed her foot. A shiver began to develop in the middle of her spine and spread, making her back and legs tingle and go cold. She hoped he would get off before her stop; travelling to the end of the line didn't give her many options to avoid him. His eyes were odd; it wasn't just the way they lingered over her body, there was a steeliness to them.

Maybe I'll get off and sit in another carriage. Her mind wove back to the news and a recent article she'd read in the local *Guardian* about a man masturbating on the tube. He was in his fifties, like the man opposite her.

The train came to a stop and the familiar whirr of the sliding doors meant she had a chance to switch carriages. She didn't want to spend the entire journey sitting opposite a man who gave her the creeps. She stiffly hauled herself up, stepped off the tube and darted along the platform at Snaresbrook.

An overwrought young mother was trying to persuade her buggy to get on the train.

'Bloody thing,' snapped the young woman as she rammed the pram in an attempt to make it move.

'I think the wheel is twisted. I'll lift it on and then you should be able to push it.'

'Thanks, that's great.'

Jess deftly lifted the pram and moved the wheel.

'Thanks, that's sorted it.' Her strong east London accent told Jess that she was local, born and bred. Jess could still hear her own flat northern vowels despite living in the capital since she left university.

She took a peek at the baby. She looked a little older than her niece.

'She's beautiful. How old?'

'Three months now. No idea where the time's gone.' The woman yawned and then took out her mobile phone, signalling she didn't want the conversation to continue.

Jess remained standing and looked at the sleeping baby. *Babies all look the same really, she doesn't look that different to my niece. Same hair colour, can't see the eyes but, still, they all look similar to me.*

She swallowed down the lump that was building in her throat and offered up a silent prayer, not to a higher force, but to her sister – *come home, both of you, come home.* She turned away from the pram.

The stations and houses blended together as the tube wound its way through the suburbs and further away from London. A handful of people remained scattered throughout the train as it reached the end of the line. Thankfully that handful didn't include the lascivious man.

Steph and Adam lived in a bungalow not far from Epping station. When Steph told her where they were buying and what kind of house it was, Jess'd teased her about becoming old before her time.

Sleepy Epping, a bungalow overlooking fields, and of course not far away from the beautiful sprawling Epping Forest. She knew it was all about Steph's vision of happiness for her future family. It was a grown-up act. It marked Steph's new phase of life while Jess remained in her one-bedroom rental in east London. Alone now, after Matt, her long-term boyfriend, had decided he needed a break from the rat race, and their relationship.

Head down, bag slung over her shoulder, her heels struck the pavement as she walked as fast as her stilettoes would allow. Thankfully it was a short walk from the station to Steph's home, her feet still ached from dancing last night.

Her phone distracted her as she walked down Bower Lane in the direction of The Orchards. It buzzed in her Longchamp handbag. She fished it out and the screen told her it was Adam. Her feet slowed down in anticipation of maybe turning around and getting back on the tube. She informed him she was two minutes away. His voice remained small, as though it was trapped in his larynx, betraying his worry. Steph still hadn't returned.

She marched onwards down the snaking road and her eye was drawn to the police car parked outside her sister's home. The bungalows all looked the same: manicured lawns and sculptured shrubs. Neat. Perfect, unlike the ramshackle

Victorian properties that clung to Leytonstone High Road. Police cars were a familiar feature of Jess's neighbourhood. But here the car made her sister's home look out of place, almost untidy, as it dominated the short sloping driveway.

Her steps slowed down as she neared the doorway. Part of her wanted to run. If she went home perhaps this would be like a child's game of hide and seek? *Seven, eight, nine, ten. Coming, ready or not!* Just like when they were kids and they'd find the most ridiculous hiding places and scare one another. Steph always made the game hard for her little sister. *An innocent game we played far too often.*

She raised her hand, paused and then rapped on the frosted glass. The obscured shape of a man's body moved towards the door. A roseate-faced Adam appeared and flung his arms around her hugging her tightly.

Jess's body stiffened. She was not used to her brother-in-law displaying any affection; even when she'd congratulated him on the birth of his daughter she remembered the awkward kiss on the cheek and then the hand placed on her shoulder keeping her at a safe distance. It had taken Jess a long time to come to understand that it was simply Adam's way. He wasn't the cuddly hug-anyone type. He always came across as reserved and cold. She patted his shoulder and hoped that this signal would prompt him to release her.

It did the trick. He stepped backwards into the hallway. She studied his face as she stepped into her sister's home. His eyes were red rimmed and the dark circles seemed to have deepened since the last time she saw him.

Jess removed her coat and hung it up. Adam led her through the small hallway into the kitchen. Several empty mugs were left on the counter. The smell of strong coffee and stale sweat filled her nostrils.

She'd often wished she didn't have such a sensitive sense of smell. It seemed particularly heightened today. She noticed that whenever she felt anxious it became keener. As though all her senses needed to become hyper-alert for danger.

Standing propped up against the kitchen counter was a youngish looking police officer. Jess watched him flick through a photo album. Presumably filled with photos of Natalie looking beautiful and cute in various poses and outfits. She noticed the grim look on his face. Incongruous with the usual reaction of viewing baby photos. He closed the book firmly and passed it to Adam.

'This is my sister-in-law, Jess.' Adam ushered her over to the police officer.

He stretched out his arm and she reached for his hand and firmly shook it. He smiled at her. He had deep brown eyes and tight afro curls which kissed his forehead, gently framing his soft features.

'Do you want a drink? Coffee?'

His voice brought her back into the present and on cue Adam began to boil the kettle, but the officer took over.

'Why don't you two go and sit in the lounge?'

Adam nodded and slowly outstretched his arm signalling to Jess to lead the way.

The February grey light had shifted and now cast a blue hue as the weak sunlight filtered through the window. A coldness washed over Jess as she entered the room. She wished she had kept her coat on. There was an odd stillness to the atmosphere, even the dust motes seemed suspended in mid-air. A thick silence enveloped her ears betraying the emptiness of the house.

The lounge was immaculate. Jess wondered where all the baby paraphernalia had been hidden. Even her sister's books and magazines, which usually littered the coffee table, were missing. She felt their absence acutely.

Goosebumps spread down her arms. Her blouse was delicately thin. Good for the stuffy office, not great for a draughty lounge. She sunk into the sofa that was enclosed by the bay window and clutched a cushion to her chest, partly for warmth but also to steady her. She needed something to stop the dizziness that was threatening to overtake her. Another symptom of anxiety, or perhaps her hangover. She didn't want to be sat here alone to face the police questions. She needed Matt to be by her side now, not across the other side of the world 'finding himself'. She puffed out her cheeks as the thought of him invaded her brain. She recognised that despite his absence he was ever present in her thoughts. The relationship wasn't over. *Not for me it isn't.*

Adam hovered by the doorway, his entrance interrupting her thoughts. Eyes wide as he stared out on to the quiet street, he looked as though he was willing his wife to walk by the window. He grimaced as he coughed to clear his throat before shuffling past Jess to sit at the other end of the sofa, resting against the arm but facing her.

She glanced at him. His hands were shaking. A wave of nausea caused her to put her head in her hands for a moment, as the shock of the news began to sink in.

Coming ready or not? Where are you hiding?

'Are you OK? Do you need some fresh air?' said Adam.

Jess pulled herself upwards, straightening her spine. She stuffed the cushion between her body and the arm of the sofa.

'No, I'm fine, it's all a bit surreal. I can't really take it all in...' She smoothed down her Hobbs cobalt skirt, brushing off a stray hair. Long, brown with a slight wave. Not her hair, one of her sister's.

'I'm sorry. I didn't want you to worry last night, when I got home and she wasn't here.' There was a tremor in his voice, his eyes were drawn to the floor.

'I thought she'd be back and when she didn't show and I found her mobile I knew that if she was with you that she'd call and you'd call...' Adam began crying. It looked as though he'd been unable to stem the tears since the police officer had arrived.

The young officer placed a cup of coffee next to Jess on a small table which housed the TV remotes and a lamp. Jess leaned back into the soft fabric of the sofa and watched him arrange himself on a chair opposite her.

The sofa was a deep purple colour and reminded her of her mother's house. She'd helped her paint the chimney in her bedroom a sumptuous plum colour. One of the few acts of support she permitted herself to do, because where her mum was concerned, it was better to steer clear, only chip in if Steph was unavailable.

It dawned on Jess that the room had many little touches which reminded her of how similar her sister and mother's tastes were. The patterned cushions resembled a bedspread her mum had owned at one time. She felt a knot form in her gut; it always did when she thought about her mum.

She reached for the coffee and hoped the movement would ease the tightness which gripped her intestines. The police officer got out his notebook. She needed to concentrate on what he was about to ask her. She needed to push every thought that didn't focus on her sister out of her head. She trained her eyes on his lips.

'I'm PC Hawthorne.'

He paused as Jess nodded and attempted a smile. Her mouth formed a line as the corners refused to budge and rise towards her cheeks.

'I've asked Adam lots of question already, but I need some more info from you, background and family history and present information, which I'll start with first.' He paused again and smiled. A genuine, reassuring smile.

'Can you tell me when you last saw your sister?'

'Last Sunday. I came over to cook Sunday lunch for all of us.'

'Is that something you normally do?'

'Not really. Sometimes the three of us would go to the pub, but I thought it would be nice if I cooked for Steph and Adam instead. She wasn't up to going out to the pub just yet.' She took a sip from the scorching coffee, winced, and hastily replaced the mug on the table.

'Not up to it yet, can you explain that a little more?' PC Hawthorne moved forward in his seat.

'She was tired, Natalie isn't a great sleeper yet, so Steph was spending a lot of her nights awake.'

She hoped he'd back her up. She traced the shape of her watch on her wrist and then clasped her fingers together as she began to feel nervous.

Adam stared at her, looking as though he was listening as intently as the police officer was, as though this information was new to him.

'We'd managed a few outings before, coffee on the high street, stroll down the lane, but as I said she was exhausted. We tended to just spend time at home and that gave me a chance to properly help her out, you know, cleaning and doing the endless amount of washing that a newborn seems to generate.'

PC Hawthorne smiled and nodded. He tapped the pen on his notebook and scribbled rapidly to reactivate the ink.

'Would you describe her as being sleep deprived?'

'Aren't all new mothers sleep deprived?'

'And new dads,' added PC Hawthorne. He smiled at Adam, but Adam seemed unable to change the fixed expression of confusion on his face.

'I've eight-week-old twins. Got my sister staying with us to give us a hand.'

Jess raised an eyebrow. PC Hawthorne looked like the epitome of youth, not a young father, but someone who had recently graduated from Police College, or wherever police officers learned their trade. Jess pushed her hair behind her ear.

'Yes, I've got next week booked off work to come and stay here with her, I couldn't take this week off and now I'm wishing I had.' The dark-stained floorboards began to swell as though they were reaching out to her, pulling her down from the sofa. The room was spinning now. Nausea reached up her throat and clawed at her soft palate.

Tears seeped from her eyes, causing her to catch her breath. The PC lunged forward to reach for the box of tissues that lay on the sofa next to her. He silently offered them to her. She dabbed her cheeks and took care not to smudge her eye make-up.

'Do you need a glass of water?'

My sister is missing. My niece is missing. It was no longer a question. It was a statement of fact.

Steph had vanished with her newborn baby. It was totally out of character for her dependable big sister. And Natalie, tiny vulnerable Natalie. Another tear slowly trickled over Jess's chiselled cheekbone.

'Coffee's fine.' Her words were barely audible.

She took another sip of her coffee, instant and not to her taste. It warmed her up; the room seemed a degree or two colder. The light shifted as though another layer of cloud had been created, further darkening the room. The white walls absorbed the odd blue-grey hue. She clasped the mug in her hands to retain its heat as the unusual blue light seemed to infuse a winter chill directly into her bloodstream. It took all her energy to make sure her teeth didn't chatter.

'I'm sorry. Where were we?' She felt her eyes narrowing to focus. She gripped the mug tightly to stop herself from shaking. Jaw clenched. Teeth jammed tight to prevent them chattering as the shock began to rattle her bones.

'Sleep deprivation – was she herself when you last visited?'

She set the coffee down again. The movement was required to free the tension, to enable her mouth to speak.

'Yes, I mean she's been a bit teary on and off, but really nothing out the ordinary. She seemed exhausted but that's normal isn't it?'

Of course it was normal. PC Hawthorne's quick hand noted her words.

'So would you say she was suffering with mood swings?'

'No. I get weepy when I'm tired. I think that is perfectly natural, especially under the circumstances. She was generally her usual happy self. OK, she didn't want to go out for lunch but that doesn't mean she was depressed. She's tired, but totally in love with her new baby and with being a mum.'

Jess bit her lip. She could confidently say that her sister was totally besotted with Natalie, but could she categorically say that Steph was happy as a mum? It wasn't something they'd discussed, it was an assumption that she'd made. Made on how smitten she was with Natalie. She could see Steph cuddling and kissing and smiling down at her perfect little bundle.

'I've never seen my sister happier. She seemed different, more relaxed, and comfortable in her own skin. She's absolutely smitten with Natalie. I guess the tears, the snappiness, it's just part and parcel of being a tired new mum.'

A scowl developed across Adam's brow.

Are you going to agree with me? That she's a knackered new mum who is a bit moody but totally at ease with her new role? Why aren't you saying anything?

She maintained her stare. His cheeks retained a rouge. She thought that was because he'd been crying, but around his hairline she could see beads of sweat forming despite the chill in the room.

Throughout the interview he'd remained silent. He was clasping his hands together and she noticed how white his knuckles looked.

Is he hiding something?

And as soon as the thought entered her mind she tried to bury it.

No. Ridiculous.

A shiver began to develop down her spine for the second time that day and she thought about the strange man on the tube.

Where are you Steph? Are you safe? Is Natalie with you?

The police officer broke her thoughts. 'So, is there anything out of the ordinary that has occurred to you? Any unusual behaviour? Anyone new in her circle of friends?'

Adam spluttered, as though he had swallowed his coffee too quickly. A coughing fit ensued. She caught his eye for the first time since the officer had begun his questioning. He glanced away, towards the phone that sat on a console table in the corner of the room.

She shook her head. 'No sorry. Nothing. I've not really been very helpful, have I?'

'Yes you have. We have to establish her character and her state of mind. We have to explore all possibilities. Rest assured that she's a high priority for us, especially as she's taken her newborn with her.'

Taken her newborn with her. Taken her child away. Not just missing. Fuck.

Jess excused herself. She needed to give herself a moment away from Adam and the police officer. In the cloakroom she washed her hands and applied some lip balm. Her lipstick had worn off and it seemed inappropriate to reapply it. Plus her hands were still shaking and she knew she'd be unable to accurately fill in the sharp points of her cupid's bow. She stared at herself in the mirror. Her skin had lost all its colour despite the fact she was wearing make-up. She ran her fingers through her nut-brown-coloured hair and then smoothed down a few sections that had become unruly. She attempted to picture Steph. They had similar eyes and noses but their lips were different. Steph had full lips with a curvy cupid's bow. It gave her a softer, more seductive smile.

Her beautiful, happy big sister. A beautiful, happy new mum. Not a mum who is depressed and struggling with the demands of a newborn. *No. That's not who she is.*

Jess flushed the toilet to make her trip look authentic and washed her hands again. The water failed to get warm. She wriggled her shoulders, stepped back into the small hallway and returned to her spot on the sofa.

PC Hawthorne was writing something in his notebook. He'd probably just asked Adam a question, but Jess couldn't recall hearing him speak as she'd exited the loo.

'So Jess, just to re-cap. Your sister was struggling with sleep deprivation, she was teary, but you put that down to her being tired?'

'Yes. As I said I get teary when I'm tired and I'm sure I'd have noticed if my sister was feeling depressed.'

'Have you seen her since Adam returned to work?'

'No.'

'Have you had any contact with her for the past few days?'

Jess's mouth automatically twisted as she felt a stab of guilt. She'd been so busy with the launch that she'd not come out of her work bubble to even drop her sister a text. She sheepishly shook her head.

'Is that unusual?'

'Yes. We text most days, but I've had a lot on at work.'

Adam coughed. 'Perhaps Steph had a lot on too with me not being home.' He half-smiled at Jess. She wondered whether that was an attempt to ease her guilt. She looked at him, hoping to catch his gaze, but it proved elusive. *Why can't he look me in the eye?*

Adam rose from the sofa and moved to look out of the bay window. He was definitely standing there in the hope she'd return. PC Hawthorne flicked through his notes. He sighed and looked up to meet Jess's eyes.

'Can I ask you a few questions about Steph's background?'

Jess nodded. Her spine stiffened and her index finger began to trace the circular watch face.

'Is there any history of mental illness in the family?'

Jess looked away from PC Hawthorne.

'No. No history of mental illness.'

'Did Steph ever experience any difficulties with her mental health?'

Adam returned to the sofa and perched on the edge of it. Poised to hear Jess's answer.

'No. Not that I'm aware of.' Jess regarded Adam. He clasped his hands tightly together as he rested his elbows on his knees.

'Adam, is there anything that we should be aware of?' PC Hawthorne's address made him jump. His grip seemed to tighten as his knuckles bulged.

'Not really. I mean, no, she got stressed about things now and again, but – no.' He closed his eyes. Jess observed his every move. His eyes remained shut for a minute. Longer than she expected them to. When they sprung open he jumped up, covered his mouth and fled the room. She could hear him retching in the loo.

'Shall I see if he's all right?' Jess asked PC Hawthorne. She wasn't sure whether she should leave the room. His questions just kept on coming. She was beginning to feel out of her depth and comfort zone. She knew questions about their childhood were probably on the horizon. She wasn't sure how to answer them, or if she could.

'No. It's the shock, perfectly usual. Just give him a moment. So, no history of mental illness.' He tapped his pen before resuming. 'Can you tell me about when you were growing up?'

Straight to the point then. Home-life time.

'Pretty standard really. Dad left when we were little. Steph coped with that better than me. That's what she's like, you know, someone who handles things well. She always looked out for me, and Mum. She took on a lot of responsibility when we were growing up but she seemed to thrive on it.'

Jess wound a lock of hair around her finger and then straightened it out again. That was true. Steph did take on a lot.

'Me and Mum, well, it was a stormy relationship throughout my teens but Steph, she was the peacemaker.'

'Apart from your father leaving the family home, your home life was pretty stable?'

Anything but stable. She breathed deeply and interlinked her fingers bringing them to rest on her lap. She glanced at PC Hawthorne before returning her gaze to her hands.

'Yes, pretty stable and standard despite Dad not being on the scene.'

Adam returned to the room. He was sweating and had no colour left in his cheeks.

'Sorry about that.' He mumbled as he sat back down on the sofa, but this time he sat next to Jess, filling in the space. A fraction too close for her liking.

'Adam's filled me in on the rest about your parents and university years. If you can think of anything else from your childhood that could be useful?'

Filled you in on the rest. He knows nothing. No one does. Time to close my childhood file.

'No, don't think so. Did Adam mention that our childhood home is vacant and currently on the market?'

PC Hawthorne nodded and then flicked back through his notebook as though he was double-checking Adam's answers. His fingers traced his writing as he silently re-read their answers. His lips moved as he mouthed a few of his sentences. He looked up at Jess and blushed. He moved to the edge of the chair and scratched his cheek with the end of his pen.

'Right. I'm getting the sense that her disappearance is out of character; she's no history of mental illness, she's sleep deprived and *possibly* struggling with postnatal depression – it makes her a high priority. This totally doesn't fit the usual missing persons' disappearance and, obviously because she's taken your daughter with her, well, they both are doubly vulnerable.'

Jess couldn't speak now. Her throat was so tight, it felt difficult to breathe. Her hand moved towards her neck. She watched PC Hawthorne's pen scribble away in the notebook again. It stopped and he flicked it shut.

'As I said, they are a high priority for us. I'll need to take her mobile, laptop and some recent photographs.' He stopped as he rose to stand. He was taller than Adam by several inches. His frame took up all the space in the room. Jess continued to stare up at him. The dizziness was making it difficult for her to concentrate. She focused again on his lips.

'I'll need her vehicle details and bank details.' PC Hawthorne looked back to Jess. She managed a brief smile before Adam led the officer out of the lounge to the kitchen.

Her thoughts looped continuously. Steph had taken Natalie. Her big sister had disappeared. This police officer thought she was depressed. Jess couldn't link those words together. It had never been an adjective she could ascribe to her dependable, never-loses-her-shit big sister. It was an adjective that she certainly could apply to herself.

No. She's not depressed. It's something else. Something has made her run. PC Hawthorne is right about one thing. This is totally out of character.

30th Jan 2017

I must get this down before A gets back from work and while Little Miss is napping. His first day back in the office and god I'm missing him. The house feels so empty. In-laws all gone back to the Costa del Retiro, and J couldn't get time off work this week, some big event, launch of a new research centre or something, wish I could retain the details. I'm finally by myself. Alone.

I was dreading A returning to work. Things have gone so well. He's bonded with N, he's great with her – she often stops crying so easily for him. He thinks she's beautiful and looks just like me. I'm starting to believe that I'm wrong.

I don't want to think about HIM. But I can't help myself, I see him in her features, especially her eyes. She's a constant reminder of what I've done.

He kept away once my pregnancy was common knowledge. It gave us a reason to end the affair and we never talked about the possibility that the baby could be his. It had crossed my mind – played on my mind – but I thought that was the guilt. And now, when I look at N, all I see is him. His features are taking over her face.

I didn't want to be left alone at home, I wanted all the visitors to keep coming because I knew HE'D be waiting. Waiting for his chance to get me alone. The attraction is strong for both of us. The lure of what we shared and what could be repeated is a temptation I'm not sure I can resist. I'm so confused. I hate this feeling of being pulled to two different sides of one precious coin.

* * *

I didn't have long to wait for a visit.

Through the frosted glass I can see a man, holding a bouquet of flowers which obscures his face. His slight frame is familiar.

As I open the door, he lowers the flowers towards me and I long to pull him close to me. Feel his body pressed against me again. To kiss him and feel my tongue inside his mouth, touching his, but I can't let the neighbours witness that, so a thank you and a peck on the cheek is all that's appropriate.

I'm in pieces. I love my husband, I do, that's the truth, and he's becoming an amazing Dad, but this man... The way he looks at me, I feel exposed. It's like he knows what's inside me, the language that my heart speaks, what my wants are before I even know them. This all sounds ridiculous but I've never felt that with A.

Practical, loveable, dependable A. The one who rescued me and put me back together.

A safe pair of hands, but with Him. Everything is different. A polar opposite... It's a symphony of passion; I'm all the instruments in the orchestra and he knows exactly how to play every one.

We talk for a while, avoiding any mention of us, N or A. Work talk, which is good because I'm missing it a little. He took on a big story about BT having less money to bid for TV Sports rights and the business editor, for the first time in months, sung his praises. His eyes shone with the echo of approval.

Time rushes away from us and I know he doesn't want to leave. I can see the sadness in his eyes, but he can't stay and we know we must end this. We must. This is ridiculous.

I kiss him before he leaves. It isn't a peck on the cheek. I can't help myself. The final kiss goodbye. He kisses me back with equal passion and I didn't want to stop. But we have to. I can't do this.

I push him away. His eyes show me how hurt and angry he is. He stands tall, as though his slight frame and height grows in an instant. As though the hurt and anger makes him swell physically. His lips part as though he's about to speak to me but they instantly close.

He leaves and I can breathe again.

* * *

I'm lucky N was napping while he was here, because if he saw her, he'd know. It was odd he didn't ask to see her. But I realised he doesn't need to ask because he must have seen all the pictures on Facebook. I couldn't not post them, could I? I mean it would look odd to everyone if I wasn't showing off my adorable baby girl.

I can't hide. The web we've spun seems to be expanding.

I didn't read the card that he gave me with the flowers, not while he was present. I wanted to read it alone, inhale each word.

But not these words.

He tells me he is convinced that the baby is his, that she was conceived when A was away on business. It was no coincidence that it has taken me and A two years of trying and as soon as our contraception failed I ended up pregnant.

'The baby is mine. The baby is mine,' he writes over and over and then tells me wants a paternity test and that he intends to tell A.

He intends to tell A. I can't take this in.

I never wanted this to be exposed. I wanted both; a secure dependable marriage and the electricity of the new and exciting world of sneaking off together and having sex. It is all over for me. My marriage, my family, our home. All because I couldn't help myself. Because I loved the thrill of affection, of the chase, the desire.

I am naïve. I know this. To think that our actions could have gone undiscovered. That it could have simply been a fling with no consequences. Because that's what it was. Sex with no strings and now the strings are reaching out to strangle me.

* * *

I'm glad Mum arrives as all sorts of possibilities are racing through my brain. I had to tell her and show her the card. It would be odd not to confide in her. She knows all my secrets like I know all hers.

Anger and disappointment. The face I've seen many times before but not worn for me. That face often greets J. But it gives way to fear too quickly. The tone of the card frightens her. She tells me not to tell A. Keep it to ourselves. She'll deal with it. Mum to the rescue as always. She gives me the usual lines of how difficult it was being a single mum and that she doesn't want me to go through this alone and how amazing A is.

She doesn't have to say what she thinks of me, I can tell, and she's right. I've been a fool. I got caught up in the moment, well several moments, and I should have said no.

I can't tell A.

It would destroy him, like it destroyed Dad.

She's right. She's been there, she's been the fool. I couldn't cope as a single mum and I don't want that for my daughter.

Missing Day One

Jess

PC Hawthorne returned to the station. He took Steph's laptop, phone, and one of the many recent photos of her with Natalie. Scrolling through them on her mobile, Jess could feel Steph's happiness, it was visceral. In each image, she had a relaxed and nurturing air about her as she cradled Natalie or snuggled next to her in bed. Whatever the pose, she looked content.

She glanced up at the clock on the wall behind where Adam sat slumped in the sofa, holding his head in his hands. Jess wondered how her office was getting on with post-launch press calls. She waited until the minute hand completed its full circle, giving her a beat before she returned to the dozens of images of Steph.

She pictured Steph cooing over Natalie, feeding her, winding her, blowing raspberries on her tummy and all the other ever-so-cute mumsy-things her sister did each time she'd visited her over the past three weeks.

Three weeks old.

The last image of her niece on her camera roll was taken by Steph. Natalie lay peacefully sleeping in her arms. She closed her eyes and felt the imprint of her niece nestling into the crook of her arm and how insubstantial she felt. Her arms had ached from the tension of the fear of dropping her.

She flicked backwards through the pictures, to the first time she'd visited Steph in hospital. The first photo she took showed Natalie's yellow-tinged skin, which had naturally worried Steph at the time, but Jess hadn't really understood the implications. She looked again at the last image. Was there still a hint of yellow tinging her niece's skin?

Where are you? Are you both safe? She shook her phone.

'Come on. Call me. Talk to me.'

Blinking back the tears that were trying to spill down her cheeks, she returned to her favourite image, the one she sent to PC Hawthorne. Steph wore her hair down spilling over her shoulders, light brown waves caressed her upper arms. Her eyes were smiling and Natalie was asleep nuzzled into Steph's now ample breast. She looked so at ease in the image. Her full lips, devoid of her usual red lip gloss, stretched in a wide smile across her face. Her features had softened with pregnancy. Somehow she was even more beautiful.

Steph had a natural maternal predisposition; something which felt alien to Jess. A vague imprint of maternal affection remained in her subconscious, lingering like the smell of a freshly opened pack of crayons that takes you back to childhood. The anger began to swell again. She closed her eyes and attempted to push away the over-played memory, but as usual it was insistent and refused to be buried.

She could see her tiny hands, a five-year-old's hands, reaching for the heavy bronze door handle, pulling it down and tentatively peering around the door. *No. Stop it. Not now.* She shook herself and arose from the sofa.

Her lithe limbs teetered in her heels which she'd forgotten to slip off. Heat spread across her cheeks as she stepped out of her shoes hoping that Adam hadn't noticed her social faux pas.

Adam remained seated in the chair that PC Hawthorne had vacated. Off in his own world, staring into space now, rather than cradling his head in his hands. She followed his gaze, her eyes stopped at the landline. He was probably willing Steph to call and tell them she was fine and on her way home.

If she's happy and has adjusted to being a mum, then why has she disappeared?

She stared intently at Adam, his eyes still fixed on the phone. For the first time she noticed a few grey hairs poking out around his ears and it occurred to her that she'd never seen him under stress. They'd probably been there a while, but she rarely spent time scrutinising her brother-in-law in such detail.

He was always calm, measured, and controlled. When she first met him, back when Steph was at uni, she thought he was an odd match for her sister. Steph's previous boyfriends were either aspiring artists or musicians, but Adam was doing some sort of financial degree.

He was caring, she'd acceded that, he had a dry sense of humour and had often caused both her and Steph to descend into girlish fits of giggles, but other than that she wasn't sure what had drawn them to each other.

She focused on his hands. A tremor. *Shock? Or something else?*

'Did you tell the police everything?' Irritation infused her tone. She was aware it was an odd question to ask, and that it was loaded with a million and one implications, but something felt off to her. She couldn't put her finger on it exactly, it was just a feeling, a symptom of her naturally suspicious nature. She'd grown up knowing that adults try to keep secrets. She knew what happens when secrets get out. Things fall apart. People implode.

Her palms were clammy. The room felt like it was closing in on them. She noted that the sweat beads had evaporated on Adam's hairline since PC Hawthorne had left, but the trembling hands remained.

'I think so, as much as I could think of. Bank details, doctors, dentist, car reg, friends, you, work, family. He asked loads of questions. I couldn't tell them what she was wearing exactly – when I left she was in her pyjamas. She's taken her long black coat but that's all I've really noticed that's missing. The police said I could look through her clothes and see what she's taken, but I've no idea, I said she normally wears jeans.'

He gingerly hauled himself up from the chair and moved again to look out of the window.

'I guess I only picture her in her work attire, but I suppose the loud print dresses have been swapped for something more comfortable?' she asked. Was she still wearing maternity jeans when Jess last visited? She was definitely wearing one of those odd breastfeeding tops.

'She normally does, it's her default uniform when she's not at work. Shit. I think I've missed loads of things.' He sunk back down again.

'Don't worry, you can call them if you remember anything else.'

He nodded before covering his face with his hands and inhaling noisily. He rubbed his forehead and then let his hands drop to rest on the arms of the chair. His fingers stroked its plum fabric, drawing tiny invisible circles, over and over.

'I didn't like him taking her things, it feels wrong to be prying.' His florid complexion faded white again and his fingers abruptly froze.

'I don't understand; I mean, I understand why he took her things, but not about anything else. None of this makes sense. I'm not missing something here, am I? I mean was she just pretending to be happy?' Jess couldn't get her head around the idea that her sister, who appeared genuinely happy and besotted with Natalie, would simply disappear.

Adam's head lolled forward as he looked to the floor. He began to rub his forehead, massaging his temples. He didn't look up when he spoke.

'She is happy. She's tired though. Exhausted actually. Worried about feeding, worried about the jaundice. I should have mentioned the jaundice.' He sat up straight now, his face colourless. 'Shit. I wish I hadn't had to go back to work, I mean these past few days, well, she's found it hard.'

'Did you tell the police that?' Jess tightened her grip on the heels she still held in her hand.

'Yes.'

'So they'll think that she's not coping. So what I said doesn't ring true?' Embarrassment wrapped itself around her. She didn't want to come across to the police officer like she didn't know her sister, or what was going on in her head.

'Yes of course it rings true. She is happy, she is coping, but isn't it normal to find it hard when you're left alone for the first time since the baby was born?'

She raised an eyebrow. 'I wouldn't know. I guess so.' The what-would-you-know card was being played. Jess refused to be baited.

She looked away from Adam. He always seemed to rub her up the wrong way. Perhaps it went right back to when they first met? How he seemed intent on dismantling their sisterhood.

Other boyfriends had often included her in plans, the kind of outings where three is fun and not a crowd, but with Adam, there was only ever room for two. She could count on one hand the occasions they'd ventured out as a threesome. She'd often include Steph in her plans. It felt natural to invite her along when she and Matt went out on dates. She never felt the need to make their dates exclusive; it was fun to all go out clubbing together or to the cinema.

Maybe it was because Adam was used to being an only child, or perhaps it was just different for Steph, she didn't need her sister around since she'd found 'the one'.

Jess had come to terms with this evolution and exclusion, it was natural and normal, but for a long time she missed her sister's companionship.

And then there was the wedding. Steph had wanted the traditional ceremony: church, friends, family, party and bridesmaids. They'd chatted incessantly about dresses and were at the point of choosing some, when Adam pulled the plug.

He didn't want this, he wanted something small, something more personal. Secret, as it turned out when he whisked her off to get married in Vegas and then straight off on their honeymoon road trip.

That wasn't Steph. That was totally Adam. Totally controlling. *Excluding and controlling. But Steph loves him and that's all that matters, isn't it? Not what I think.*

Jess sighed abruptly. Her anger towards her brother-in-law was gently simmering again. Recently, she'd felt differently. Having Natalie meant that all the family had to be included and involved again. Not pushed to the periphery.

She stood up and marched to the hallway to place her shoes near the door, then strode to the kitchen to get a glass of water. She began to load the dirty cups into the dishwasher. A streak of blue caught her attention. A couple of blue tits pecked at the fat ball hanging from the holly tree in her sister's garden. Even in winter the garden looked alive and welcoming. The holly tree's leathery emerald green leaves contrasted with the yellow-tinged leaves of the shrubs that sat in the borders. Another blue tit landed on the fat ball, scaring the other one away. Jess smiled as she pictured Steph hanging out the fat balls; she'd always had a thing for feeding the birds.

A breeze caressed the nape of her neck sending a cold shiver down her spine, as though a window had just been pushed open.

Adam's footsteps brushed against carpet. A scuffing of plastic and a faint beeping sound alerted Jess to the fact that he was making a phone call. He was using the landline, not his mobile. She leant against the kitchen counter and pushed a tendril of hair behind her ear, tilting her head to one side as she strained to hear his voice.

She couldn't make out any of his muffled conversation. She heard the handset being slid back into its cradle and the sound of his footsteps nearing the kitchen.

'I'm going out. Drive around a little. See if I can spot our car. I can't sit here any longer and do nothing.' He turned abruptly to leave, but before walking down the hallway he paused. 'Can you stay here? I mean, she may call.'

'Or come back while you're out?' Jess put on a fake smile of encouragement.

'Yes, yes, let's hope so.'

She was glad to see him leave. She listened for the purr of his car engine firing up and then rolling away before she went back to the lounge to pick up the landline.

She hit the redial button. Three number tones sounded. Then, an automated voice, telling her that 'at the third stroke, the time, brought to you by Sky, will be...' But she knew the time. And what's more she had heard Adam speak to someone, a brief conversation but a conversation nonetheless. *Did he call the speaking clock to cover up the number he dialled? And why would he do that?*

She slammed the handset down but found her feet didn't want to co-operate with her urge to flee the room. She took in the immaculate lounge. The lack of her sister's detritus worried her. This room always seemed so welcoming. Newspapers or magazines would be left on the coffee table and since Natalie's arrival there had always been a baby book, or cuddly toy, or packet of baby wipes left on the sofa. The neatness now seemed incongruous.

The police had taken things that they thought would be useful. PC Hawthorne had said that at this stage they wouldn't search the house, but if she remained missing that would be a possibility.

She found herself going through Steph's work papers which resided in a box file on the bookcase. Payslips, official letters and loads of clippings of her stories from *The Mirror*. Jess still loved to see her sister's name as the by-line. She was proud of her. The first clipping was of an article on Brexit and consumer rights. She flicked through the rest. *These must be the ones she's proud of. Keeping for a portfolio? Maybe. Always having one eye on the future.* A few of the articles had a shared by-line, but mainly Steph's name featured. Jess flicked the folder shut and slid it back on the shelf next to a couple of other files. She fought the urge to search through Adam's papers. *I wish I'd inherited the organising gene.*

Jess wandered into the bedroom. She didn't want Adam to notice that she'd been searching through her sister's things. She resisted rifling through her drawers; unlike Jess, Steph probably wouldn't store little keepsakes underneath clothes or at the back of drawers. She knew her sister would have a special place for them. A box, or a file; something. Not like her own mementos which she'd secrete throughout her flat.

Steph's jewellery box lay open next to her make-up mirror on the chest of drawers. A few pairs of her favourite marcasite earrings and matching necklaces sat together in the velveteen lined box. She had a thing for retro jewellery.

They had both enjoyed meandering around Portobello market when Jess first moved to London. Steph adored the heavy marcasite necklace that she'd spotted on a stall one Friday night. A flower in the middle: gems for petals and a freshwater pearl for the centre. The silver was cold to touch as she smoothed out the necklace on the top of the drawers. Her fingers pushed around a few earrings but she couldn't see anything of interest in there.

Mum had given Jess her wedding ring and Steph her engagement ring. She'd kept them for years after Dad had left, only taking them off once the divorce had come through. Neither of them wore the rings, but the engagement ring wasn't here. Jess couldn't remember her sister ever wearing it. Its absence was conspicuous.

Next to the box was a photograph of her, Steph and Mum. The frame was plain, unlike the beautiful frames that were covered with ornate flowers and patterns carved into the wood, which adorned the walls. Each frame was filled with photographs. Weddings, holidays and one now full of images of Natalie. Jess smiled, she was pleased that she was present in at least one of the photographs in each frame.

Jess lifted up the necklace and gently positioned it to snake around several pairs of earrings and flicked shut the jewellery box lid. She sunk down onto the bed tucking her hands under her thighs. The empty Moses basket stood by the window. A solitary blanket remained. *Thankfully she's taken some blankets for Natalie. Has she taken some clothes for her? Enough nappies? At least she doesn't have to lug around bottles and powdered milk.*

Jess shook herself. Pins and needles were beginning to spread into her fingers as she'd sat on her hands for some time, a habit which she wanted to break but was so natural and comforting in an odd sort of way. She withdrew her hands and shook her wrists in an attempt to reactivate the blood flow.

'What is this actually achieving?' she asked the four walls of the bedroom.

She returned to the kitchen, boiled the kettle and took out her phone. Scrolling through the phone book she stopped at Matt. Three months and two days since he embarked on the longed-for trip he'd decided to take without her.

It had been so hard to say goodbye. She missed his steadying influence and so much more. Where was he now? Thailand. In a week or so he was going to Oz. Her finger hovered over his name. She desperately wanted to tell him how much she missed him and how she needed him back home right now to help her get through this. He was so practical and down to earth, he'd know what to do, what to say. He'd make sure she'd tell the police officer the important details, and prompt her to remember the things she'd missed as her anxiety addled her thinking. But he had gone. He had left her. And the bitter taste of resentment stung her tongue because she'd always hoped he wouldn't go through with it.

The landline began to sing a strange birdlike song. Jess ran to it. She lifted the handset to her ear abruptly and held her breath. It was the same soft tones she'd heard earlier: PC Hawthorne.

He'd tried to get hold of Adam but he wasn't answering his mobile. They'd got some CCTV images of Steph at a petrol station, the one just around the corner, and of course they'd got the last transactions she'd made on her card. A substantial amount of cash had been withdrawn. Her number plate has been flagged so they should pick the car up on traffic cameras. And did we have any family outside of London that she could be visiting?

Jess found herself writing these notes down on the pad by the phone. Steph always had a notepad to hand; it came with the territory of being a journalist and being super organised.

The pen stopped.

Her voice became thin as she explained that they had two cousins, Martha and Jacob Ellis, one lived in Scarborough and the other in Manchester, but they hadn't seen them since their aunt and uncle's funeral and that was way over ten years ago.

PC Hawthorne asked for her cousins' full names and thanked her for the details. She slid the handset back into its cradle.

They will find her. She's leaving a trace. Could she really be going to visit her cousins, or even our childhood home? She couldn't stop her mind from looping back to the past. Their cousins. They tried to appear before her but she didn't want to see their mournful teenage faces in her mind's eye. Jess attempted to swallow but her throat tightened further.

I couldn't visit them. What would I say? But then again, I still don't know what my darling sister knows or doesn't know about our cousins.

Goosebumps prickled her arms again. The short-sleeved shirt wasn't keeping her warm. In the doorway, hanging up next to her coat was one of Steph's cardigans. She slipped it on and pulled it tightly around her.

PC Hawthorne had asked her to get Adam to call him when he returned. She hoped it would be some time before he did so. She was gradually convincing herself that he was hiding something.

No one calls the speaking clock to hear the time do they? TV, mobiles, watches even, surely in this day and age you don't need the speaking clock? And he spoke to someone. He definitely spoke to someone. And then the words 'substantial withdrawal' hit her ears again.

Where is she planning to go? Jess's train of thought couldn't be continued as the sound of a car engine came to a stop outside the door.

31st Jan 2017

I cried as soon as A left for work. I can't bear to be alone. I know I'm not alone, I know I have my beautiful gorgeous girl with me, but what protection does she offer me? And what protection can I offer her?

I'm exhausted, after feeding her and tending to her all night. I think I managed an hour's sleep at the most and I can't get him out my head. I think back to the last time we made love, just before I found out I was finally pregnant.

Like teenagers, we snuck off to the forest after work, we raced each other, dressed in our running gear. Who would suspect? Me running ahead of him, giggling and feeling the thrill of anticipation.

The forest has many paths, but we didn't stick to them. We found a secluded area, densely packed and where the snapping of twigs and the crunching of bark would alert us to someone's presence. I loved the danger, the possibility that someone could catch a glimpse of us. It all adds to the excitement and the ecstasy of the chase.

I remember his fingers caressing my lips. Tracing my neck until it found the fabric of my top. He pushed down my leggings until they trapped my ankles. I pushed off my trainers and freed my feet so I could wrap my legs around his hips. And against a tree, slowly and tenderly and then quick, hard, passionate. HIM holding me, his breathing quick in my ear. I can still feel his hands on my breasts – and now I can see his face as his body relaxed, and that's how I want to remember him. With tender eyes and desire lingering on his lips.

But the message in the card has created another person. A new side to him and I spent most of the night panicking that he'd come back. Every sound in the house, the creaking of expanding pipes, the wind rattling in the chimney, and even A's movements in bed set me on edge. Shit. I can barely keep my eyes open as I write.

The post arrived with a thump and even that made me tremble today. As I walked towards the door to pick it up I could make out a shape moving down the path. The outline of a man was steadily forming as it moved closer to the door.

I instinctively ducked down and crawled towards the post, hoping I couldn't be seen through the glass. I scooped up the mass of magazines, envelopes and junk mail and held it close to me, hugging myself for protection.

I sat against the wall to the side of the door and closed my eyes. I could hear the footsteps approaching. Large heavy footsteps of a man. They stopped. He was here.

The letterbox clicked and I opened my eyes and watched it slowly open.

Through the gap he bellowed that he knew I was alone. That he would, if necessary force me to take N for a paternity test. That he would return when A was here and tell him.

I remained silent. I held my breath. Before he left he added that I needed to be careful. Perhaps I shouldn't go for a walk today.

My stomach lurched. He's been watching us, watching as I take her out in the pram to send her off to sleep. I wanted to poke something sharp through the letterbox. Make him go away, but his quick steps told me he had left.

I crawled back down the hallway, just in case he was standing at the end of the path watching.

N was just waking up from a nap. She deserves so much better, she deserves someone who will put their family first and not me. Not me. I've destroyed everything that I dreamed of. I must protect her. Keep her safe. We won't be going out today.

* * *

By the time Mum had arrived I had worked myself up into a frenzied state of anxiety. I told her about the threats. I want to go to the police, but she's right, I don't have any evidence because I destroyed the card. I had to. I couldn't bear the words hanging around in the house. I should have got rid of the flowers too.

And what would I tell them? She still believes I shouldn't tell A the truth, but she thinks that he needs to know about the threats.

I'm not sure what to tell him, how can I explain the threats without confessing to the affair? Mum says I need to stay calm. She'll think of something, she'll sort it out, just like she did when we were kids, she's always been good at solving problems.

I wish she and A got on better, it would make things easier for all of us if she could stay over, but he likes his space and doesn't like her 'interfering'.

Missing Day One

Jess

Jess raced into the kitchen and flicked the switch on the kettle. She needed to look busy. Reaching into the cupboard beneath the sink she pulled out the Dettol spray to clean the sink and add authenticity to her cover-up. Poking out of the bin which clung to the cupboard door was a bouquet of flowers. The heads were in full bloom and she wondered why they'd been unceremoniously shoved in the bin.

A few squirts of Dettol sent a lemony scent into the air and mug rings disappeared in a wave of a cloth. As she replaced the spray, the flowers slid to one side and the lid of the bin removed itself as the door opened. They were still beautiful, delicate pink and white flowers. *Why are they in the bin?*

She measured out the coffee grinds, carefully, so not to spill any, like a test to make sure her hands weren't trembling. They weren't. They were strong and steady. Steam swirled around the top of the cafetière as bronze bubbles lined the surface of the black liquid.

The sound of a key biting the lock announced Adam's arrival, boots were slipped off and his feet padded down the hallway into the kitchen.

'Coffee?'

'Yes. Good job I won't be sleeping much anyway. I've lost track of how many cups I've had today.' His mouth attempted a smile, but only one corner managed to rise. He edged towards the kitchen table and slumped into a seat.

'I'll be wired tonight, too. I assume you didn't find anything? I mean, on my way here, I kept thinking that this is a mistake and she ended up staying at a friend's, and because she hadn't taken her mobile she couldn't tell you. She'll turn up and be all apologetic about the panic she's caused.'

'Wishful thinking. I'm pretty sure she knows my number and yours too; I remember seeing her filling a form in recently and I was impressed that she'd remembered my number. I don't recall hers.' His face crumpled a little, he was clearly recollecting the moment.

'Yes, I'm pretty useless at remembering numbers. Don't need to, do you?' She placed the coffee in front of him. Steam danced around the lip of the mug.

'I know it was futile driving around here, I mean she's probably miles away now, but I just needed to go and look for myself and driving has always cleared my head a little.'

'The police called.'

He was about to take a sip of the hot black liquid but paused and set the mug down again. She wondered whether the mention of the police would set the shaking and sweating off again.

'Yes, I saw the missed call while I was driving, so I stopped and called them back. At least they are letting us know when they find things. I want to know every detail of what they are doing to find them. I don't feel like I'm in control of anything, you know?'

'We have to assume they are doing all they can. He asked about visting any family we have outside of London. I doubt she'll visit our cousins.'

Jess found herself wiping down the surfaces again, removing the new rings caused by the mugs and coffee pot. Her hand lingered on the pack of baby wipes left amongst the kitchen the detritus.

Just because there is no way I'd visit our cousins, doesn't mean that Steph wouldn't. She was close to them when we were growing up, closer to them than I was.

A memory attempted to form, of her, Steph and their two cousins running through long grass, poppies everywhere, the four of them laughing. *Not now. Not now.*

The feeling that she'd wake up at any moment kept pricking her subconscious and everything she did seemed to be part of an automatic response system, or a choreographed dream. She stopped cleaning and moved towards the table and stood opposite Adam.

He put the coffee down and sighed. 'She wouldn't go and stay with them would she? I mean she's never mentioned them, I think they sent cards, but I can't remember.'

Another picture of her cousins formed in her mind. Jacob and Martha, transformed from frolicking in meadows into forlorn and pale-looking figures clad in black. Then their Victorian house began to materialise. She could see their door, but she wouldn't let her mind enter *that* house, not now, not today.

'Probably not, I think she's more likely to go and stay in a hotel; she withdrew a load of cash according to the police.'

'Yeah, I don't get it. Shit. None of this makes any sense.'

He pushed his chair backwards and a scraping sound made Jess wince. He ran the tap and filled and drained his glass of water. Jess watched his hands. They weren't shaking like before. He confidently set the glass down on the kitchen worktop.

'Are you sure we haven't missed anything?' She searched his eyes, he seemed unable to make eye contact whenever she asked him a question.

He looked out of the kitchen window and rubbed his temple. 'As I said, she was exhausted. She was on edge.'

The shadows below his eyes seemed to have darkened another deeper shade of purple. His square jaw moved from side to side and his deep brown eyes darted around the room as though he was looking for something that he had physically missed.

'On edge?'

'Yes, I guess, because she was tired and because it was the first time she'd been left alone. I mean, it must have been hard for her, you know. She'd had me, family and friends round nearly all the time since we came back from hospital. She told me it was a huge adjustment, to have all those people around and then nothing. She... oh god, Jess, where is she? Where's my baby girl?'

Silent tears fell onto his chest, leaving perfect circles on his black sweatshirt. Jess moved towards him and embraced his muscular frame.

She pictured Matt encircling her in a protective embrace as he had done so on many occasions, and despite the anger she'd felt towards him when he left, now all she wanted was him by her side, telling her things would be all right.

She held him until his crying ceased and then released him. Taking a step away she placed her hand on his shoulder to restore a distance between them.

'Come on.' She shepherded him to the dining room and pulled out a chair for him, which he sank in to.

In the corner of the room she could see Natalie's baby stuff. Her playmat was neatly folded, and placed on top of it was her bouncy chair filled with stuffed toys. All her comforts. Steph hadn't taken any. A tear wove its way down Jess's cheek into her mouth.

'When was the last time you ate?'

'Ages ago, I'm not hungry.' Adam replied.

'I'll make you something anyway, you need to keep your strength up.' She winced at the trite phrase.

She left him alone and went to prepare lunch. She tried to picture her sister in a hotel room; perhaps she's lying on the bed feeding Natalie, perhaps... but the picture wouldn't form. She felt disconnected. *There's so much I don't understand. A puzzle piece, or several pieces are missing, along with my sister.*

She carried the sandwiches she'd made through to Adam who was still slumped in the chair and staring at the table, frozen exactly in the same pose she'd left him in. She followed his gaze to the sideboard under the window which was filled with 'congratulations on your new baby girl' cards.

'So many cards,' Jess murmured. 'And that bouquet of flowers in the middle there. They are beautiful.'

'From my office. Yeah, so many cards. Steph was popular. Is popular. Fuck, I can't start talking about her in the past tense, can I? I mean she's just having a moment, right? Things have got too much for her and she's having some sort of breakdown. The police are right, aren't they? That's what they think.'

Jess nodded, barely acknowledging him, shunning his panic. She moved towards the cards and began to read the inscriptions.

'She, she wouldn't do anything silly? I mean, she's exhausted, not thinking straight, but...' He shook his head and then covered his face with his palms.

Jess tried not to laugh, the word 'silly' seemed so inappropriate, and came as a shock. A shock that he'd verbalise his jump to a conclusion.

'Something silly, like what, commit suicide? Fucking hell Adam, are you really suggesting that?' She remained standing and realised she'd raised her voice and probably appeared a little aggressive. She dropped down into the chair next to him.

'I can't think straight, my wife and newborn baby have disappeared. I mean, what else am I supposed to think?'

'I didn't like your choice of words, that she could have done something silly. She's having a meltdown. She needs a break.'

The colour drained from his face. When he finally looked up he stared directly into Jess's eyes.

'Yes. I'm starting to think that she couldn't cope and that's why she's gone. She's trying to escape herself.'

Jess shook her head. 'Escape herself? Do something silly? No. Not Steph. Needing a break? Showing us all that she's not coping. Yes. That makes sense to me.'

Her sister was the classic elder sister. The one who always coped. Who not only mopped up Jess's tears in a crisis, but also their mother's. It had always been this way. She was their go-to, their port in a storm.

Jess could even feel her arms around her now, cradling her, just like when Matt left, wiping her tears and putting her to bed after she'd drained a whole bottle of wine.

She could hear her sister's voice whispering to her, telling her that she'd be OK, that he'd come back and that he needed some space to clear his head. That he'd forgive her accusations and her silly suspicions. Space and time would show him what he was missing. *Some space. A whole world's worth to be exact.*

Her sister's hypnotic soothing voice lingered in her ears. She was strong. Steph didn't just crumble in a heap.

She perused the cards and contemplated the photographs of Steph with Natalie. She desperately tried to focus on her image of Steph, the strong big sister who always came to the rescue, and not the image of a new mum struggling with the weight of responsibility of a newborn baby.

Jess took a bite of her sandwich and the bread lodged in her throat. Like Adam she wasn't hungry, either. The uneaten food sat on the mahogany table, a rich deep colour which today seemed to suck all the light out of the room rather than warm it up.

Clearing away their uneaten sandwiches, she slid the plates into the dishwasher. She heard Adam leave the dining room and plod through to the lounge. She stuck her head around the door.

'Do you want me to stay tonight? I'll need to pop home and get my stuff.'

'Would you stay? That would be great. I'll run you home.' He made eye contact, briefly.

'Yes, I'll stay. But I need some air, and a tube journey always helps me think. Plus, you should stay here in case Steph comes home. See you later.'

He nodded and she heard the TV kick in as she retreated to the hallway. She pulled on her coat and slipped on her heels. There was something sharp inside her left shoe. She bent her foot towards her calf and took off the shoe and vigorously gave it a shake.

A stone flew out, bounced on the wooden floor and came to rest next to a small piece of paper which looked like a receipt. She picked it up with the intention of popping it in the bin, but the date and time stamped in the middle of the paper stopped her.

It wasn't a receipt. It was a parking ticket. It was dated today, and the time read just after one. Adam was driving around, looking for Steph during this time, but the parking ticket suggested otherwise. Other than the date and time and the name of the company who operated the scheme, there was nothing else to tell her where Adam had parked. *Has he given up already? Did he simply just sit in his car and hold his head in his hands as he's done since PC Hawthorne left?*

Slipping the ticket into her pocket she left the house without saying goodbye. Her footsteps quickened as she walked down The Orchards in the direction of the station.

31st Jan 2017

The relief I felt when A returned from work was indescribable. Imprisoned in our home. Awaiting his arrival. I know he'll tell A. It's only a matter of time.

I keep hearing his words in my head over and over again. And then Mum's words about not bringing up N alone. It was hard for her. Being a single mum back then was difficult. And she's right. I'm not strong like her. I couldn't cope alone. I need A. He's always protected me.

I know I should tell him about the threats. The fact that he's been watching us come and go will persuade A to keep us safe. I need to tell him something, something that will convince him to help me, to stop the intimidation. Something which will make A rescue me again like he did before.

I must be the victim. He is the pursuer, the stalker, the one clearly in the wrong. A memory keeps pushing itself forward. Emails. Horrible, disgusting emails. I pictured the emails from before. Before maternity leave. They spurred me on.

* * *

I told A that my colleague had a thing for me. That nothing happened but he'd been following me. Turning up when I was out interviewing people, researching stories. Making sure he got the same tube as me on the way home from work and insisting that he'd accompany me home even though it's out of his way.

I explained I hadn't said anything before because I felt sorry for him. He was having a difficult time at work and his fiancé had just left him and I was sure he didn't mean to scare me. He said he was in love with me and I knew his behaviour was wrong, but I didn't want to cause him any trouble.

He then took to constantly emailing me, horrible, disgusting, sexual emails.

A listened intently. I watched him clasp his hands causing his knuckles to bulge. He's angry that I didn't do anything about it.

He wanted to go to the police. I told him that we should tell work first, that he needs help, not police involvement. I don't want to criminalise his actions. I described how he'd threatened to tell him that we were having an affair and how he said he'd been watching me when I was taking N out in the pram.

I explained what he'd written in the card that he gave me with the flowers.

I began to cry when I told him about the letterbox incident. I could feel the fear seep into my bloodstream again. His vehemence came back to me, his hideous words attacked me all over again. I couldn't stop shaking and sweating.

A began pacing, the muscles around his jaw began to twitch.

He said that coming to our home and threatening us isn't the behaviour of someone who is simply obsessed with me. He needs more than just 'help'.

He reassured me he wasn't going to the police, he wasn't sure what they'd do or if they'd help, but he needed to go and see him. To scare him, just like he was scaring us.

This was the last thing I wanted or expected. The fear of A discovering the real truth engulfs me. He knows so much about me. Things only someone intimate would know.

I couldn't stop him. A said he needed to protect us and make him understand that if he comes near us again we will go to the police. He wasn't listening to me. There was a coldness in his eyes, like a light had faded.

* * *

When A returned he said they'd exchanged words and that he denied everything, but he didn't think he'd be bothering me again.

He held me, he was shaking. I wasn't sure if he believed me.

He didn't tell me what was said.

He couldn't look me in the eye.

I know he knows the truth.

Missing Day One

Jess

Jess's key slid into the door. Pushing it open, she felt the familiar brush of the draft excluder swishing across the coconut hair mat. Those sounds always comfort her, signifying that she's back to safety after a long day's work. Safe. That is what she felt here, so unlike the gradual creeping dread that had filled her blood at her sister's home.

On the doormat lay a postcard. The second one she'd received from Matt, and this one pictured an enormous temple in Thailand. She imagined him taking in the sights and being a tourist. Was he enjoying his time alone? Or was he missing her as acutely as she was missing him? The postcard was a welcome diversion.

She pressed it to her nose and inhaled deeply but she couldn't pick out his scent. He'd worn the same aftershave since university. Subtle spicy aromas with a hint of something floral and musky.

She could almost smell it as she pictured the first time he confessed he loved her. Closing her eyes, the memory of him sitting opposite her in the dingy student pub back in her hometown of Sheffield began to play.

* * *

As usual he was fiddling with a beer mat, spinning it, fraying the cardboard edges. Normally he'd chat while destroying it, but today he was uncharacteristically silent.

'Get your poker face on,' he grimaced and drained the last of his wine. 'I've split up with Elaine.'

Jess kept very still, she made sure that the corners of her mouth didn't break into a smile, she began to worry that she actually had something on her face as Matt stared at her so intensely that she had the urge to rub her cheek.

'Good. Good poker face.'

'Wow. That's a surprise.'

'Is it?'

'Well, the last few weeks of the semester you were both pretty vocal in the bedroom, so I assumed that all was pretty rosy in the garden of shag.'

She'd had to endure Elaine's vocalisations nearly every night, the walls in their run-down student house were paper thin.

'Why do you always make a dig about my sex life?'

'Because if I had the same amount of men visiting my bed as you, I'd be considered the university bike. And I'm jealous of your sex life compared with my non-existent one.'

She hoped that he hadn't noticed her blush. She refilled their wine glasses. 'So, what happened?'

'I don't know, I was kind of spellbound by her for a while. She was different to the others. But, it wasn't right, something was missing or in the way. I don't know,' he sighed.

Jess bit her lip, she hoped that her desire wasn't etched into her eyes.

'But when it got to the summer she wanted to come and stay with me and I realised that I'd been looking forward to spending my summer the way I wanted to. Alone, or with Dad or Mum, and with you.'

Jess looked out of the window. She couldn't trust herself. If she met his eyes she knew she wouldn't be able to resist telling him how she really felt.

'She didn't really get why I wanted to spend time with you,' he continued. 'She seemed jealous and she was always at ours, always wanting me to do everything with her, so I really needed the holidays to myself.'

'Have you not seen her at all then?'

'Saw her at the start of the hols.'

'Please tell me you didn't end it by text?'

'God you really don't fucking think much of me, do you?'

'Bloody hell Matt, chillax. I'm sorry. I know that's not your style.'

'Sorry, I just feel – oh anyway, no I called her and met her earlier today. I told her that I'd had fun, I really liked her, the sex was great but I thought she was looking for more commitment and I wasn't looking for that.'

Jess glanced towards the bar. The low ceiling made the bar always appear so drab and uninviting. Today only a few other people occupied the odd seat scattered around the pub. Mostly men, making pints of beer last for ever while staring up at the screens that currently showed the cricket.

Jess shifted awkwardly in her seat. 'Did you tell her that you were coming to mine for the weekend?'

'No. She cried loads. I'm crap with tears. I've only ever seen you cry, and it's normally not my fault.'

'True, you normally make me laugh.' She pictured Elaine and felt sorry for her; she was besotted with Matt, she followed him around like a puppy, was always at his side, too much for him, not his style at all.

'Feel quite flat though. Flat bordering on down. That was the longest relationship I've had. Three months.'

Jess couldn't help but smirk. '"Flat, bordering on down."' She made quotation marks with her fingers. 'You are allowed to be sad even when you do the dumping.'

She paused and took a slow sip of wine, 'Do you think she loved you?'

She held his gaze for a moment but returned to her view of the street. Her eyes followed an odd-looking man wearing a ridiculously oversized hat. She prevented a grin from forming.

'She never said it but I think she did. Fuck I didn't mean to hurt her. I kept thinking that perhaps I should keep seeing her and then maybe eventually I'd end up falling in love with her.' He turned his head to look out at the street, too.

'I'm pretty sure it doesn't work like that, not that I know that much about love.'

Jess tried very hard not to blush, she traced the circular base of the wine glass with her index finger. Sunlight streamed into the pub and she scrunched her eyes to shield them from its glare.

'No, it doesn't work like that. I know that. I know what love feels like.'

He was sounding increasingly defensive and his voice sounded strained. Jess finally looked at him. His cheeks were burning up.

'Do you? Have I missed something? Who have you been in love with other than your beloved Arsenal?' Her fingers froze and she felt the tension spread throughout her body. She wanted him to say it, to tell her.

'You.'

Jess felt her cheeks tingle as the heat spread across her face and down her neck. 'Me?'

'Oh for fuck's sake. Yes. You. It's always been you. I know you don't love me, well not like that, you see me as the brother you don't have. I know you're not interested in me in that way.'

A giggle escaped her lips.

'Great. You really are something.' He stood up abruptly and the wine glass wobbled as he used the table to steady himself.

'No, no.' She supressed her laughter. 'Sit down, I'm sorry, I'm sorry. Don't go.'

He stood still for a moment, his face stern, but he couldn't resist the urge to stay. He slunk back down into his seat.

'I'm laughing because it took me a while to realise it too. I don't love you like a brother. I love *you*. I never thought you'd be interested in me. Best friends, nothing more. We've always made that pretty clear, haven't we?'

'Yes we have.'

She reached across the table and took his hands.

'I love you, not as a brother, and more than a best friend.'

She stood up, walked around the table and sat next to him. She held his hands again and gazed into his eyes.

'I love you.'

She leaned in and kissed him, gently pressing her lips against his, and teasing her tongue inside his mouth. After the kiss they kept their eyes closed and rested their foreheads against each other's, staying still and silent in the moment.

* * *

Jess opened her eyes and touched her forehead. Despite the memory feeling like it was a lifetime ago, she could still feel the touch of his head against hers.

I'd love to go back to before we started living together, before my inability to trust anyone took over. Why did I accuse him of having a fling? Why do I always have to screw things up?

The feeling that she'd pushed him away was ever present, always lurking in the background, colouring her perceptions, driving her anger inwards.

She stared at the postcard. Re-read the words. Yes, he was having a good time, but these weren't the words she really wanted to hear. She wanted him to tell her that he was on the next plane home. That he was wrong. He shouldn't have run. He should have helped her face her demons together. Now her sadness was fading as the anger built.

He left me. We could have worked things out, but he fucked off and is keeping me on hold. I know I should have been more open with him. If he could have given me just a bit more time, then I would have opened up, told him about my childhood, and explained it all.

She stuffed the postcard into the recycling. She didn't want to see the stunning Buddhist temple staring at her, mocking her. The knot in her intestines was squeezing ever tighter.

She kicked the recycling box before retreating out of the kitchen to her bedroom to pack an overnight bag. She stuffed her clothes into a large navy weekender bag and hurled it into the small hallway. She wanted to eke out more time alone before returning to the oppressive atmosphere of her sister's house. She flung herself onto the sofa and checked her work emails. Her deputy had efficiently answered the urgent emails and highlighted the non-urgent ones. Jess sighed, at least one facet of her life was under control. She squeezed the on button of the remote and the TV sprang to life as the local news was just beginning. A&E waiting times were at their highest, an item about a team of women cyclists raising money to help the homeless, and a police appeal for information about a man who was assaulted in his home.

She half expected to hear the newscaster ask for information about her sister. Not yet. That will be next. Tomorrow morning she'd have been missing for forty-eight hours. So far the police didn't have much information to piece together about her whereabouts. They were all vulnerable.

She flicked off the TV and put her coat back on. Her trainers lay upturned in the small hallway; wearing them she could at least run to and from the station to ease the anxiety that held a firm grip over her. As she straightened up, a gentle creak of a floorboard sounded in her bedroom, a stone's throw away from where she stood. She opened the cupboard in the hallway to check the heating. The old converted flat often creaked and groaned whenever the heating was on. The timer indicated that it would be another hour before the heating was due to kick in.

She tentatively pushed open her bedroom door. This morning's detritus was left untouched. An odd blue haze enveloped the room as the late winter sun began its descent. She stood in the doorway, listening intently. A noise from the lounge then made her spin around. The small flat made it easy for her to see from the bedroom doorway straight through to the floor to ceiling windows in the lounge. Of course there was nothing there. No movement. Just a stillness that reminded her how alone she was. She shook herself and reassured her anxiety riddled brain that it was simply a noise from upstairs.

She tightened her laces and stepped out again onto the street, retracing her steps back to Leytonstone tube station. Once on the train she put her headphones on and shut her eyes for the entire journey. She didn't want to see or think about anything.

The February gloom clung to the streets of Epping. The wind had long since stopped hurling rain at the commuters and now the clouds brought darkness as the invisible sun sank low in the sky somewhere west over central London.

Her trainers provided a welcome respite from heels as she jogged from the station to her sister's house. She pulled the hood over her head and felt her pace quicken as the music sped up. It was a short run, but enough to release some tension.

Breathless, she rang the doorbell. Adam slowly made his way towards her, she could make out his body shape through the terrible frosted glass.

'I don't know why you two haven't changed this door. I hate the frosted glass. It's so old fashioned and kind of creepy.'

The colour drained from Adam's face. 'Funny, that's exactly what Steph said. Near word perfect. You are so alike, not just in appearance but your tastes—'

Jess interrupted him. 'Our tastes are very different. I think it's a female thing, you know we prefer either to see clearly or be hidden.'

Slipping off her shoes, she pushed them neatly under the dresser and followed Adam into the lounge. He sat in the chair next to the phone, his legs spreading to take up the space.

She wondered if he had consciously positioned himself next to the phone, so he could leap on it as soon as the police called. Her body felt devoid of energy as she slumped down on the sofa and tuned into the TV. *More news. Normally I'll absorb as much news as possible but today I want to hide from it.*

She looked at the phone now, hoping that the only news she'd receive would be via that handset, telling her that her sister was on her way home. She noted Adam's frame. A trace of muscle tone lingered on his arms, but his gut was becoming loose; if he wasn't careful the working long lunches would give him a paunch.

She thought of Matt's physique. Not muscular, but toned from the running and cycling they used to do together. She closed her eyes in order to fully appreciate the memory of her absent partner.

Adam's voice broke her musings.

'I'm not surprised you feel that way about doors. I mean where you live, well it's not as salubrious as sleepy Epping. So many burglaries and attacks in Leytonstone.'

'Oh thanks, you know how to make a single woman feel safe.'

He winced. 'Sorry, I didn't mean to – oh you know what I mean, you knew what it was like when you moved there.'

'Yes, the not so trendy neighbour to Wanstead and South Woodford. I don't know why me and Matt have a soft spot for it, but we do. And actually I do feel safe there. OK, I wouldn't walk home by myself at night, but you know, shit happens everywhere doesn't it? I saw a news item earlier about a man who was attacked in his home here in Epping.'

He stood up abruptly and she heard him audibly swallow.

'Yes, you're right, shit happens everywhere. Glass of water?' She nodded and leaned forward to reach the remote to change the channel. She'd had enough of the news today.

Part Two

Adam

Adam fumbled in the darkness, his hand exploring the carpet down by the side of the bed to retrieve the phone. Eyes still closed, fingers finding the cancel button, he silenced the alarm. He stretched and looked over at Steph, expecting to see her eyes softly closed, but she was awake. Eyes wide. He moved towards her and kissed her on the forehead.

'How did Monday happen?' he asked.

'It comes after Sunday, it's inevitable.'

Steph smiled, it didn't encourage him to want to get out of bed. He stroked her forehead, teased out a strand of hair and began to twist the brunette lock around his finger.

He was about to put the tendril back, trace his fingers down her neck and stroke her breast, but he stopped. Sex had not been put back on the agenda yet, and she'd never been keen on morning sex not since the early days of their relationship.

But still, a man can hope? He glanced at her heaving cleavage before rolling over and hauling himself out of bed.

'Ugh. Suppose I best go iron a shirt.'

A warm smile spread to his eyes as he caught sight of his daughter enveloped in a deep slumber. Her little arms were raised above her head and her hands made two tiny fists. She had surrendered herself to sleep. Finally. He recalled rolling over several times in the night to find that his wife was absent from his side.

He wanted to kiss her forehead, but instead he crept away from the Moses basket to the en suite hoping the sound of the shower wouldn't wake her and she'd allow Steph to get some much needed rest.

But, of course, the noise did wake her and when he slowly opened the door he saw his wife sat up in bed peacefully feeding Natalie.

An automatic smile spread across his thin lips. They both looked so beautiful; a perfect little unit.

Pulling on his dressing gown he registered a hint of the coldness that would meet him when he left for work. He tightened the cord in an attempt to shut out the chill and picked out a powder pink shirt. He'd always worn pink, but being surrounded by all the baby girl outfits and pink teddies, it seemed all the more fitting to wear it on his return to work.

The kitchen was still and the clunking sound of the ironing board folding down shattered the peace. The iron hissed to life as the steam blew through the holes indicating that it was ready to use. Adam wondered what Steph's day would be like without him as he stretched the shirt across the board. As the iron smoothed over the material he wished that he could have just one more day savouring the cuddles with his beautiful Natalie.

The creases were efficiently removed and he returned to the bedroom to dress. He watched Steph winding Natalie on her shoulder, and made a mental note not to hold her when dressed – pink shirt he'd get away with, baby sick down his jacket, would not do.

He slung his jacket over his shoulder. 'Cup of tea?'

'Just a glass of water. I'll be out in a minute.'

He noticed the catch in her voice and moved towards her wrapping his arms around her waist. He kissed Natalie on the top of her head and inhaled her newness and wondered when that smell would disappear. He acknowledged that with every amazing moment of babyhood there was a hint of melancholy as time marches forever forward towards the ascent of adulthood. A lump formed in his throat.

He'd miss her terribly; he'd enjoyed two weeks of quiet cuddles and the rush of love which continued to wash over him like lapping waves, a tide of love building, not to a crescendo, but a steady constant swell.

'You'll be fine. Honestly, what use have I been?'

'True,' she attempted to smile, 'but I'll be lonely on my own.'

'Phone a friend?'

'All my friends are at work.' A tear made its way down her cheek. He put his finger in its way and gently made it disappear.

'Your new mummy friends from NCT, silly. I know Sally's in hospital, but the others haven't dropped yet, so give them a call. You should pay Rachel a visit as they've been over to us. You can drive over can't you? Be good to get out and about.'

Adam moved in to kiss her, she returned it, but with less enthusiasm. He recognised there wasn't anything he could do to fix how she was feeling, and resisted suggesting anything else, as he knew all too well that despite his urge to problem-solve, all she wanted was a shoulder and an ear. He'd listened. That was enough.

Breakfast eaten, coffee poured into his takeaway cup and shoes on, he kissed Natalie, told her to look after Mummy and to keep her amused. He kissed Steph and whispered that he'd call her at lunch.

Door closed. Headphones on. Tie in briefcase. Adam was ready to return to work. Yes, he'd miss his wife and beautiful daughter and the longing to stay was strong, but he was also beginning to miss the camaraderie of his team, and his emails told him his clients were missing his attention to detail.

His office was filled with gifts: flowers, shiny gift bags and a bloody balloon. He tried to hide his natural irritation at the prospect of lugging the gifts back on the tube plus the balloon.

'Hello there, Daddy!' The familiar tones of the team secretary hit his ears and he turned around to see Roseanne entering the office with her arms full of post and paperwork. 'You actually look like you've managed to sleep during these past few weeks. Congratulations. The pictures you sent of her, oh she's so gorgeous. Looks exactly like Steph.'

Roseanne moved towards him and gave him a congratulatory kiss on the cheek.

'Thanks Roseanne, she is adorable.'

'How are you finding it?'

'Good, bit knackering, but you know all good.'

'And Steph? How's she doing?'

'She's besotted, tired, and emotional, but she's loving the feeding and cuddles. I'm not loving the nappies.'

'At least you are doing your bit. Now I've put a couple of files on your desk that I think you should check out after you've gone through your emails, if you get the time today of course.' Roseanne was a larger than life presence in the office. Her voice boomed around the room even when she was attempting to conduct a discreet phone call.

'Thanks. All been good here?'

'Yes, sorry I can't tell you that the wheels have fallen off in your absence,' she chortled.

'Thanks Rose, I can see I'm dispensable. Perhaps I should take a career break?'

'Oh god don't do that. I'm not sure I can cope with Malcolm's ego or constant grumpiness.' Roseanne glanced behind her to check that Malcolm hadn't just walked through the door.

'Just kidding. Thanks for managing without me.' He smirked and raised his eyebrows. Roseanne returned the smirk and returned to man the desk by the office door.

After the initial flurry of other colleagues popping into his office to congratulate him and bestow more gifts, Adam's day continued as it always did and he soon found himself ready for lunch.

He was a private person, generally personal phone calls were made outside of the office, so he walked through Minster Court towards Fenchurch Street, hoping to grab a few minutes without bumping into anyone from the market.

It wasn't easy, Adam knew so many faces; he'd worked in insurance since he'd left university and despite it being a large industry he was well known.

The wind sliced through his coat and made people quicken their pace in order to retreat back inside, there were no familiar faces queuing for coffee at the stand in the courtyard outside the station, it was too cold to hang around today.

He turned his back to the wind, touched Steph's name and smiled in anticipation of her answering. Her mobile rang until it went to voicemail. He called the landline, again she didn't pick up. It surprised him, he'd expected her to answer, especially as it was her first day on her own and she said she'd feel lonely.

Maybe that was it, she'd taken his advice and was out with her NCT friends. He called her mobile again and left her a message. Pulling up his collar to shut out the icy wind, he marched back to the warmth of his office.

Lunch, meetings, drinks and home. Day one at the office done. And he couldn't wait to get back to Steph and Natalie.

The ache of longing to hold his daughter was a surprise to him, he felt butterflies in his stomach and that rush of love that kept on growing whenever he pictured his newborn daughter's face.

It was a surprise to him, because he hadn't felt paternal throughout the pregnancy, but as soon as he held her, saw those searching eyes, it had kicked in. He was a dad. And he loved it. Every minute of it. Even the sleepless nights when he rocked her back to sleep after Steph had fed her. The morning snuggles in bed. The fight with the kicking legs when trying to dress her. Bath time, carefully pouring water on her hair avoiding her eyes and then wrapping her up in the hooded towel and cuddling her dry. All of it. He wanted time to stop so he could appreciate it and hold every moment in his mind.

He arrived back home laden down with presents for Steph and Natalie. Before moving down the hallway he gently set the gifts down and he could hear Steph singing lullabies to Natalie and assumed she was getting ready for bed. The balloon attempted to tangle itself around his arm. He batted it away.

He hadn't thought about what time to get home and now realised that he might only get five minutes with his daughter before she went to bed. He took off his tie, draped it over the dining chair and traced his footsteps back a few paces to the bedroom.

Steph didn't turn around as he entered, her eyes firmly fixed on Natalie wrapped up in a blanket in the Moses basket. She stood still, singing a lullaby in barely audible tones. He crept towards her, slid his arms around her waist and nuzzled into her neck as he joined in with her low singing.

Natalie's eyes were unable to resist sleep. He pushed the mobile of stars which hung over the basket, and it rotated in a soothing motion. Together Adam and Steph silently slipped out of the room.

'I hadn't really thought about how I'll only see her for a few minutes each day when I'm back from work,' he whispered as they paused outside their bedroom to softly close the door. He held her hand and squeezed it gently, a sign to her that he needed reassurance.

'Yes.'

Steph sighed and walked away from him. She didn't squeeze his hand back as she usually did. He followed her to the kitchen where she began to stir something bubbling on the hob. It wasn't the response he was expecting, he thought she'd at least offer some comforting words.

'How was your day? Did you go and see friends?'

He poured himself a glass of water and leaned against the counter watching her tend to supper. The aroma of garlic and spices wafted his way causing his stomach to rumble.

Steph didn't look at him, she just continued to stir the food.

'No one was free today. I took her for a walk out in the pram but I found that exhausting. We stayed at home, just relaxed.'

'Probably for the best, you still need to rest. Not too lonely though?'

'A little.'

Adam moved towards her and caressed her upper arm. Her muscles tensed as her body stiffened.

'But you were OK, I mean you would have called me back if you needed a chat?' He traced his finger down her spine and stroked the small of her back.

'I'm fine. It was so quiet without you. We did miss you.' He noticed that her eyes brimmed with tears.

'Here, go and sit down, I'll finish this. The chilli smells amazing.' He took over the stirring.

Steph complied and sat down for a moment before getting up again to remove the plates from the cupboard and free the rice from the rice cooker.

'Honestly, you sit. I'll sort.'

'It's fine. If I sit down I'll fall asleep.' There was a detached edge to her voice.

Together they readied their evening meal, a dance of silence, movements mirroring each other, both unable to reach out to the other. They carried their plates to the dining room. It was a habit they both insisted on; evening meals together in the dining room, away from the kitchen even though they could sit at the cosy kitchen table – it transformed supper together into more of an occasion. To Adam, the kitchen table said, grab a bite to eat and then run. The separate dining room made him think of leisurely lunches, a place for conversation as well as eating. A place where they'd always catch up on each other's days.

Supper was consumed in silence. Only the sound of forks scraping against the plate ruptured the peace. Steph ate a little, but she pushed most of the food around the plate.

Adam felt a despondency wash over him. He'd expected her to greet him with excited chatter. Ask how his first day back had been, and though he reasoned that she was tired, he'd expected her to register at least some interest. It's what they'd always do after a day's work and he didn't think that returning home tonight would be any different.

Yes, looking after a newborn is a little different, but still, they'd have things to catch up on and he wanted to know what they'd been up to because he couldn't be part of it. He pushed his chair away, it scraped the wooden floor and he began to noisily clear away the dinner detritus.

Steph remained seated. She seemed distracted, like there was something on her mind. It was the same look he'd seen on her face before she started writing an article. A look of concentration and confusion. Normally the laptop would be positioned in front of her, fingers poised before she wrote the cut and thrust of her next story.

Heavy footed he mooched back to the doorway to retrieve the gifts. He hoped to lift her mood, but when he placed the gifts down on the table her face didn't show any sign of being pleased by the generosity of his colleagues.

Together they opened the gifts and Adam found himself giving a one-way conversational commentary on each item.

'And the final one is from Liz, our MD.' He pushed the large box towards her. It was immaculately wrapped in shiny gold paper, bound up with a chunky satin red ribbon, quite unlike the other presents which conformed to the standard pink and cutesy baby wrapping.

Steph carefully removed the paper and laboriously opened the box. She took out a pair of leopard print booties for Natalie, a red coat with matching gloves and hat, and a dressing gown for her. It was silky, and thankfully not leopard print. Adam grimaced as he picked up the booties.

'I always think leopard print is tacky.'

The booties were suede and as he handled them tenderly his expression softened. 'But these are rather sweet and not tacky at all.'

'There's a card.' Her voice held one note.

Steph passed it to him, her face showed no glimmer of excitement or gratitude.

'"For when you really hear the patter of tiny feet." Cute. Best put them somewhere safe for when the time comes when she's walking. What a lovely sentiment.'

He smiled at her again, no response. Nothing. Not even a flicker at the corners. He sighed.

'Darling, perhaps you should go to bed? I mean you've hardly raised a smile at any of these gifts, so I can only assume that you've had a tough day on your own and you're exhausted.'

At this she began to cry.

'Shit, I'm sorry, that came out wrong, I mean, I know it must be hard here on your own. I missed both of you terribly.'

She remained silent. She wiped her tears away with the tissue that Adam had passed her and disappeared off to the bathroom.

'That went well,' Adam murmured as he put the cards on the sideboard along with the others and returned to the kitchen to place the large bouquet of flowers on the window ledge, next to another smaller bouquet of pink and white chrysanthemums. Steph emerged from the bathroom and hovered in the doorway.

'Did these flowers come today?'

'Yes. They're from my colleague, Jason.'

Adam thought for a moment.

'Jason – he doesn't live far away does he? Didn't we go to his house-warming?'

He paused and noticed the colour seep out of her cheeks.

'Are you OK? Have you had enough to eat today? I mean you hardly ate a thing at supper.'

'I'm exhausted, too tired to eat.' She sighed and dipped her head. 'Yes, that's him. He dropped them in earlier today.'

She abruptly turned on her heels and retreated to their bedroom. Adam stared at the space she'd vacated. Again he reflected on how it wasn't the home-coming he'd expected. He thought she'd be desperate for conversation and that she'd show him how much she'd missed him. She seemed so preoccupied and remote.

Nearly a sulk. Like I've done something wrong.

Yes, she's not sleeping well, but he'd thought she'd relax a bit more now the visitors had stopped descending, and she could do her own thing, but the house was immaculate. And that wasn't like her either; she liked a clean home, but it always looked lived in, not like a Dettol sparkling show-home. Nothing was out of place. He noticed how the usual clutter had even been tidied away, like she was attempting to preside over order and gain some control.

He remembered how she was when they first met at uni. They lived in the same halls of residence, they liked the same music and both loved an argument about politics. Him conservative, her labour. But then all that changed after what happened to her. She became quiet and withdrawn, with an immaculate room. He sighed and pushed aside the other image of his first real love, the image that haunted him throughout his university years but had since been consigned to the past.

Adam stood by the sink and waited a while for Steph to re-emerge. But as she failed to re-materialise he realised she must have gone to bed. He wasn't tired, but he wanted to be with Steph, he would forgo the usual fruitless channel surfing. Pouring himself a glass of water, he regarded the bouquets of flowers. The office one dwarfed the one Jason had bought her. He picked up the vase and returned to the dining room. He made a space for it on the dresser in the middle of the cards. He didn't want the bouquet to dwarf the kind gift her colleague had taken the trouble to drop by.

He slid into bed beside her. He knew she was awake as her breathing was steady and lacked the depth of someone asleep.

He held her close to him and whispered in her ear.

'It's OK to have found today hard, you know. And it's also OK for you to just relax and rest and enjoy your time with Natalie. I mean, the house looks immaculate, but you're hardly sleeping and you need to rest when you can. It's important to rest.'

'I'm resting now.'

'I know, but how many times are you feeding in the night?'

'Every two hours.'

'Yes, and how much sleep are you getting in between?'

'Not much.'

She rolled over to face him. 'It was hard today without you here. I did miss you. I'm sorry I was off with you tonight. Everything is just... you know, exhausting.'

He moved towards her to kiss her, but she turned away from him again.

'You're right. I should try and sleep during the day as I'm not getting any sleep at night.'

Missing Day Two

Jess

'Thousands of people in the UK are searching for a missing loved one.' Jess found herself reading the line over and over again.

She scrolled through the thumbnail pictures of missing persons. Some photographs looked like passport images. Some were holiday headshots and others looked more like police mugshots. The images just kept on loading as she scrolled to the bottom of the homepage for Missing People, a charity that she hoped she wouldn't have to use. She didn't want to add Steph's picture to this gallery.

All the images showed adults, or teenagers. Not a single image showed a mother and child, let alone a mother and her newborn baby.

Her laptop flickered in the grey light of her sister's kitchen. The sun remained hidden behind thick billowing cloud. Rising from the table, she switched the light on and her eye took in a teddy bear resting against the white brick-shaped tiles at the back of the worktop. Rosebud pink with delicately sewn eyes and mouth. She scooped it up and held it close to her.

She returned to the laptop and sat the teddy next to it. She felt the need to go through Natalie's things. Make sure Steph had taken enough clothes for her, nappies, and those funny muslin cloths, but the images of the missing faces stared back at her, stopping her from leaving. Some appeared to have pleading eyes and they seemed to be asking her to search for them too. Others stared back defiantly. A challenge. They didn't want to be found. Which category did Steph fit into?

She became aware of Adam standing behind her, she'd not heard his slipper-less steps pad through the hallway.

'Jesus. Look at how many people are on there.'

'There's probably about three hundred pictures on their homepage.'

A shiver raced down her spine. She hovered the cursor over an image and it showed the person's name, date they disappeared, and a reference number. She moved to the page which detailed how the charity could help.

'We should call them.'

Her voice didn't sound like her own; small, child-like.

'Maybe. Let's see what the police have to say today, they might tell us to get them involved.'

In contrast, Adam's voice had recovered some of its confidence, but his pallor revealed how little he had slept. Bleary-eyed Adam began to make coffee while she continued to look at the site.

She wanted to get them involved. She wanted to get everyone involved. The whole country needed to be searching for Steph and her niece, not just the two of them and a few police officers.

The police's involvement seemed minimal and remote, there wasn't much they could do yet, she knew that, but she felt frustration surge around her body. Her fingers jabbed the arrow keys as she scrolled back up the page.

She'd spent all night trying to think of all the places her sister would go. Perhaps somewhere they'd visited when they were little? She thought about their aunt and uncle's house. Money had always been tight, so summer holidays were often spent with their cousins and on day trips to the beach.

She pictured the four of them roaming the fields at the end of their cousin's street. Climbing the trees at the far corner of their garden, or running on the sand into the sea on the several day trips they took together to Bridlington or Cleethorpes. Typical northern seaside towns. Amusements and candyfloss and usually very little sunshine despite the fact it was the summer holidays.

She could almost hear their squeals of delight and surprise as the North Sea splashed up their legs and told them a swim was out of the question, but they ignored the cold for a while and plunged in together for a quick dip while their aunt and mum watched from the beach, always wrapped up and ready with towels to dry them off.

Happy memories, not like the one she could not entertain. The one she attempted to keep locked away. That memory seemed to have a habit of resurfacing particularly at times of stress.

Not today. All my thoughts need to be focused on Steph and the here and now.

'Penny for them? You look so much like Steph. You're so alike, and you sitting there, like she often would at her laptop … for a moment this morning when I saw you from behind I thought it was her.'

'Yes, we are physically similar, but she's much prettier than me. I was thinking about when we were little. I've been trying to think of places she might go. I mean if she was still in contact with our cousins then I guess she might visit them?

I've been on her Facebook page and written a list of friends who she could possibly stay with, but in all honesty Adam she would have called by now, wouldn't she? She'd tell us who she was staying with. It's not like she's got anything to hide.'

Adam turned away from her and moved back to the sink. The tap had been dripping a little, he tightened it and began to straighten up the washing-up liquid and hand wash.

'Yes, she would. She would call us and no, she's got nothing to hide. I've made a list of people, local friends, that we could speak to.'

'Maybe we should put something on Facebook now? Get all our friends involved?' asked Jess.

Adam remained at the sink, staring out to the garden. 'I don't feel comfortable with doing that. It makes me feel like people are picking over our private life, like we are broadcasting our problems. The police will appeal for information and I'd feel much more comfortable seeking help when they get the word out.' He sighed heavily before adjusting the blind.

'Why wait? The police will be broadcasting our problems soon enough.'

'You're right, but let's wait, we don't want the police to start getting loads of calls when they aren't ready.'

'Surely that's their job and they'd welcome information.'

'Look, I hate anything that draws attention to us, to me, or anything. You know I'm a private person, it's just my way. But, I guess you're right. I'll put something on my page. I'll tag you when I've done it.'

He still didn't turn to look at her. Jess had become aware of how rarely he gave eye contact, and this, although a miniscule behaviour change, had begun to alarm her. Adam, ever the negotiator, usually made strong eye contact. The kind of eye contact that was straight out of a management training module. Open, direct, honest. The eye contact that got him the perfect deal.

Here and now, his avoidance frustrated her and his confrontational tone was making her hackles rise.

'What about work colleagues?' She refocused the conversation back to the search for information.

Keeping his back to her, he took out a bowl and a box of cornflakes from the cupboard. Cornflakes rushed out too quickly and Jess noticed how his hands were steady as he scooped the extra flakes back into the packet.

'Yes, I made a list for the police. She's close to a handful of people at work but again they'd call us or get her to call. I can't see anyone wanting to hide her or help hide her – I mean they'd have her best interest at heart and know how distraught we'd be.'

He moved to the fridge and poured out the milk. His movements were quick, light, and not laboured like they were yesterday. Today he seemed to be feeding off adrenaline and not shock.

'Have you still got the Mini?'

Finally, he turned around to engage.

'If I could borrow the Mini, maybe I could visit a few of her local friends and even work colleagues to see if they can help us, because I don't feel like we've got the true picture here.'

'I do, not driven it for a few months, it should still go. So how about you visit her friends and I'll visit work colleagues – that way we'll get it done more efficiently. You're right, we should do something rather than sit here and wait for news.'

Jess nodded. She'd been hoping he'd let her take the Mini. She was toying with the idea of driving back to their childhood home. Just in case that's where she'd gone. Back to Sheffield, not because there was anything there for her, but because it was somewhere else to hide.

That word again. It kept popping into her head. *But from what? Why would she need to hide?* Jess had spent all night trying to piece things together, but nothing readily fit, and today she just wanted to do something; she couldn't bear to sit around Steph's house and do nothing.

Steph and Natalie had now been missing for two nights. Two cold nights. At least the clouds today suggested no frost later; Jess shuddered at the thought of them both sleeping in the car if she wasn't able to find a hotel. How would she manage the driving with sleep deprivation? Her mind started to visualise her sister's car crashing into the barrier that divides the carriages of the motorway. Or her not checking her mirrors and being crushed by a lorry. Jess wanted to shake herself. She wished her anxiety would loosen its grip on her and stop playing out every worst case scenario.

The landline sounded and Adam dashed to answer it. She could hear him answer a few questions. She wanted to hear more but when she got to the lounge he wasn't speaking, just listening. He thanked PC Hawthorne and replaced the handset.

'He wanted to check in with us. They will do an information appeal later, so the word will be out soon. He said they've tracked her on the A1 and they are going through CCTV images at a service station just outside of Newark-on-Trent. So she's still alive.'

His shoulders trembled and he wiped his eyes. His hand had gripped the handset, causing his fingers to turn white. He replaced it and turned to look out of the window. Jess wished her sister's car would pull up on the drive and end all of this now.

'I keep imagining them calling and telling me they've found a body. I keep telling myself to stop thinking the worst, but the longer she doesn't call or walk through the door, well, I can't stop thinking she's done something terrible.'

He began to sob. Jess walked towards Adam and stood next to him. She still didn't feel comfortable with putting an arm around him and she didn't want to. He'd mentioned it again. The possibility that she could have taken her own life. She didn't want to engage in this conversation again.

'Where's she going? Does she know anyone in Newark? I mean it doesn't ring any bells to me. I could have a look on Facebook again?'

Adam nodded. 'Yes, let's have another look.'

Returning to her laptop, she painstakingly scrolled through her sister's Facebook friends list. Only a handful of them had their details on display for anyone to see, most of them had their profiles locked down. *Sensible, but if only they weren't so cautious*. There was no one in Newark.

Jess opened up Google Maps and looked at the A1. She could be going to Sheffield, it's not the route Jess would choose, but it was possible. She could even be heading towards Scarborough, that would make more sense to travel on the A1 and then head over to the east coast to visit Martha.

Both her and her sister still sent Christmas cards, unlike so many of her friends who sent out emails, or Facebook posts which included links to charities that they'd donated to instead of sending physical cards. Jess knew Steph still had her cousins' address.

She wished she had her cousin Martha's number, but what would she say? They disappeared from their lives, probably when they needed them most, after their cousins' parents had died. Years had passed and she hadn't wanted to reach out to them, she needed to keep them at arm's length, away from her and her sister. But perhaps for Steph things were different? Maybe motherhood had triggered something in her, a need to reach out to family, renew ties?

The laptop beeped as a Facebook notification appeared on screen. Jess struck the cross at the top of the page. She wasn't interested in what her friend was selling today.

'Adam, do you know where Steph's address book is?'

She called through to the lounge as Adam hadn't moved from his spot, she'd expected him to follow her to her laptop. A shuffling noise announced that he'd eventually come through to the kitchen. She noticed a slight tremor in his hands as he stood by her side.

'No one in Newark, although I can't find out where everyone lives,' Jess told him. 'I suppose if I had her password for Facebook I could search more.'

'Don't know it, thought of that myself and had a go at hacking into last night with all the possible combinations I could think of. No idea where her address book is. Shall I look for it?'

'I don't know if it will help. If she's going up the A1 she could be going to Martha's, maybe she has her number? I've not heard her mention her in years. Do you think the police have called people in her phone book?'

As Adam continued to stare blankly at her, she felt the knot of anger squeeze her intestines and she stood up abruptly.

'I can't sit here all day waiting on the phone. I feel so fucking helpless. Let's go and visit a few of her friends like we said we would.'

He nodded and disappeared to his bedroom.

Jess retreated to the spare room. She picked up her mobile and read the reply from her boss. Again, mercifully, his response was reassuring as he permitted her another day of personal leave.

She pulled on a pair of black skinny jeans and her favourite jumper to keep out the February cold. She stared at herself in the mirror. She looked tired and pale, and the dark circles under her eyes were no longer thin crescent moons; now wider and a deeper shade of violet, they made her high cheekbones seem more prominent.

Today would require extra caffeine to keep her sharp, and water as her skin was looking dry and tired. Her glands felt swollen as though she was coming down with a virus. She dug out her make-up case and blended foundation across her cheeks. She covered the dark circles. They could be hidden.

As she emerged from the bedroom she found Adam hovering in the hallway. He thrust a piece of paper into her hand.

'Why don't you have a chat to some of the NCT mums. Here's the list of addresses one of them put together. Maybe there's one she's become close to? Told her how she really feels about being a new mum?'

Jess refrained from telling him that Steph would never confide in someone she barely knew. That wasn't her style. If there was anything to confess she'd have told her, or at least attempted to confide in her. She stared at the piece of paper and retreated back into the spare room to allow Adam to leave before her.

Is this really a good idea? Turning up on someone's doorstep unannounced. She didn't want to upset the other women, they were about to go into labour in the not too distant future, or were new mums themselves.

She also wondered whether it was OK to go and question them; maybe she should contact the police, push them to get more personnel involved. The words of a recent research paper whirled around her head. She'd helped an academic get his findings out into the press. Analysis of crime statistics and the correlation between rising crime and declining police numbers. *Fuck it. I have to do something.*

She slipped her coat on, locked the door and put the spare key in her pocket. As she did she felt the now crumpled parking ticket. She fished it out again. No location; it was probably from a street parking meter. She thought about the phone call he made and how he'd called the speaking clock. That still seemed odd to her. The shaking and sweating could be signs of stress and shock, she reasoned, she'd felt her hands tremble too and she couldn't stop swallowing down an acrid taste. But why call the speaking clock? She put the ticket back into her pocket. Keeping secrets, finding out secrets, continued to haunt her adult self. Her suspicious nature coloured her judgement. She sighed heavily in an attempt to push aside her tendency to point the finger.

The garage door lifted to reveal the racing green Mini. Typing the address into Google Maps she turned the key in the ignition. It spluttered into life.

Steph and Adam had lovingly kept the first car that they'd bought together despite them both owning another car each. In the past, Jess had half expected this little car to be gifted to her.

As she drove she rehearsed her speech. *What do you say to someone who you've never met before? Not easy to strike the right tone, if there is a right tone for this situation. Of course it's alarming. Disappearing with your newborn daughter, how can this situation not strike fear into her new NCT friends?*

The sat nav announced that the house would be on her left. She slowed up the car and it abruptly came to a halt. She glanced at herself in the mirror and attempted to arrange her interview face, the one she used at work when gathering information for a press release. Business-like but understanding.

The house was set back from the road up a short pathway. She strode up the grass verge, the steep camber forced her to take long wide strides; her ankle wavered as she pushed on to the pavement. She stopped still and rotated her ankle, feeling the strain pull across her foot.

Tentatively she reached for the catch on the wrought iron gate which creaked as it swung open. She paused, checking for signs of inhabitants. No lights shone out into the grey day, no sounds emitted from the small Victorian terraced property.

She rang the doorbell a couple of times. No answer. She wanted to peer in through the window, but realised that was inappropriate. She jogged back up the path, returned to the car, and set off to the next address. Jess blasted herself with warm air as the morning chill found its way through her coat and she became aware of her heart pounding in her chest.

This doesn't feel right. I'm not sure I'd be keen to let in a complete stranger. She gripped the steering wheel hard and pushed her doubts from her mind.

The next address wasn't far away, nestled on Epping high street, and in a rare moment of luck, a car pulled out of the space in front of the house she required.

Flicking the indicator she pulled in. This time there was no grass verge, or garden gate. The house had no boundary separating it from the street.

It was one of those Victorian terraced cottages – railway cottages – from a more gentile and less complicated era. She pushed down the old-style car door locks and double-checked her pocket for the car keys before slamming the car door shut.

She rapped on the door gently with the silver knocker and within a few moments a heavily pregnant woman stood in front of her.

Jess took in the figure before forcing herself to give a warm smile. She didn't want to worry the young woman. She was well aware that she was in a delicate state.

'I'm terribly sorry to bother you. I'm Jessica Morely – my sister is Stephanie – Steph Henderson. Adam, her husband, gave me your address. It is Rachel, isn't it?'

'Yes it is.'

She peered at Jess as though she'd forgotten to put her glasses on and needed to squint slightly to focus.

'I see the resemblance, you look just like her. Is everything OK?'

The woman began to stroke her swollen belly. Her soft round face displayed a look of concern.

'Yes, it is, but could I come in and have a very quick chat. I won't take up too much of your time.'

'Sure.'

Rachel waddled back inside slowly. Jess noticed that her breathing was a little laboured. She showed her into a dark lounge where Rachel sat down on a huge exercise ball.

The room seemed cluttered despite every surface being clear. White wallpaper with black velvety fleurs-de-lis. Combined with the dark furnishing and carpet the room felt as though it would close in on itself. Jess shifted her weight uneasily. She sat opposite Rachel on the small hard sofa.

'I won't stay long. I'm just wondering whether you've seen my sister recently?'

'Only when me and Andrew popped in to meet Natalie just a few days after they got home from hospital. Is everything OK?'

'Not really. She's gone missing and has taken Natalie with her. The police are looking for her, but I wanted to speak to a few people who she may have been in contact with over the last few days.' *There's no easy way of broaching this, is there?*

'Oh my god. I'm so sorry. That's crazy, I mean, I've never known anyone to go missing. And she's just had a beautiful girl.' Her bottom lip wavered and she again began to stroke her belly again.

'We exchanged a few text messages over the last few days. You know, moaning about being pregnant, me that is, and of course how things were going with Natalie.'

'And how did she say things were going?'

'She said she was adorable and amazing and that all the things they told us about sleep deprivation were ten times worse.'

'And that was that?'

'Yes, nothing really out of the ordinary. I did call her on Monday when Adam went back to work to see if she wanted to come over and keep me company, but she didn't answer her phone or call me back.'

Rachel began to rub her back and breathe even more heavily despite sitting down on the large exercise ball.

'Thanks, that's been really helpful.' *What is the point of this? What did I expect to find?*

She got up abruptly. Jess wasn't sure what she had expected to hear. She felt comforted that Rachel didn't have any information that could suggest anything out of the ordinary, but she had hoped for something. Just a crumb of a clue to set her off.

Rachel staggered off the ball and stood bolt upright. She grasped her bump and leaned forward. The ball rolled backwards to the fireplace, hit the marble hearth and then rolled towards Jess. She stopped it with her hand and stared at Rachel whose previously red cheeks now looked ashen.

'Shit. I think that was a contraction.'

'Don't look at me, I can't help you with that – you need to time them don't you?'

Jess winced at her clumsy response, this was the last thing she wanted.

'Yes, I don't suppose you'd stay until another one happens? My husband's at work so it would take him an age to get back here and I don't want to bring him home if it's a false start. I know I don't know you, but just until the next one happens and then I'll decide what to do.'

Jess nodded. She had no idea what to do, this was well out of her comfort zone, she didn't make it in time to see Natalie being born, and she wasn't going to stick around and help a stranger give birth. She'd stay, just until the next one came along.

'Well the time is 9:30, so we'll clock-watch.' Jess tried to smile, but her mouth refused to co-operate. 'Can I get you a glass of water?'

Rachel shook her head, her cheeks flushed back to their original rouge and her breathing seemed to become more raspy.

'I'll text my husband once I've had another. I mean, it might be a false alarm, but it feels different to Braxton Hicks.'

'Braxton whats?'

'False contractions – it's your body gearing up for proper contractions.'

'Oh. Good to know.'

Jess realised how little attention she'd actually paid to Steph's pregnancy. She'd talked non-stop about what her body was going through, but Jess had been too preoccupied with the fallout from Matt leaving and, as she had no inclination to start a family in the near future, or perhaps ever, she had switched off whenever Steph talked about her pregnancy.

'You've not got kids then?'

'Not yet.'

Rachel smiled at her, she was gently swaying. Jess recalled Steph doing that, rocking the baby in utero, she still did that even when she was no longer pregnant. A new habit.

'So you've not heard from her at all?' Rachel's question broke the silence.

'Not at all.'

'Jeez, Adam must be going out of his mind with worry.'

'Yes. The police are doing all they can, they told us to sit tight, perhaps she wanted some time away, they think she's depressed, that's often the trigger for people to go missing.' The words fell rapidly from Jess's mouth. She was beginning to regret the visit. She was alarmed by Rachel's size. Her bump wasn't neat like Steph's. It was huge. She couldn't take her eyes off it and that embarrassed her.

'She didn't seem depressed to me.'

'Me neither.' Her tone was detached. She didn't want to come across as being too friendly now. The thought of accidentally ending up helping this woman give birth unnerved her.

Keeping her answers short would also save her from spilling out more detail than she wanted to. She didn't want to talk about the possibilities and the what ifs with this woman who Steph had only known for a few months. She was beginning to regret her amateur detective efforts.

'Woah... oooh.' Rachel let out a low moan.

Jess tapped her watch. 'Ten minutes since the last one.'

'I'll call the midwife.'

Rachel calmly spoke into her mobile.

Jess already understood the gist of what was coming next.

'They want me to keep timing the contractions, but they'd like me to come in. I'm so sorry to ask this but can you drive me? There's no way I can my drive myself there. Never thought it would happen when my other half wasn't around.'

Jess nodded. Her head wanted to shake from side to side. She hoped the irritation which flooded her bloodstream wasn't written on her face. She knew she had no choice but to help, but seriously, this was the last thing she wanted to be doing.

'I'll call my husband while I get my hospital bag. Just drop me off there, honestly, I don't need you to be my birth partner.'

Jess felt the tingle of a blush spread across her face.

'I'm sorry, of course, of course.'

She stood alone in Rachel's lounge. She could hear her going through things upstairs and talking excitedly to her husband. Her heavy footsteps gradually got louder as she emerged in the doorway, still red-faced and breathing heavily.

'He's on his way, he'll be about an hour.'

Jess jumped forwards and took the large bag from Rachel, who giggled nervously as Jess's arm was pulled to the floor by the bag's weight. She struggled to lift it.

'Be prepared, I've got all sorts of stuff in there.'

She laughed again as Jess went to the door, slowly lugging the bag. She unlocked the car and stuffed the overnight bag into the boot. Rachel awkwardly lowered herself into the seat. It wasn't easy for her sit in the mini. She took up most of the space in the passenger seat and placed her hands on her bump to stop the seatbelt digging into her.

Princess Alexandra Hospital was only a short drive away, otherwise Jess would have insisted on calling an ambulance. It would only take thirty minutes out of her search time and she noticed that one of the other addresses wasn't too far away from the hospital.

Jess glanced at the sky before pulling away. Wall-to-wall cloud hung heavily above them. It looked like a sky full of snow, but it wasn't cold enough today to encourage the clouds to scatter their contents on the road ahead.

'How are you doing?' she asked as she stopped at the first set of traffic lights.

She noticed that Rachel's breathing had slowed down and become more even; she was staring into the distance as though she was focusing the pain away from her.

'Good actually. All a bit weird down there, but won't go into that.'

'Yes, I had enough of the gory details from Steph.'

Jess slowed almost to a stop to manoeuvre the car over the speed humps, she didn't want anything to speed this labour up or cause Rachel any more pain.

'Adam gave me a list of all the NCT mums' addresses. I went to Justine's first and she wasn't in.' She attempted to keep her voice casual, as though she was attempting small talk rather than fishing for information.

'She messaged last night to say the baby came at midnight. I'm the only one left now.'

'Oh, I'm sure Adam said there was only one other mum who had given birth so far. Maybe he got confused.'

'Yes, easily done what with having the baby early and now this … I'm so sorry for both of you. I mean, you must both be going out of your mind. I'd be roaming the streets too looking for my sister if she disappeared.'

'Yes. Adam searched yesterday. I couldn't wait in again today.'

She blinked back a tear which was attempting to form. 'I must admit, I was worried about coming across as some kind of oddball – I was half expecting you to tell me to go away.'

Jess hoped to lighten the mood a little and give Rachel something else to concentrate on as her face was taut and losing its colour. Rachel shifted oddly in the passenger seat and reached her hand up to feel for the internal handle, there wasn't one. She kept her arm up regardless, pushing against the curve of the car roof. Her body filled the passenger seat and Jess had been worried that the seatbelt might not have been big enough to stretch over Rachel's protruding abdomen. She'd had a thing about seatbelts ever since her aunt and uncle's car crash. Not that a seatbelt would have saved them, but the thought of being safely strapped in, especially in an old car like this, gave her a speck of comfort.

'Me and my sister don't look alike at all. She's a redhead and half the size of me, even when I'm not blown-up to the size of an elephant.' Rachel's thin laugh vibrated hollowly around the car. 'Hopefully it won't come to this, but it will work well if the police need to do an appeal and you can be in the reconstruction.'

Jess didn't respond, this wasn't the silver lining she was looking for. Irritation made her breathe deeply.

She stared at the road ahead and began to slow down as she approached the hospital entrance. As she turned to enter the car park, Rachel wailed in pain. Jess stopped the car and automatically reached across to her and held her hand.

'You're doing really well, I just need to park and then I'll make sure we get a midwife to take over.'

Rachel nodded, she had tears in her eyes. Jess was about to drive on when her eyes were drawn to a familiar white car exiting the car park.

She watched the man slowly pull away, pause at the roundabout a few yards in front of them and then exit quickly, wheels screeching.

It was Adam.

She had plenty of time to take him in, there was no mistaking it.

Her heart thumped in her ribcage. She closed her eyes and inhaled deeply; she looked at Rachel, but she was looking out of the passenger window. She couldn't ask her if she'd just seen him, she assumed if she had she would have said something.

She jumped as a horn sounded behind her and her foot slipped off the clutch causing her to stall the car.

'Sorry, coming here has, well, it has reminded me of visiting Steph and my niece.'

Rachel simply nodded, her face contorted with pain.

'Let's get you in there ASAP, you're going to be fine. I think you need to breathe more.'

Turning away from Rachel, she felt acutely inadequate; unable to respond with comfort, or know whether the advice she was giving was useful. *Just drive now. Get her in there and get the fuck out.*

Jess followed the road signs and parked in the maternity car park. She dug some change out of her purse and paid for the parking.

After helping Rachel out of the passenger seat she hauled the overstuffed maternity bag over her shoulder. Rachel's phone began to ring, her husband was fifteen minutes away, much to Jess's relief. She held Rachel's elbow, and together they waddled into the maternity unit.

Jess had imagined a rush of nurses and women shrieking in pain, but the reception area was quiet with just a few couples sat in the waiting room silently glued to their phones. Rachel leaned against the counter and gave her details to a fresh-faced nurse who deftly entered them into the system.

Twisting her hair around her finger, she looked around at the posters on the walls advising her where to get help to give up smoking during pregnancy and what to do if you were feeling like you couldn't cope with your newborn.

Rachel put her hand on Jess's forearm. 'Thank you so much for your help. I'm sure Steph will be back, I'll pray for her.'

Rachel twisted the crucifix which hung over her chest and Jess placed the ridiculous oversized maternity bag at her feet.

'Thank you and good luck. I'm sure I'll be seeing pictures of your wee one with Natalie when they return.'

Jess hoped she sounded sincere. The offer of a prayer freaked her out, it made it feel inevitable that Steph wouldn't return. Praying never gave her comfort, it reminded her of her mum and her recently acquired blind faith.

Blinking away the tears she left the maternity unit in search of signs for the main hospital entrance. She tripped over her own feet as she rushed towards the main doors.

The doors revolved to reveal a busy waiting area and reception desk full of nurses and admissions staff talking on phones or filling in forms. Waiting in line to talk to the receptionist gave Jess enough time to compose herself and rehearse her speech. She didn't want to get emotional. She wanted to remain in control.

A large lady with a ruddy complexion waved her hand for Jess to approach the counter. She had the phone pressed to her ear and was obviously waiting for another department to answer.

Jess stepped forward, she felt the blood rush away from her head as a darkness settled over her eyes. She grabbed hold of the counter to steady herself. The woman blankly stared at her. Jess tried not to stare back.

The receptionist had a sponge-like nose which looked as though someone had squashed it flat against her face; it seemed to spread out unnaturally across her cheeks.

'Hi, my name is Jessica Morley, I'm wondering if you could tell me whether my sister Stephanie Henderson has been admitted? She went missing two days ago – she's not been in contact and I just wanted to double-check that she's not…' Jess paused, swallowing down the lump which was beginning to form. 'That she's not been involved in an accident. She has her three-week-old daughter with her too, Natalie Henderson.'

The woman slowly replaced the receiver.

'Stephanie Henderson. Date of birth?'

Jess stated all her sister's details and waited as the woman typed them into the computer.

'Sorry, system has been down this morning and it has been crazy. Got a whole pile of admission forms to enter in. Hang on, it's getting somewhere now.'

Jess crossed her fingers. Maybe the CCTV images were wrong. Maybe her car had been stolen. Perhaps she'd been injured in a random car-jacking and she's— the loud Essex accent stopped Jess's thoughts.

'No. Nothin'. No one of that name here. I'll check to see if the baby has been admitted.'

Jess gave her Natalie's birth date, but she knew that her name would draw a blank.

'Nothin' again. I'm sorry. Assume you've alerted the police?'

Jess nodded solemnly.

'They do an amazing job Miss, I'm sure she'll be found in no time, especially as she's got a baby with her, she'll be a top priority.'

Jess managed to thank her, before running back to her car.

Through the windscreen she took in the pristine white parking ticket sitting on the dashboard. There was something strangely familiar about the ticket. She'd seen it before. Her fingers twitched before they found their way into her coat pocket. She pulled out the now dog-eared ticket. She pulled out the dog-eared one from her pocket. They were identical.

Adam

Adam poured a large glass of Merlot for himself and one for Marcus. He carefully set the bottle back down and ran his fingers through his light brown hair; he pushed it to one side, hoping the few strands of grey were not visible. If they were, Marcus was bound to comment. He never missed a sign of weakness or aging.

'Cheers,' Marcus said, raising his glass. 'To your new family. May nappies and sleepless nights be something you get out of.'

He wore his usual self-satisfied smirk, it rankled others, colleagues and clients, but Adam was used to it. It was well-worn and Marcus couldn't help that smugness was his default setting.

'Don't let Steph or Miranda hear you say that.'

Adam sipped his wine. 'Good wine as always.'

'Miranda never let me change a nappy or do a night feed. She was a control freak back then, well, she still is come to think of it. Plus I was pretty hopeless. Don't get much out of the baby stage.'

'And you should know, you've had four babies now.'

'Yes. Four. And I'm sure Miranda would keep going until the menopause strikes. Babies bore the hell out of me if I'm honest and I'm never really sure what to do with them. I actually prefer it when they can talk. Well for a bit, until every sentence involves a demand.' Marcus sipped his wine.

'Really? I loved my two weeks off with Natalie and I'm sure I was beginning to get her, you know, we kind of found our own way to communicate.'

'Yes, she'll be advising you on negotiating in no time.'

Again the smug grin spread across Marcus's face.

'You know what I mean.' A waiter appeared and took their order, steak and fries, rare to medium for Adam, well done for Marcus; their usual order. They often ate in the Archway. It was quiet, the food was good and quick, and more importantly the wine list was extensive.

Adam had known Marcus since they'd first worked as assistant underwriters in the same syndicate; both worked as graduate trainees and both excelled at what did they did, but in very different ways. Adam was meticulous and a hard negotiator. Marcus was a charmer. He had a neat way of getting what he wanted and Adam had never been sure how he managed to wriggle his way into the most difficult position and then miraculously get out of it.

'So, will I be needing to renounce the devil in the not too distant future?'

Adam's eyes widened. The corners of Marcus's mouth quivered, but he managed to keep his smile at bay.

'Surely you'll be returning the favour and making me a godfather?'

He raised his glass in anticipation of a toast.

Adam laughed and wondered how Marcus never seemed to miss a beat.

'Godfather? I won't be making you an offer you can't refuse any time soon. Seriously, you and Miranda had everything mapped out from day one? I mean, for the past few weeks it's been good to take one day at a time – actually that's such a novelty for me – I've kind of enjoyed it.'

'Don't get too comfortable, you'll lose your edge, although I do fancy a change of scenery. The view from your office is better than mine.'

'It is a great view but I'm not sure your ego will fit through the door.'

Marcus raised his glass again.

'Still sharp then. I remember hardly sleeping for months after Scarlett was born. I couldn't string a sentence together.'

Marcus sipped his wine then thoughtfully scratched his beard. That beard was grown way before the hipster fetish had taken hold of some of their colleagues. Adam took the piss out of his friend for growing it, but now it made him look more serious and gave him a more distinguished look. Marcus had an air about him which suggested that you were in good hands. He'd look after your interests as well as his own. Maybe it was the soft, slightly plummy accent, or the way he clearly hung on every word, and had a photographic memory for detail that impressed fellow brokers. Whatever it was Adam had to work twice as hard to equal the success of his friend. And that's exactly what he did.

He sat back in his chair and felt his shoulders slump a little. Steph's frosty demeanour had continued at breakfast despite her attempt at an apology before he fell asleep. Her mouth seemed set in a line and she barely said two words to him. He couldn't push her coldness from his thoughts today and he was glad to get out of the office for lunch in the hope that Marcus would provide a welcome distraction, but he still couldn't shake off his misgivings. He shifted awkwardly in his seat.

'I know it's early days, but Steph was a bit off with me last night when I returned from work.'

'Ah. The return to work sulk. The "you've-no-idea-what-it-is-like" whinge. Honestly every time I returned to work she'd trot out the same refrain and yet she still insisted we had four. Four kids. I think I'll go for the snip. She had that glint her eye again last night. Cheeky minx.'

Adam slowly shook his head. Marcus was playing to his audience of one.

'I never get a look-in though really, we never get a look-in. I should have taken her offer up as I reckon the last time we managed a bit of sex was when we conceived Quinn. Stop at two mate, sooo much easier.'

'Come on, you wouldn't change it for the world.'

The waiter arrived with lunch, causing Marcus to draw breath before replying.

'Oh I would. I often daydream about how much quieter and how simpler our lives would be. Maybe I'd have taken early retirement. Rather than sitting here with you I could have been swinging a golf club in the Algarve.'

Marcus began to look around the restaurant. Adam saw his eyes drawn to two young women who were leaning against the bar, deep in conversation.

'Simpler, less complicated.' He nodded in their direction. 'I can dream, no?'

Adam took another slug of wine.

He was used to Marcus's musings. He wasn't serious, he'd chat up every good looking woman in sight. He was charming and women were drawn to him, but he was all talk.

And despite his protestations he adored his kids; he was one of the few fathers who took time out to attend the various school events and Adam knew he spent most Saturdays ferrying the boys around to numerous sporting activities, not because he had to, but because he wanted to.

This version of Marcus was not the genuine article, it was his favourite role, the role of a man who wanted a change; a different view to the one he'd built.

Adam smiled at his meanderings and felt a little relieved to hear that he wasn't alone in receiving a frosty reception.

He toyed with talking a little more about it, but he figured that she needed time to adjust; it must be similar to taking on a whole new role at work and one which someone had lost the job description for and no one really could tell you what to do.

He checked his watch before shovelling the last piece of steak into his mouth.

'Really sorry to leave you and run, but I've got a conference call and I'd like to shoot off a bit earlier today.'

Marcus was mid-mouthful, he nodded and waved.

Adam put some money on the table and strolled out of the dimly lit restaurant. His eyes quickly adjusted to the late January gloom. It was only a fraction brighter outside. At least today the wind had eased and there were a few figures hanging around indulging in conversation or vaping.

Adam slipped into his office and returned to his desk. Just a few hours left. Head down, fingers aggressively striking keys, phone calls made and answered, and time spiralled away, pulling Adam to the tube and finally to his door.

His key crunched the metal lock and he pushed the door open, revealing the noise of Natalie's cries. High-pitched, cat-like, demanding instant attention.

He placed his briefcase down and moved to the source of the cries. Lying on the changing mat, on their bedroom floor, Natalie was arching her back and screaming loudly, he couldn't believe that something so small could omit such a loud, excruciating sound.

He picked her up and held her close to his chest, her skin was covered in goose bumps. Her screams ceased immediately once she was in his arms. He rocked her, holding her close to warm her up. 'Steph?' He called out into the stillness.

Natalie's eyes searched his face. He stroked her brow and admired her tiny perfect features. Her beautiful lips, just like Steph's. Her bright blue eyes. A striking colour. Unlike his own or Steph's, but he'd read somewhere that it takes a while for eye colour to settle. The lumious blue suited her, he hoped it would stay. He began to sing a lullaby-like version of 'Wonderwall'.

Adam felt a breeze behind him signalling that Steph had swept into the room. He turned to see her looking dishevelled, wet patches marked her top where her nipples should be. She folded her arms and clutched a packet of baby wipes to her chest.

'I couldn't find the new packet. I thought I'd put them in here, and then, for the life of me, I couldn't think where they were. I can't think about anything when she cries.'

'You could have carried her with you rather than leaving her squawking on the mat.'

Adam knew his words would upset her, but he was simply stating a fact. The wipes dropped to the floor next to his feet.

He returned Natalie to the changing mat. His gaze remained trained on his daughter. He started pulling silly faces at her and walking his fingers up her tummy and tickling her. He put on a new nappy, smoothing down the fastenings and straightening them up. He'd learnt the hard way how easily these things leaked. He picked up a vest and stretched the neck to ensure it slipped effortlessly over her head.

He finished dressing her and hoped his intervention would divert Steph's attention from the remark, but he could feel her frostiness whip the back of his neck.

Steph stood still behind him, silent. He didn't need to look at her expression, he could feel it, mouth fixed in a pout, glowering with petulance.

He put the clean babygro on which Steph had laid out by the mat. He fought the kicking legs and carefully slid her tiny arms into the sleeves and finally attempted to push the poppers together, which he managed, for the first time, with ease. For the past few weeks his fingers had changed to thumbs whenever he attempted to push the press studs together.

He could feel a tingling in the back of his neck where his hairline ended and his neck began; he knew Steph was glaring at him.

He lifted Natalie up into his arms and stood up to face Steph. Her face didn't look as he had pictured. Instead she was ghostly pale and silent tears kissed her cheeks.

Sitting down on the bed, he patted the space next to him. Steph complied and sunk into the soft mattress, resting her head on his shoulder.

'I don't really know how to explain this. So don't interrupt, just let me talk.'

He noticed how her whole body vibrated and how she had to hold her own hands to prevent them from shaking.

'I will, but you're scaring me. You're reminding me of how you reacted when you told me what that bastard did to you at uni.'

She squeezed his hand before moving to the window to draw the curtains. Adam stroked Natalie's wispy hair. Steph smoothed the curtains together. A funny little tick of hers. Unnecessary. It irritated him, her preciseness. But today he couldn't be irritated with her, she looked so white and the frostiness had been swapped for something else. Fear flickered in her eyes.

She returned to the bed, but sat a little away from him.

'I should have told you about this before. I'm sorry.'

He watched her clasp her hands together tightly, her knuckles became white with the pressure she exerted.

'It started about a year ago. Jason from work, he, he had a thing for me.'

Adam felt his jaw tighten. He had promised not to speak, he gritted his teeth, unsure what was coming next. He kissed Natalie's hair and inhaled her scent, hoping the act would ease his tension.

'Our work has some crossover, so sometimes we'd work on a few similar stories. I found him to be a bit over-familiar. You know, one of those people who has no concept of personal space, but I didn't think anything of it at first.'

He reached for her hand in order to reassure her and press her to go on.

'He often made a point of waiting for me so we could leave work together; at first it was work chat, but after his house-warming he started to ask questions about you.'

Adam's brow furrowed. 'Me? Why?'

'I don't know. It started off friendly enough, but then he started to tell me that you weren't good enough for me. He said you were one of those selfish city types who travelled away on business and that you were probably shagging a colleague or two while I was sat at home alone. I told him he was being ridiculous and that I didn't like the tone of our conversations anymore and it would be better if we didn't get the train home together again.'

Adam realised that Natalie was now asleep. Her snuffles had stopped and she was silent on his chest. He stood up and carefully laid her in the Moses basket then watched her wriggle to get comfortable. Her eyebrows arched as she pursed her lips as though she was getting ready to feed.

'So, did he leave you alone then?'

He kept his voice low, he didn't want to disturb his daughter. He stroked her forehead, bent to kiss her goodnight and then returned to sit by Steph's side.

'No, he apologised the next day. Said he was being an idiot, that his dad worked in the city and was a womaniser and that you had reminded him a little of his father – he said, you looked a bit like him and had the same swagger. He gave me a little bunch of flowers and seemed genuinely sorry for mouthing off.'

Adam began to feel uncomfortable talking in front of Natalie.

'Shall we go to the kitchen? I'm starving. And we can leave Little Miss in peace.'

He stood up and walked through the short hallway to the kitchen, he needed a bit of space to process what he'd just heard and clearly there was worse to come. He reached up to the top shelf of the cupboard for a glass and poured himself a large Cabernet-Sauvignon and a water for Steph. The velvety liquid warmed his throat and the tension in his jaw loosened.

'So, I'm guessing he didn't leave you alone?'

'No. For a while I avoided leaving work with him and thankfully we didn't have many stories to work on together, so I managed to not see much of him for a few weeks. We had an event together and I don't know why, I guess I'm too polite, but I agreed to go for drinks with him afterwards.' She took a sip of water and he noticed how the glass shook in her hands.

Adam pictured the two of them together, laughing over a drink. He didn't want this image in his head. He wasn't sure he wanted her to continue.

Steph groaned and replaced the glass on the kitchen counter. She leaned against the worktop and stared out into the darkness, twisting a thick curl of hair around her finger. She moved towards the window and pulled the cord of the blinds which squeaked as it slowly lowered towards the windowsill.

'He told me he'd fallen in love with me and didn't care that I was married, he wanted us to be together. I told him I didn't feel the same and that this was the last time we'd see each other outside of work. I called a cab and left him in the bar. After that he started to send me nasty emails.' Steph began to cry.

Adam drained his glass and put his arms around her. He kept his voice even.

'Emails? What kind of emails?'

'They were horrible. Calling me a whore. Telling me I shouldn't have led him on. Telling me what he wanted to do to me and how he'd make you watch. He sent loads of them. All similar in tone and it went on for weeks and I know I should have said something to HR, but I was scared of him.'

'Fuck, he's well overstepped the mark. Why didn't you say anything? I could have helped you. And yes, you should have told HR.'

Adam refilled his glass. He was keeping a lid on his feelings. What he really wanted to say was he'd love to have popped around to Jason's and punched his lights out.

'You're too nice for your own good.'

He sighed heavily. Why was she so secretive? They'd been together for years, he'd helped her through worse, why didn't she say something?

'So, he basically was obsessed with you and then when you rejected him, he lost it?'

'Yes. Yes, that's it.'

She paused and began to move around the kitchen, putting away anything that had been left on the work surface, restoring order while she continued.

'There were a few times when I left work before him and he appeared on the same train as me and followed me home. He'd never get too close to me. Always at a distance but he'd be there, watching me. Standing at the end of the road, ugh, I feel sick thinking about it.'

She began to sob.

'We could have got the police involved. Fucking prick. I'm pretty pissed off you didn't tell me any of this.'

'I, I didn't want to, we were having problems weren't we, we were both so busy with work and the stress of trying for a baby ...'

He pulled her close to him again and held her. His mind drifted back to the months before Natalie was conceived.

Work had been hideous and the scheduled sex had left him feeling cold and remote, he knew he'd shut himself off from her. He wanted to shut her out. Shut out the idea that he was imperfect.

The fertility tests were incredibly stressful; waiting to see which one of them was defective. Adam expected it would be his fault. He'd put off making the appointment for as long as he could, and ironically on the day his results came through, Steph showed him the pregnancy test confirming that, in fact, neither of them were defective.

He never did tell her his results, they didn't matter. One of his more motile swimmers had hit the jackpot. The doctor said it wasn't impossible, just a bit trickier. Steph was so ecstatic she never pushed him on the finer details of his results. He told her that he was fine. As far as she was concerned neither of them had a problem. It had just taken longer than they'd anticipated.

'I don't know what it was, but after discovering we were going to have a baby, I got braver. I printed out all the emails and put them on his desk and told him that I was pregnant and that if he sent any more, or followed me home, I'd go to HR and the police. And it worked. He left me alone until this week.'

'What?'

'He brought the flowers over. I didn't show you the card. He threatened me.'

Adam spluttered and began to choke on the gulp of wine he'd just taken. He listened intently to Steph as she explained what he'd written in the card and how he'd returned the following day and shouted abuse and more threats through the letterbox, and that he was watching the house.

He downed the last slug of wine. It didn't quell the anger that had begun to bubble in the pit of his gut. It fuelled it.

How dare he? How dare he threaten my wife and come to my home. My home. The sick fuck.

He closed his eyelids, inhaled and then exhaled a long deeply drawn breath. Steph was still shaking. He pulled her into his chest and held her tight, in the hope that the shaking would stop.

How dare he do this to her. How dare he? I promised her no man would ever hurt her again. Bastard.

He kissed Steph on the top of the head, and without saying a word, grabbed his house keys, bounded down the hallway and slammed the front door shut.

1st Feb 2017

A was up and out before we were out of bed. He was so preoccupied, he kissed us goodbye but he seemed so cold. A kiss on the forehead. No tenderness, perfunctory. What was required and expected.

HE must have told him. Maybe A is biding his time? Deciding whether to believe him and then confront me? Two men now out to hurt me, hurt me and my baby. I don't mean physically, but to inflict the same emotional pain that I have meted out on them.

And who can blame them? Wouldn't I want to inflict hurt upon the one who caused me pain? Of course I would.

* * *

Mum thinks I need to get away. Not for good, just for a few days, give myself some space and be ready to tell A everything and rebuild our marriage. She's been my rock, always turning up when I need her the most. Giving me advice, helping me see clearly.

The thought of my husband wanting to take N away from me hangs in the air and feels like there could be some truth to it. If it was A who had been cheating on me, then yes I would leave him and take N with me. I'd take everything. Mum is right, it's the only thing I can do now. Run.

Missing Day Two

Jess

Adam's car hadn't returned yet, the drive remained empty, so Jess eased the Mini onto the sloping concrete. When she reached the front door, she struggled to get the spare key to turn. Partly because it didn't bite as it should, and partly because her hands wouldn't stop trembling.

She couldn't shut out the image of Adam exiting the hospital car park. Maybe he was double-checking with the hospital. She would have to ask him about it and explain that she saw him, it was the only way forward, but she couldn't put aside her fear that he was hiding something or trying to cover something up.

She was aware of her naturally suspicious disposition; it was ingrained into her psyche, etched into her soul. She knew it coloured the way she reacted to Adam, she needed to keep a lid on her mistrustful temperament, but when it came to Steph all she ever wanted to do was to protect her. Keep more secrets. Keeping secrets stopped bad things happening. And she'd become acutely aware of the signs shown by others who kept secrets, too.

The door opened and the house was still. The air hung heavy with anticipation, but of what, Jess was unsure. A shiver rippled down her spine. She caught sight of herself in the mirror and noticed how pale she looked. Her hair was scraped back into a tight ponytail. She took out the band and tipped her head forward, bending at the waist.

When she straightened up she could feel a tightening at her scalp. A ghost of a ponytail. She ran her fingers through her shoulder-length bob. She instantly noticed how it softened her face; the pallor was still there, but her hair framed her features and made her look less unwell. She made a mental note not to wear her hair up.

The smell of coffee lingered in the hallway pulling her towards the kitchen. Filling the kettle, Jess stared out of the kitchen window into the early February gloom. The garden looked bare, no signs of spring yet, just the evergreen shrubs providing a splash of colour along with the spongy-looking lawn. A flash of blue flew past the window and landed on the bird table. The blue tit picked at the remaining seeds. Jess wondered where Steph kept the bird seed. Just like Mum, Steph loved feeding the birds.

Another shiver took over Jess's body. A deep one which spread over her thighs making her grab hold of the edge of the sink to steady herself. Flicking the switch on the kettle, she closed her eyes and let her memory play out.

* * *

She could see the birds feasting on the bird table, they were oblivious to the watchers. The two little girls sat wrapped up in blankets and drinking hot chocolate while their mum attempted to sketch a couple of the birds as they were busy feasting.

Bacon rind. The birds loved it. And then, they suddenly took flight as Dad arrived home. He emerged through the gate.

His face, beaming from ear to ear as he scooped up the girls in a huge daddy bear hug.

* * *

It was her last memory of her father before he left. Never returning. No contact. Gone.

Unlike the other kids whose fathers had disappeared off with the 'other woman', dad vanished into oblivion. No weekend visits, no arguments about who had who and when. Nothing.

The rumbling boil of the kettle snapped her back into the present. Boiling water splashed up the sides of the mug and onto her fingers. She winced as the pain seared her skin and she swore as she ran them under the freezing cold water.

Making her way back to the front door, she scooped up her handbag. She pushed the contents around: receipts, her purse and an umbrella blocked her way. A scowl naturally worked its way into her brow. Why couldn't she place her phone back into the specifically designed pocket? She found her phone, pulled it out and typed a text as quickly as her fingers would allow. Just plain emotion.

She needed Matt. She needed the voice of reason to cut through the fog. Her emotional barometer swung between anger and – something she didn't want to admit – need. Needing him to be here. Needing to hear his voice and feel his arms wrap around her and calm her anxiety. He alone could do that. His absence increased her worst-case-scenario tendencies.

She returned to the kitchen and watched a jay hop over the grass. Its shock of blue feathers streaked through the air as it abruptly took flight, frightened off by something.

The sound of metal forcing its way into a tight gap and the click of the lock told Jess to ready herself for Adam's entrance. She reached up to the cupboard and got out a mug.

'Coffee?' she yelled as he slammed the door closed, making her voice sing-song like.

'Yes. That would be great, thanks.'

He sat down at the table and let out a long sigh. 'Any news here?'

Jess winced. 'Shit. I didn't check the voicemail when I got in.'

'I didn't mean that, but I'll have a listen. I made a few phone calls to some of her colleagues and visited one of them, Bethany Chambers. She had her second baby a couple of months ago, so I thought Steph might have been in touch. Actually she said she was surprised that she'd not heard from Steph, she seemed a little upset that she hadn't got in touch. It got me thinking a little.'

Adam paused, he looked at Jess as though he was checking if she was still listening. Jess mixed the instant coffee granules in Adam's mug and added milk to hers. The white swirls of milk invaded the brown liquid. She had lost count of how many cups she'd had today. She wasn't sure if the caffeine was required; cortisol had been fuelling her body and priming her thoughts all day.

Jess slid into the wooden chair opposite him. She pushed a stray strand of hair back behind her right ear.

'She never talked about many people from work. We didn't socialise with them. Did she ever mention anyone to you?'

He was right. Steph would talk about work, talk about the stories she was planning or pursuing, but she never gossiped or even complained about anyone at work. Jess on the other hand always had plenty to say about everyone she worked with. It was her life. She loved her job; her colleagues weren't just her colleagues they were her friends.

'No, I don't recall her talking about anyone really, or socialising with them.' She tried to picture any of Steph's colleagues but none sprung to mind.

He stroked his chin and Jess noticed he hadn't shaved today. 'You and me, we're more alike when it comes to work aren't we? You know, some might think we are obsessed by it, but it's just us giving it our all and if that includes socialising with colleagues and enjoying getting stuck into the politics and gossip, well that's the way we like it, right?'

Adam sipped his coffee and stared at Jess; she realised he was waiting for some kind of response. His face appeared strained. A few more fine lines crept across his forehead today, plus his clutch of grey hairs seemed more visible.

She wasn't going to respond to him. They were not alike in the slightest. She scraped up her hair into a tight ponytail again. As she stretched the hairband, it snapped. She scrunched it up in her hand and squeezed it tightly.

'What about you? Find out anything useful?'

As she sipped the coffee she felt the warmth infuse her.

'Me? Oh yes, well the only NCT friend around was Rachel – the others have all had their babies.'

'Really? I guess the dads leave it to the mums to make the announcements. I know Steph was in the WhatsApp group but that was only for the mums.'

He sounded genuinely surprised.

'Rachel hadn't heard from her and, well, she went into labour during my visit and I ended up taking her to the hospital.'

She concentrated on Adam, waiting for him to mention his visit to the hospital. Today he seemed more able to look at her directly. She glanced away to check out his hands. Nothing. No shaking yet. He drank more of his coffee and sat back in his chair.

'So, yes, I drew a blank too. Did you have another drive around then?' Her voice maintained a casual even tone.

She wanted to hear him detail what he'd been doing this morning.

'Yes. I drove around a little and then I thought I'd check the hospital. Nothing. I know the police have rung around, but I needed to do something. Also I'm wondering whether I should go through her things and see if she's kept her passwords to Twitter and Facebook anywhere. I told the police I didn't think she did, but I now recall seeing her write in a notebook a couple of times, but I've never seen it just lying around with all her usual clutter.'

Jess scrutinised his face.

'That was a good idea to check out the hospital, funny, we might have been there at the same time.'

His face remained unreadable, expressionless.

'Fancy you ending up ferrying some woman you've never met before to the labour ward.'

'Yes, I was a bit worried I might have needed to help her give birth in the hospital car park.'

He wasn't going to tell her what time he was there. He'd admitted to going there. And why wouldn't he? There was something that wasn't right about his behaviour, she couldn't quite put her finger on it. Keeping secrets, carrying around guilt from her childhood made her naturally suspicious. She knew he'd done very little to arouse her doubts but she couldn't help herself. She'd grown-up questioning everything her mother did, everything her dad did. It was only natural that she'd continue to question everyone who was close to her.

She wanted to press him further about how he'd spent his day, but she knew it was futile and besides, what evidence did she have other than a gut feeling that he was hiding something.

Her phone vibrated. She pushed her chair away from the table and crossed the kitchen to place her cup in the dishwasher. She looked at the text.

'It's from Matt.' She wanted to smile but her mouth refused and grimaced.

'Ah. I'll let you read it in peace. I'm going to have a look for those notebooks.'

Hey babe. Got your text. Of course we can chat. Not had a chance to get online since I got here. I've made a friend so will borrow his laptop and Skype later, say 6.30 p.m. your time? Missing you. Has my postcard arrived? Loads to tell you. XXX

As usual his texts were short. No change there, even at the start of their relationship he'd send only a few lines. Since he'd been travelling he'd texted sporadically. Jess didn't mind his lack of communication, after all they were on a break and she'd not needed or wanted him to constantly update her on all the things he was experiencing without her. But now she felt differently. She needed to talk to him. Even if he couldn't do anything to help her, she needed someone who was away from all of this, who had both a literal and a physical distance, to give their perspective. For the first time since he'd left her it wasn't anger that she felt when she thought of him. She wasn't sure yet what she felt, she didn't want to name it, she didn't want to feel vulnerable again. Not now, definitely not now.

An open bottle of wine stood invitingly on the kitchen counter. It was far too early to have a drink but she needed something to take the edge off, to stop every minute detail jarring her nerves.

She picked up the glass she used earlier and ran the tap. Wine would flow later. Water would have to do now. A jet of water surged into the glass and straight out again, splashing out over the side of the sink. She couldn't spot a tea towel hanging in the usual place on the radiator so she opened up the cupboard under the sink. As the door opened the bin lid slid open automatically. It still puzzled her why fresh flowers had been plunged into the bin. At the back of the cupboard stood a few rolls of kitchen paper. She mopped up her spillage and moved to the lounge.

She slumped into the sofa and flicked on the TV for the first time that day. The local news kicked in. No mention of Steph yet. That would be the police's next move. It wouldn't be long before it all became public knowledge. She closed her eyes. *Fuck, our lives will be under the microscope.*

When she opened her eyes there was a reporter standing outside a house. Police tape cordoned off the driveway of the average-looking property.

The reporter explained that the police were appealing for witnesses in connection with an assault which had taken place at the victim's home. The victim may have been known to his attacker as there was no sign of forced entry.

A photograph of the victim appeared on screen as the reporter detailed his name, age and occupation. He was a journalist for *The Mirror.*

Her attention fixed on the screen at the mention of her sister's place of work. The man was found on the night before Steph had gone missing. The photograph lingered on screen a second or two longer than necessary.

Steph's colleague? Did he know her? Could they have worked together? It's a huge organisation, possibly their paths didn't cross?

A policeman appeared on screen asking people to remember if they had seen anyone looking suspicious in the Epping area, around Amesbury road.

Shit, he lives nearby. He was attacked the night before she disappeared. Their paths must have crossed at some point. They probably got the same tube into work.

She became aware of someone watching from the doorway. She glanced at Adam. His hands were shaking and beads of sweat glistened around his hairline.

He wiped his brow and moved to sit on the sofa opposite Jess.

'I'm not feeling great. Think it's the stress of it all. Keep sweating and shaking, like I'm coming down with something, and I keep seeing Steph and Natalie in the car rolling and rolling into a ditch.'

His cries caused his whole body to shudder. Jess awkwardly got up and sat next to him and tentatively draped her arm around him.

'We need to stay positive. My mind keeps doing the same thing. Playing out the crisis version of every event. Matt's always telling me I catastrophise.'

Adam moved out of her embrace. 'You're right. We need to be positive.'

Jess shuffled over into the corner of the sofa and hugged a crisp white cushion to her chest for warmth.

'Did you see that news report? The one that was on when you came into the room?'

He looked away from her. 'Yeah, I just caught the end.'

'That man is a colleague of Steph's – he's local and works as a reporter for *The Mirror.* Do you know him?'

Adam scratched the back of his neck and looked out of the window.

'Like I said earlier, she never talked about anyone from work.'

'Not even someone who was local? I mean they could have got the tube home together. It's possible isn't it?'

Adam stood up. 'Yes it is possible, but it's a big workplace and, well, he could be a sports reporter or something and she wouldn't know him as their work wouldn't cross over.'

'I guess not. Just a coincidence that he was attacked the night before she went missing.'

'Of course it fucking is, I mean, it's not like Steph could have gone and attacked him is it? What are you trying to say? Do you truly think it is out of the realms of possibility that she is depressed?'

Jess was taken aback by his vehemence. The veins in his neck pulsated. He wasn't trembling now; his hands were perfectly still, everything about his stance and the way he held his head, slightly cocked upwards so he was looking down his nose at her, all suggested that he was perfectly in control.

'I'm not suggesting she'd attack him. For fuck's sake as if she's capable of that! And no it's not out of the realms of possibility that she's depressed. It's just ... it's just that for me, as her sister, why wouldn't she tell me how she's feeling? She had plenty of opportunity to tell me if she wasn't coping, but she never said, or behaved in any way to suggest she wasn't coping. I'm trying to piece together why she's run away and taken Natalie with her and I'm sorry if you think I'm trying to put two and two together to make five but I have to. We have to. We have to find her. We have to think of everything.'

He sat down and put his hand on her knee.

'Jess, do you know everything about your sister? Do you know all her deepest, darkest secrets?'

'I'd like to think I do.' She bristled. Of course she knew.

'Do you know what happened to her at uni?'

'Nothing out of the ordinary that I recall.'

A memory surfaced as she recalled times when she'd walk in on Steph and Mum talking quietly.

Steph was always on the verge of tears and Mum would stop talking and ask Jess to go and fetch something or make tea, and even though she knew there was something that they were hiding, she had assumed that Mum had finally told her the truth about why Dad left.

She knew if it was something else Steph would have told her. They'd always told each other everything. Steph was her confidante. Steph knew nearly all of her secrets. But now, thinking back, this confidence was rarely reciprocated. It was a one-way listening street.

Jess bowed her head. She rubbed her temple and sighed deeply.

'Perhaps I was usually the one telling her my deepest darkest secrets. I'm not sure she readily shared all of hers and so I guess, well, I assumed she didn't have any.'

He took her hand.

'At uni she was raped by her ex-boyfriend.' He paused, letting the words fizz around the room. The beige wintery light faded as a heavier cloud took up its position in front of the already obscured low sun. Further layering the cloud, plunging the room into shadow.

'She was so traumatised by it that she hid in her room for a week. She should have taken the morning-after pill, but she couldn't bear to be seen by anyone. She was in shock.'

'Wait – slow down. She was raped by an ex?'

'They weren't together long. Steph ended it, he was a bit overbearing, but he seemed fine with the break-up. Anyway, she took some CDs back to him, he lived in a different halls of residence to us.' Adam cleared his throat before continuing. He held Jess's hand tightly. 'He invited her in for coffee. Locked her in his room and forced himself on her repeatedly.'

'Jesus. She didn't tell the police? He ... got away with it? Did you know him?'

'Yes I knew him. Yes, the bastard got away with it.' He spat the words out and she noticed how the veins on his neck stood out as his jaw jutted forward and his nostrils flared.

Adam stared into her eyes, but now she couldn't even look at him. She wanted to throw up. She couldn't believe what she was hearing. Her mouth had fallen open, she wanted to speak, but what could she say?

'As I said, she was so traumatised and in shock that she didn't leave her room. She knew that because she didn't go to the police straight away that there was no evidence. No witnesses. She entered his room of her own free will.' Adam coughed and released Jess's hand. 'It would be her word against his and she couldn't cope, she couldn't cope with going over and over the rape details again. Things got worse...' He took a deep breath. 'She found out she was pregnant. She had to have a termination.' Adam eyes became watery.

'She ... couldn't live with herself. She couldn't live with the fact that she never told the police. That he could do it again to someone else, and she couldn't cope with the termination. She took a load of paracetamol and we found her, me and her best friend Anna.'

Jess's face remained fixed in an expression of disbelief. She couldn't process this. Any of it.

'That's why she took it so hard when we couldn't conceive.'

He got up and walked to the window. He kept his back to her.

'I've been trying to convince myself that the mood swings and tearfulness are normal – like you said, par for the course when you're a sleep-deprived mum. But there's been this nagging doubt, that perhaps she wasn't coping, perhaps she's more fragile because of what she went through. Perhaps I've missed something?'

He turned to look at Jess. She nodded slowly.

'I should have taken more time off work. The little signs I noticed I shouldn't have ignored. Like it couldn't happen again because there's an us now, there's our history and she's happy and things are different now. Fuck, she couldn't do this to us, could she?'

Why didn't she ever say anything? How could I not know?

'Adam, this is too much. I could have been there for her, helped her through it. I can't even imagine going through anything like that. At least she wasn't totally alone.' She half wanted to thank him for saving her, she knew that's what she should say, but she was struggling to come to terms with what he'd revealed. It was too much.

She got up from the sofa and moved to stand by his side. As she put her hand on his shoulder she became aware of an ache in her armpit, swollen glands, like a virus was hitting her.

'I think I need some time alone by myself. Do you need me to stay here tonight? If you do it's fine, but I'd prefer my own bed.'

She managed a smile, hoping it looked pleading enough to secure her escape, because for some reason, and she couldn't put her finger on it, she felt captive here. There was a heaviness to the air in the house, something oppressive, which made her feel trapped. It was freezing standing here by the window. The air temperature plummeted several degrees. The heavy cloud suggested sleet.

'Maybe I'm coming down with something too, I feel chilled to the bone.'

'I think its stress, and of course you can go home. I didn't anticipate you having to stay another night ... I'll call you immediately if I hear anything from the police. Go and get some rest.' One corner of Adam's mouth moved in an attempt to give Jess a smile.

'Thank you.' She moved to the doorway but something stopped her from leaving the room. 'Adam, why didn't you tell PC Hawthorne this?' She turned to face him. This time he couldn't look her in the eye.

'I ... I couldn't. You were here. I didn't want you to find out like that. And I wanted them to be properly looking for her. Not immediately jumping to the conclusion that she's disappeared off to kill herself. I wanted them to be searching for my wife and daughter and not scouring well-known suicide spots.' He covered his face with his hands.

'But maybe that's where they should be looking.'

'No! Fuck! Everything's such a mess.' He dropped to the floor. 'I'm sorry Jess. I just want them home. I need them to come home.'

Jess moved towards him and eased herself down to the floor to sit beside him.

'I know. That's all we both want.'

She remained at his side for what seemed like an hour. Pins and needles attacked her toes.

'Come on. You should try and get an early night. That's what I'm going to do.' She felt awkward. What was she supposed to say to him? Everything swam around her head. She couldn't hold any of her thoughts still. 'I need to go home and sleep in my own bed.'

Adam remained on the floor as Jess retreated to the spare room. Gathering her things she felt like her movements were on autopilot. Her brain attempted to process all the details Adam had shared with her.

He was right. She thought she knew her sister better than she knew herself, but the truth was the opposite. It was Steph who knew her thoughts, hopes and desires before she did because Jess was an open book to her sister.

She was the little sister who sought her big sister's approval as a child and her counsel as a teen and adult. It was one-way traffic and it had never dawned on her until now that Steph never leaned on her.

Mum was her confidante. It was another way to exclude her. Steph was the one she'd lavish affection on, take out shopping, play with when they were really little, do everything with. While Jess was left at home alone, or banished to her bedroom, or sent to the neighbour's house when Mum had had enough. A strange taste flooded her mouth, like bitter coffee. She flung her bag over her shoulder and shook off the image of her sister and mum deep in conversation and stopping whenever she entered the room. It was a scene that had been repeated throughout Jess's adolescence. Leaving her, as always, thinking that she was the subject of their tête-à-tête.

She dragged her feet towards the bedroom door and trudged into the lounge.

'Just one thing before I go. You checked the hospitals today. Did you check yesterday?'

'No. I drove around yesterday, useless I know, but I needed to keep searching, and you're right I should have checked yesterday.'

'It's OK, I only thought of checking myself when I took Rachel there earlier. I'll see you later.'

She slipped on her coat and felt for the ticket in the pocket. It was still there.

She peeped around the lounge doorway. 'Actually, can I borrow the Mini again?'

'Yeah, sure. You can keep the spare key too. See you tomorrow?'

'Yeah. See you tomorrow.' She rubbed the ticket between her fingers.

My sister is missing. My sister was raped. I feel sick and so ashamed. Ashamed that I couldn't be there for her; to help pick up the pieces afterwards. And I'm angry. Why didn't Adam sort out the evil bastard who did this to her?

Her thoughts spiralled and refused to stay still. She scrunched the ticket up in her fingers. *Maybe I should tell the police now. Maybe they should know what she did, what she's capable of.*

She gripped the steering wheel, checked her mirrors and reversed erratically off the drive. Focusing solely on the road ahead helped her push her thoughts to her subconscious where she hoped they would stay for a while to give her some peace.

Missing Day Two

Jess

Jess ended the call. PC Hawthorne wasn't at his desk and she felt uncomfortable divulging her sister's biggest secret to someone she'd never spoken to before. They said he'd call her back as soon as possible. Her laptop clock said 6.29 p.m. A minute until she could speak to Matt. A numbness settled in her chest. There was so much she needed to say, but now wasn't the right time, not the right time to discuss their separation. Not that there ever would be a right time. He was on an adventure while she remained left behind. Left behind so he could have some space. Space away from her. She shook herself and inhaled her favourite perfume; the one Matt loved too.

6.30 p.m. Skype told her he was online and she pressed video call. The line clicked, the funny bubbly ringtone sounded and then there was a crackle, the video screen fired into life and Matt was sat opposite her.

His face was illuminated by a funny little pink lantern hanging above his head. He was sitting at what looked like a bar, but he was the only thing lit up. Darkness surrounded him. She couldn't help but smile at his newly sun-kissed skin which peeked out from under an odd little straw hat that looked cool despite being a little too small for his head.

'Thailand calling England. Are you there England?'

Matt put on a 1940s wartime reporter's accent, well-worn to her ear, which usually made her grin, but today the smile refused to form.

'England is here, you idiot.'

She watched the smile spread across his face as he squinted at the screen.

'Not been easy to stay in touch in these parts, but off to Oz next week so should be way easier. Had to charm the barman here to borrow his laptop and I'm actually working a shift as we speak in payment for this luxury.'

The familiar smirk appeared.

'Seriously, since when have you been able to pour a pint, did you mention you got sacked from your local pub?'

'Don't panic, there's no beer on tap here. I've been pouring ridiculously large measures of spirits and making up stupidly named cocktails. Might call one the Jess Special. Gin and white wine. Beer heads are safe tonight.'

Jess snorted as she recalled his trial shift where he was unable to pull the perfect pint, she had never seen so much froth and she couldn't understand how he managed to be so awful, although part of her suspected he had done it on purpose as it wasn't the summer job he wanted.

'So how are you?'

They delivered the words in unison.

'You go first,' said Matt.

A creeping unease spread throughout her body, and the chill she'd felt on and off at Steph's house seemed to rise up from the floor and settle over her, causing her to sit up and pull the throw around her, making Matt snigger.

'Bit cold back in Blighty?'

'It's February. You know how I hate February. Cold, cloudy, damp and miserable.'

'Well you know the answer to that don't you?'

'I can't just up and leave and join you. You know I can't.'

'You can. You just don't know you can.'

Matt picked up a drink and raised the glass to her, a signal to begin. She wished for a glass of white wine to be in her hands, but she needed to stay sharp.

'OK, things have gone a little crazy this week.'

She bit her lip in an attempt to prevent the tears flowing. She exhaled the words.

'Steph is missing. She's taken Natalie with her. We've no idea where she's gone. The police are looking for her. They are putting out an appeal this evening as she's been missing for forty-eight hours now. They think she may be struggling with postnatal depression – mental health issues cause many people to go missing. I ... I don't know what to do Matt. I feel so helpless.'

The soppy grin vanished as his expression darkened. He put down his drink and put his finger to the screen.

'Shit, Jess, that's bloody terrible. Missing? Shit. Surely if she was about to have some sort of breakdown Adam would have noticed?'

She nodded as cries choked her, preventing her from continuing. She reached for a tissue from the box on her bedside drawers, wiped her eyes and noisily blew her nose. Matt slightly tilted his head to one side. Patiently waiting for her to go ahead.

'Adam says she was a little weepy, and he's right. I've been there when her moods were erratic but I thought that was totally normal. The hormones, the adjustments, the sleep deprivation; Adam backs all this up and told the police that she didn't seem depressed. But today he dropped a huge bombshell.'

She no longer felt comfortable on the bed so she picked up the laptop and walked out of their bedroom to the lounge, placing it on the small dining table.

'You needed a view change. Flat is still looking lovely, but let's decorate when I get back, be nice to have a change. Reckon the landlord will like us to spruce it up a bit.'

'I hear your not-so-subtle attempt to reassure me that you are coming back.'

'Jess, I know you feel like this was going to be the end of us, but it is what it is.'

He paused and she could hear a slight hint of exasperation in his voice.

'It's me needing to have a pre-midlife crisis and find myself. And yes I need some space away from us, but there still is an us.'

He smiled that warm Kit Harrington-like smile which always made her knees weak, but today she didn't feel the usual reassurance or the jelly legs.

'OK, but I'd like to keep the lounge blue, I love the two contrasting tones.'

Matt laughed before draining the last dregs of his drink. He took off the daft straw hat to reveal a sandy mop of hair, sprinkled with blonde flecks. It was in need of a decent haircut. She inhaled, wishing she could take in his smell and wrap a strand of his hair around her finger.

She'd done enough to curtail any more chat about their relationship. Under normal circumstances she would have talked through all the things she'd left unsaid. The words that hung around the flat. Permeating the atmosphere, making her want to sink under each day.

But today there was something bigger than the both of them which took up all her mental energy, something acutely more terrifying than the possibility of the loss of her lover.

'So, Adam told me that Steph had a hideous time at uni and became so depressed she attempted to kill herself. I was getting upset about the idea that she could be suicidal. I know he was trying to give me the full picture, but – oh shit – I didn't know about this, she shut me out from so much.' Jess slammed her hands down on the table.

She felt the blood drain from her head, dizziness took hold of her and she held onto the table in case she fell off her chair.

'Did he say if there was a trigger for her depression?'

'Matt, he says she was raped. She didn't tell the police, she ended up pregnant and she had a termination. And I knew nothing about any of this.'

She paused and watched the horror wash over Matt's face. 'Words fail me. I feel like I've let her down because I didn't know. I mean, she had Adam to help her through it, but to deal with all of that alone and to take a shit load of paracetamol with the intention to kill herself … I don't even know where to begin, or how to even attempt to process any of this. I'm starting to feel like I don't know her at all.'

Jess stared beyond the laptop over to the bookcase. Her eyes glazed over. *Steph was raped by an ex-boyfriend. She got pregnant. My sister tried to kill herself. Shit. Is this happening over again?* She shook her head and re-focused on Matt.

'I know he wanted to give me the full picture, but his timing seems off – we'd had a similar discussion the previous day, why didn't he tell me then? And now I'm thinking that what if getting pregnant and having Natalie has triggered all the trauma that she's been holding onto. What if she has run away to kill herself?'

'Do the police know about the suicide attempt?'

'No, Adam didn't tell them because he wanted them to focus on actually finding her alive and not looking at local suicide spots.'

'Er, surely they can do both?'

'Yes, I'm sure they can do both. I've asked the officer to call me back as I need to tell them, even if Adam doesn't want to. Oh Matt. I'm so frightened for her and for Natalie, surely she wouldn't do this now? And then, there's ... Oh it doesn't matter.' A pained expression spread over her face.

'No, go on, what is it?'

'There's something not right about Adam, his behaviour feels off. I sound paranoid, don't I? I'm not saying he's involved in her disappearance in any way. I mean, he absolutely, utterly adores Steph and is besotted with Natalie, but I found a parking ticket for the time period he said he was out driving around and then I ended up taking one of Steph's NCT mums to hospital.'

Matt raise his eyebrows, the non-verbal cue requesting the full story of the hospital trip. 'Yes, I know, but that's a story for another time. I saw Adam leaving the hospital car park as I was entering. He didn't deny he went today. The ticket could be from there, he could have been there checking two days in a row, but honestly why waste time going there in person? He could have just phoned. And, I don't know, he's constantly shaking and sweating. Both signs of stress which could be caused by being out of his mind with worry, but – ugh, I'm probably being ridiculous but something doesn't feel right.'

She slumped in the chair. She knew she'd rambled and that she sounded ridiculously paranoid. She half knew what Matt was going to say next.

'So he's what, lied about his whereabouts and the stress of the situation is manifesting itself physically? I think you are clutching at straws. You're letting your feelings towards him cloud your judgement and your lack of trust in general is controlling the way you think.'

She sighed and stared at his grainy image. She knew he'd be measured, deal with the facts. But for her facts were slippery, fluid and could take on the colour of lies. She thought through her worries about Adam.

The speaking clock. The ticket. The shakes and the revelations. Am I seeing a puzzle where there isn't one? The speaking clock.

'Did I mention he called the speaking clock?'

'Adam called the speaking clock? That's not a crime though, is it?'

'I know, but who does that? Who needs to do that? And I heard him speak to someone and then he called the speaking clock to cover it up.'

'Or maybe he didn't know the time, couldn't be arsed to go and get his mobile and yes, most people don't do that these days, but it's another big straw you're clutching at.'

'You'd clutch at everything and anything if it was your brother who'd disappeared. You'd do anything to find him.'

'I would, but I wouldn't start suspecting his partner. I'd be practical.'

She wiped her eyes with her hand and instantly regretted the application of mascara as the black lines streaked the back of her hand.

He moved a fraction closer to the laptop camera. His voice was softer, more intimate. 'Are you sure there's nothing you've missed?'

She sighed deeply and leaned back in the chair again and folded her arms.

'Like what?'

'Something from your childhood?'

'Our childhood?' She sighed noisily and dug her fingernails into her arms.

'Yes, the closed book of Jess and Steph's childhood. Dad leaves. End of. You hate your mum. You trust no one other than Steph. You don't even trust me.' He drained his drink. 'Cheap shot, I know, but you not trusting any one is making you paranoid.' He put his finger to the screen. 'You need help, you have to let me in if you want me back and maybe there is something in your past – in Steph's past – that has driven her away. Something that you need to get out so you're not so fucking angry at everyone.'

'I'm talking about my sister being raped, attempting suicide and now she's disappeared with my niece and you're talking about us. This is bigger than us!'

'I didn't mean to belittle what's going on, but I—'

'No. I can't talk any more. I was hoping to feel better talking things through with you but we are back going over old ground.' She moved the cursor over 'end call'.

'You always react like this when I mention your childhood. I'm sorry, but seriously, maybe there is something from the past that can help you find her. I know I shouldn't have thrown us into this equation. It's not the right time. I'm sorry. I'll go.' He massaged his left temple. 'Ugh, I don't want to leave it like this. I do love you. I miss you.' He stroked the screen with the index finger of his right hand.

'You've a funny way of showing it.' Her finger twitched as the cursor moved away from the cancel sign. She thought about all the arguments they'd had, all the accusations she'd flung at him, all of them were unfounded. All of them a defence mechanism. Stop her from getting hurt. Pushing him away before he had the chance to hurt her.

Eyes closed tight, a child's hand – her little hand – pushing open a door materialised in her mind's eye. Always when she felt under pressure, always that memory pushed its way forward. She inhaled deeply. *No. I won't see this.*

'Now push aside your natural tendency to leap to conclusions and catastrophise, and think positively. She'll come home. They'll both be safe.' His words shook her back into the present.

His smile wasn't convincing, it was all he could do to pathetically attempt to reassure her.

'I love you Jess.'

'I'll call you when there's news.'

She ended the call. A blank screen appeared. Nothingness. Silence. A black hole, like the one he left behind. Anger replaced the numbness now. Talking things through hadn't cleared the mist engulfing her thoughts, it had deepened it to a full fog.

Leaving the laptop open, she trudged to the fridge to pour herself a large glass of white wine. Returning to her seat she checked her Facebook page and looked through Steph's too. It seemed eerie that the photos of Natalie had stopped. She abruptly closed the pages down.

Once the media appeal went out she'd put a link to it on her and Steph's Facebook pages and on her Twitter account too. She'd meant to do it earlier, but time seemed to race away and there was so much buzzing around her brain.

She pondered Matt's words 'the closed book of Jess'. She knew he was right. She needed to deal with the rage and the paranoia she let flow freely through her veins. But to tell him about her mum and what she did. Would he believe her? The only time she had confided in someone they did nothing. Assumed she was attention-seeking. Her primary school teacher Mrs Livingston didn't believe her.

She remembered staring at her teacher's spindly long fingers, hands covered in liver spots. She told her that she didn't have a PE kit. She always borrowed the spare things. Her teacher said she needed to ask her mum for one and when she said her mum refused to give her a kit she'd laughed. She remembered her legs giving away from under her as she cried and told her teacher how her mum never bought her new things, that she'd often shut her in her bedroom, that she'd go out places with her older sister for hours and leave her home alone with nothing to eat. Mrs Livingston didn't write anything down. She simply told Jess to come back in tomorrow with a PE kit. She thought she was making excuses up. After all Mrs Livingston knew her mum. She knew the version of Mum that came on every school trip, the one who helped out at all the school fetes, the one who heard the children read. Not the real Mum who lived in her house. The one who frequently locked her in the cupboard under the stairs as punishment. Punishment for telling the truth. Would Matt believe her? Or would he think she was catastrophising again, making a mountain out of childish hurts.

She found herself browsing through some of the old photos she'd scanned in a while ago. She'd chosen a collection of images from their childhood, ones she loved, or were significant to her, and she'd taken the time to laboriously scan them in.

Her and Steph on Steph's seventh birthday with a new bike. Red, glittering in the summer sunlight.

The two of them with their cousins holding hands and jumping together over the tiny waves. She could almost hear their squeals of delight and the squawks of the seagulls overhead.

Lots of pictures of Steph, Jess recalled trawling through a heap of old photos. Mum had taken picture after picture of Steph. But when it came to Jess the images ceased when her Dad left.

She winced at the recollection and scrolled through until she came to a picture that she had taken of her sister. Steph, about sixteen, sat at her desk in her bedroom with the awful girly pink and white walls. She held her hand up towards the camera. Her heavy fringe hovered on her forehead. She was making a face saying no.

Jess had kept the image because she liked the drama of the scene and because it was one of the few times she'd managed to borrow the camera. Steph had a pen in her hand and it was paused in the act of writing in a notebook.

She stared at the image of Steph writing. It was a memory that flickered to the surface of her subconscious. It was an image she'd seen repeated time and time again.

She kept a diary.

She was always writing in it and then hiding it away, quickly if she was disturbed, or sometimes more leisurely as if the act of diarising her day wasn't important.

But it was. It was something she'd done for years. And what did Adam say? He wondered if she kept her passwords written down in one of those funny little notebooks he'd seen her with.

And they were funny because they were small, thin and dull looking, just like school exercise books. She'd probably pinched them from school as a teen. Thin enough to hide easily.

They need to be found.

She smiled, it felt like a small triumph, something tangible that might point her in the right direction, as long as Steph hadn't taken them with her on her mysterious road trip. Jess's brow furrowed. No, she wouldn't have taken them, there seemed a lack of order to her disappearance evidenced by the fact that she'd hardly taken any clothes with her. The only act of order seemed to have occurred when she withdrew all that cash. Jess suddenly felt a sense of purpose, instead of feeling that she was flailing around in the dark, or putting two and two together and making five.

Where would Steph hide her diaries?

Missing Day Two

Meadowhall Railway Station, Sheffield

PC Jenkins surveyed the platform. Two witnesses were huddled together on a bench under a shelter. One wrapped in a shiny blanket. Shaking, despite their layers of clothing.

Jenkins was pleased she didn't have too many witness statements to process; the couple and five other members of the public.

This couple had called the British Transport Police, unusual, but Jenkins saw a poster displayed on one of the advertising boards telling the couple exactly what to do. Normally people ignored the posters and dialled 999.

It wouldn't take long to get their statements. The CCTV would tell them what happened and the poor unsuspecting shoppers would add a little more information and that's all she'd need.

Suicide. She glanced at the tracks and winced. This was the second one she'd been called to this month and the thirteenth in her career. The last one was a young lad aged nineteen who threw himself in front of a high-speed train near Barnsley. Identification had been difficult.

Rain began to fall more heavily and there was a crispness to the air which made her wish she'd slipped another layer of clothing on under the uniform. The fluorescent hi-vis waistcoat failed to provide additional warmth. She stiffened up in an attempt to retain heat.

She approached the couple as the paramedic finished checking them over. Jenkins nodded at the medic who grimaced in recognition.

'Thanks,' said Jenkins, a brief acknowledgement of the work they'd undertaken here.

Moving towards the couple she introduced herself, explaining that she'd like to take some details and a statement if they were up to it. She took out her notebook. Took down their names and contact details and proceeded to discuss what they'd witnessed.

'Can you tell me what you saw, starting before the incident occurred?'

The woman looked at her husband, as though she needed his permission to go ahead. He nodded.

'We were just sitting here and she arrived a bit after we'd sat down. She stood very close to the edge of the platform. That's what drew my attention to her, you know, I was expecting her to sit down on the bench or at least keep away from the edge, but she just stood there.'

The woman pointed to an empty space on the edge of the platform.

'She didn't have any shopping bags either, but she held something close to her. It could have been a baby. She held it like one, like she was supporting its bottom and legs with one hand and the back of its head with the other. But if it was a baby it was asleep or content, no crying. No movement.'

The woman began to sob loudly, her husband pulled her close to him and gently rocked her. Jenkins waited until her cries quietened.

'It's OK, you're doing really well. Take your time.'

The husband took his wife's hand and held it, gently stroking it in an attempt to soothe her. Jenkins wanted to smile at his tenderness but refrained; inappropriate, remain solemn.

The woman took out a large handkerchief and dabbed her eyes before continuing. 'There was an announcement about a high-speed train coming through on our platform.' She began again. Her voice still had a wobble to it. 'I expected her to move back and sit down since it wasn't her train coming next. It was all so quick, one minute we could hear the train approaching, the next minute she jumped and then the train hit.'

The woman, who was in her late sixties, had one of those faces which had begun to sag around her mouth making her look constantly melancholic. She stared at Jenkins, as though the officer could tell her why someone would do this, to herself and possibly her baby.

Jenkins knew the look well. 'Thank you Mrs Colton, you've been really helpful. Did you notice anything else about her? Did she seem distressed or agitated?'

'No, not really. She just stood on the edge and looked forward all the time. I couldn't see her face because she wore a hood. She seemed calm, just standing there.'

The witness broke down again. Her husband intervened and asked if he could take his wife home.

'Did you see anything else, sir? Anything that might help?'

'Not really. I didn't take much notice to be honest. I saw her near the edge and then I wasn't really looking at her. I was watching the pigeons, they were courting one another, I was watching the chap do his dance, sorry, I'm bit of a bird enthusiast not a people watcher like my wife.'

'Thank you Mr Colton, if you do remember anything, or you or your wife need to speak to me, here's my card.

You've both been a great help. Here's another card with some numbers in case you need some help processing today's event. It has been very distressing for the both of you.'

Jenkins waved over a member of the station staff and asked him to call the couple a cab.

The discovery that the young woman may have not only taken her own life, but also the life of her baby, had shaken her.

Once out of the way she texted her mum, asking her to give her daughter an extra hug and a kiss. She'd seen enough suicides to understand how desperate people became, but to kill yourself and your baby? She couldn't comprehend it. She took out her notebook again and began the same process with the other witnesses.

Missing Day Two

Harlow Police Station

Sergeant Browne yawned, stretched, and refocused her eyes on the flickering monitor. She was always tired these days, and the night shifts seemed to take more of a toll on her body. Ageing and motherhood, she mused, an exhausting combination. She finished some paperwork and began to check through the ongoing concerns.

An ANPR alert had come through. They'd flagged the missing mum's number plate and her car had been picked up near Sheffield. Notes showed that Hawthorne had made contact with South Yorkshire Police confirming that her car had entered and remained in the Meadowhall shopping centre car park.

Browne looked over the statements of the missing woman's sister and husband. The girls grew up in Sheffield, although no family members lived there at present. It was feasible that she might still have a connection to the area, an old friend perhaps, pondered Browne.

She took off her glasses, opened her desk drawer and pulled out some Optrex dry eyes spray. She blinked as the mist clung to her lashes. Replacing her glasses she continued to go over the notes.

Information had been circulated to local media, including a striking image of Mrs Henderson and her baby. Browne stared at the image. *Why has this new mum disappeared?*

Hawthorne had said that it seemed odd that none of her close family thought she was depressed, just the usual baby blues. Browne recalled the first few weeks after the birth of her son. She was either crying or on the verge of tears, but she wasn't depressed. What would her family have said about her back then? Emotional? Unstable? Moody. She wasn't sure they could have provided a clear answer.

The picture was haunting. The woman smiled for the camera, a natural proud smile as she held her perfect daughter in her arms. A very emotive image. Browne sighed.

Hopefully there'll be a sighting of her soon and she'll be returned to her family in the next few days and be able to get help, surely she needs help, otherwise why the hell would she disappear?

'Coffee anyone?' Browne asked the handful of colleagues hunched over their desks. Luckily, no one said yes. They were deep in paperwork and took little notice of her.

The noise of the kettle seemed extraordinarily loud in the quiet kitchen, just a few more hours of peace before Friday night kick-out time, thought Browne.

The evening had started off far too quietly for her liking, it always unnerved her: the calm before the urban shit-storm erupted. She always felt like she'd drawn the short straw when she had to work a Friday or Saturday night shift, and recently she'd begun to dread it.

The drunks, especially the women, really wound her up. Her patience and tolerance levels declined in tandem with her sleep.

As she returned to her desk the phone began to ring. At the end of the line a soft northern accent explained that he was calling from South Yorkshire Police.

'We've a sighting that possibly matches your misper Mrs Henderson.'

'Good, go ahead.' Browne flicked open the file on screen and hoped to be adding good news to her notes.

'Earlier today British Transport Police responded to a completed suicide at Meadowhall shopping centre train station where ANPR last sighted the misper's car. CCTV shows a woman fitting the description of the misper standing on the edge of a platform before leaping in front of the high-speed train.'

Browne stared at the image still on her computer screen. She offered up a prayer to anyone who would answer. *Shit. Not this news. Please don't let it be her.*

The voice continued and Browne began to take down the details being fed to her.

'The woman was holding a bundle, a witness thought she was holding her baby.'

Fuck no! Browne held her breath as she tried to absorb the information.

'CCTV hasn't captured her face because all the time she stood on the platform she had her hood up and her head was down, staring at the bundle in her arms.' The voice paused.

Browne's thoughts went into overdrive, she visualised the mum hugging the newborn to her chest, head dipped as though she was inhaling the baby's scent or kissing its head. She was desperate for this woman not to be the beautiful woman who was smiling at her from the photograph on screen.

She needed CCTV to show Mrs Stephanie Henderson entering the station or the car park at the shopping centre or any place where an image showed her face clearly. DNA evidence was needed to confirm identity and this was not going to be easy.

Again on the end of the line a soft Yorkshire accent spoke far too quickly into her ear. Browne was thankful she wasn't speaking to a colleague in Merseyside; she always seemed to struggle with fast-talking northerners. She knew her colleagues took the piss out of her slow Essex drawl, but at least no one required her to slow down or speak more clearly. She scribbled down the contact details of the officer in charge of the investigation.

'Can you find more CCTV images of our misper? Any to confirm that she enters the station? Can you find her in the car park and leaving it? I need all her movements showing her leaving the car park, entering the train station and that it is her standing on that platform holding her baby.'

They'd get back to her in the morning. *Fuck*. She slammed the phone down and uncharacteristically her hands trembled. She'd been an officer for thirteen years now. Things didn't used to rattle her. It was her job, she took the horror in her stride, able to put it in a box and lock it away, but this case got under her skin in a way she'd not experienced, or allowed a case to do, before. Motherhood had weakened her guard.

This woman was the same age as her. One child. One baby. It could be her. She felt an odd connection, something she'd not felt for some time. This was the first time the station had been involved in searching for a misper like this. Normally it was suspects known to the police, teenagers, or people known to social services.

Not a white middle-class female with a newborn baby and with no history or baggage. Someone like her, or like her sister. She checked the time. Maybe she should text Hawthorne, he'd probably want to know that there was a high probability she'd killed herself and her child.

Missing Day Two

Jess

Jess put the glass down on the coffee table and switched channels. She wanted to see the police appeal. She'd thought about noting down some of the words they used so she could repeat them in her own Facebook post.

BBC local news. The usual stories, politics, a stabbing south of the river, a man charged with robbing several teenagers in Hackney. And then the picture she'd taken appeared on the screen. She drew in air through her teeth and held her breath, her hands automatically rose to cover her mouth and goosebumps ran down her arms.

The presenter detailed when she'd last been seen, what she could be wearing and that she'd taken Natalie. A solitary tear trickled down Jess's cheek. The disembodied voice went on to say how worried police were because Natalie was only three weeks old. The female presenter shared the usual phone number.

Jess took in the presenter's concern. It looked real, not rehearsed, but in reality she'd probably read out a missing person's report many times in her career, but maybe not like this one.

The presenter moved on to a lighter piece and just like that her sister was forgotten. She turned off the TV and threw the remote onto the floor. The back fell off and skittered across the wooden floorboards coming to rest before it disappeared under the TV cabinet.

Her whole body shuddered as she hauled herself off the sofa to take a seat in front of the laptop at the small dining-room table. The Ikea table had seen better days. The laminate was beginning to peel away from the corner. She pushed it back into place. It held for a moment before springing back.

Jess opened up Facebook. Her fingers froze. She knew what she needed to do, but it really was the last thing she wanted. She was used to shaping the news, not being part of it.

'Get a grip.' She chastised herself and feverishly began to type a message asking for help, appealing to friends to look for her. Telling them that Steph hadn't taken her phone and that anything they recalled might help. Along with tagging in her sister and Adam, she tagged a few old friends from Sheffield who knew them both, in the outside chance she might turn up on their doorstep. She linked it to Essex Police's website where details of her sister's case now appeared.

The pointer hovered over the post button. She puffed out her cheeks and blew out air. Pressing post would get her message out there, but it would encourage the Facebook voyeurs to look on and make judgements at a distance and not comprehend the pain she and Adam were going through. She re-read the message several times. This was the most important post she'd ever write.

The weight of it made her head spin. She put her hand to her forehead and read it one more time. Every word. No typos. All made sense.

Fuck. Click post.

Gone.

She saw her post appear. And then the comments began. The disbelief, the 'I'm so sorry what a nightmare' comments and the 'we'll help look for her and share this post' to the ones with emojis and kisses. It wouldn't seem real to them, just another thread to comment on.

One of Steph's school friends from Sheffield posted and reassured her that she'd keep an eye out for her and she'd share the post, too.

Jess thanked the old friend. *Perhaps not everyone sees this as just another meaningless status update.* She walked away from the screen to pour herself some more wine.

The initial flurry of comments had ceased for the moment but she couldn't step away from Facebook. Its addictive pull held fast.

It could help, it's getting the news out there. Someone may see her, a friend of a friend in Sheffield may spot her, as her car was heading up north. She might be hiding there.

Only one of the Sheffield friends had commented so far. She clicked through to another school friend's page. She had checked into the Leadmill, but another status update caught her eye.

Stuck at work. No trains cuz someone jumped in front of one!

After the status update there was an angry face emoji. An angry face, not a sad one, mused Jess. Further comments ranged from sympathy to a total lack of empathy.

But one raised alarm bells.

'I heard it was a woman holding a baby. OMG. How could anyone do that? WTAF?!'

Jess re-read the comment several times before searching the local newspaper. *The Sheffield Star* gave a short report:

> A woman, who died after being hit by a train, has not yet been identified. A British Transport Police spokesman said: 'We were called to Meadowhall station in Sheffield shortly after 4 p.m. on Friday 3rd February, after a report that a person had been struck by a train. Colleagues from Yorkshire Ambulance Service also attended, but the woman was pronounced dead at the scene. Officers are trying to identify the woman, whose death is not being treated as suspicious.'
>
> The police could not confirm reports that the woman was holding a baby when she jumped in front of the train.

It couldn't be. Would she go back home? She never hankered after the north, or if she did she never talked about it. But what do I know? I'm wondering if I know anything about her any more.

Jess drained her wine. Her head was already spinning and her eyes were so sore it was difficult to see the screen on her mobile as she searched for the number for Epping Police. She had to know if they'd heard anything, if they had any evidence to stop her brain jumping from one conclusion to the next.

A woman answered, not PC Hawthorne. The Essex drawl wrong-footed Jess as she attempted to explain what she'd read, her words didn't seem to come out right, but she'd said enough.

'Miss Morley, we are aware of the report that you're referring to. At present we need to piece together the exact movements of your sister. I can confirm that her car is parked in the shopping centre car park, but the woman on CCTV, she doesn't look at the camera on the platform. We can't confirm that it is your sister, we need more time and, as well as additional CCTV images we require DNA evidence to establish the identity of the victim.'

'But her car is in the car park. The woman was holding a baby!'

'Miss Morley, until we can absolutely confirm that the woman on the station platform was your sister we are still conducting a missing persons search. I know this is an extremely difficult time for you, but until we can absolutely confirm the identity of this woman we will stay focused on finding your sister and your niece.'

Jess coughed before speaking in order to free her voice from her closing larynx. 'I'm sorry, it's just too much of a co-incidence and …' she paused, she wanted to tell her about what Adam had told her, but his words stuck in her head because this officer had said something similar, 'they'll stay focused on finding your sister and niece', they will still keep looking until they find her, if they believe she's dead then the search is over. *I don't want it to be her. It can't be her under that train.* 'I'm sorry, I just want them home safe and sound. Thanks for updating me.'

'No problem. As soon as we get any more information we will update you and your brother-in-law.'

She placed her mobile on the table and slammed her laptop shut as a lurching sensation gripped her body causing her to run to the loo. The wine she'd drunk flooded into the basin. She had to cling to the fact that they couldn't absolutely confirm that it was her sister. There was still hope, still a chance that DNA evidence would prove it wasn't her. *A faint hope.*

Adam

The door slammed closed behind him. He replayed Steph's words. This man, this fucking little oik had threatened his wife. Scared her witless. It's one thing to have a crush which leads to an obsession and a string of nasty emails, but to come to their home and shout abuse and threats through the letterbox.

No. No fucking way.

His thoughts raced. In his mind he rehearsed his speech. Threats to counter-threats. In no uncertain terms Jason would know he couldn't set foot on their road. If he came anywhere near the house, the police would be informed. He'd make sure that Jason knew he'd do anything to protect his family. Anything to keep this unhinged man away from his wife. He must be deranged to carry on like this. To shout threats through a letterbox. *Fucking coward, but I'm glad he didn't ring the doorbell and insist he be let in. Why didn't she tell me ages ago and put a stop to this? Feeling sorry for people gets you nowhere.*

But as his steps slowed down as he strode up Bower Hill, his thoughts mirrored his footsteps. He needed to be calm. Focused. He'd simply threaten to go to the police and report his verbal assault if it didn't stop. Adam pondered whether he should head straight to the police station now, but he wanted to put the wind up Jason in the same way he'd scared the shit out of his wife.

He needed a dose of his own brand of medicine. He needed him to know that his secret was out. The stalking, the emails, he wanted to make him squirm, put the frighteners on him enough to make sure he'd think twice about doing it again.

He couldn't go to work tomorrow worrying about whether some sicko was going to stalk his wife. Watch her and Natalie. No. He couldn't wait for the police to intervene, it needed to end now.

Tuning into his steps helped calm his nerves, stem the flow of adrenaline or testosterone or whatever it was that was propelling him forward and making him want to take the fight to this wanker.

But his feet seemed to quicken. He became aware of his sharp intakes of breath. He stopped. He needed a moment for his lungs to recover and allow his brain the chance to rehearse his speech. How would Jason react to him turning up out of the blue? Would he remember his face? *If I'm supposed to remind him of his dad then he'll probably recognise me.*

His thoughts jumped back to the house-warming. Had there been any clues? He recalled how Jason was incredibly chatty. He asked lots of questions, but then all Steph's colleagues did. It was their job after all; it became a way of life.

But yes, come to think of it, Jason had asked a few odd personal questions, one about what Steph got up to while he was away on business. At the time it had made Adam cringe a little. It was his tone, almost leering, suggestive that she could and would get up to something in his absence and he recalled excusing himself to escape him.

As he approached Jason's address he took in the details of the street. The road was quiet. No residents stirred or cars approached. He could hear a dog barking in a back garden, but other than that the occupants were probably busy with their evening meals or watching TV.

He checked behind him, no one appeared in the darkness. He strode up the short driveway breathing deeply to stop his racing heart thumping loudly in his ears. He straightened his spine and pushed the doorbell. Tinny-sounding chimes announced his arrival.

A clatter of claws on wooden floors could be heard accompanied by loud deep barks. Adam recoiled from the step. He disliked dogs with a passion, he thought back to the party, *what type of dog did he have?*

The door opened slowly to reveal the answer. A golden-coloured medium-sized dog barked at him. It was the sort of bark that suggested he distrusted the person in front of him, but feared him, too: deep and low, turning into a rumbling throaty growl. Adam looked nervously at the spaniel, but quickly pushed his fear aside.

Jason stared at him with a puzzled expression on his face. Adam knew he didn't recognise him.

He peered over Jason's shoulder down the hallway. He could hear the TV blaring out from the lounge.

'Sorry to bother you, but I need a quiet word. I'm Adam Henderson.'

Adam noticed a glimmer of recognition flash across Jason's face, but it quickly faded to a deadpan expression revealing nothing more.

'Can I come in?'

Jason shifted the weight from one foot to the other.

'Er, what's this about?' He scratched his head.

Adam found his fake puzzlement irritating. He knew the name, he probably did recognise him now. He wanted to have it out with him right now on the doorstep for all to see. But his natural leanings to keep calm and keep things private stopped him.

'My wife has told me a lot about you. I'm not sure you want me to detail all the stalking you've been doing out here on your doorstep. Perhaps you'd prefer to talk more inside?'

Jason grimaced and assented. As Adam advanced through the doorway the dog backed away and proceeded to lie on its back in a submissive pose.

Missing Day Three

Jess

Jess yawned and stretched, reaching upwards towards the kitchen ceiling before bringing her arms down in an arc. She rubbed the sleep from her eyes and on autopilot she made her way to the kettle to make herself a coffee.

She was exhausted. Running on empty. Her sleep had been restless, waking from dreams of Steph drowning in the North Sea, but the Steph of her dreams was the child of the photographs, not her fully grown sister. She reckoned at the most she'd managed a couple of hours' sleep.

Fag lady, as Jess had dubbed her, emerged from her back door and stood at the top of the stairs blowing smoke into the cold air. The thought of being outside caused Jess to pull her dressing gown tie tighter. Fag Lady put out a cigarette and instantly lit up another. The curls of smoke climbed skyward, gradually dissipating.

A blackbird darted across the lawn. It drew her attention away from Fag lady and made her think of Steph.

She checked the news article again on her phone before opening her contacts list and letting her finger hover over it. No. Adam can wait; she wished she'd not seen the article. It could be anyone. It could be a coincidence.

*But she's already tried to take her life.*A creaking sound emitted from the lounge which stopped her thoughts in their tracks. It sounded like the floorboard near the window, it always made that noise whenever you stood on it to draw the curtains. Jess tentatively moved towards the lounge doorway.

The curtains were wide open. She rubbed her brow, she was sure she drew them last night and she didn't recall entering the lounge this morning. She must have forgotten to close them. All her actions were on autopilot. Her body was following the usual routine while her mind was plunged into darkness.

Quickly showering, she got dressed and layered up as she couldn't shift the chill that continued to rinse over her skin. She was glad she could jump in the Mini and drive to her sister's house, avoiding being further exposed to the seasonal nip.

She hoped Adam was out; she knew she couldn't keep the news article from him but she wanted to search for Steph's diaries in peace, it wasn't something she intended to share with him, not yet, or maybe not ever if they revealed nothing. It could simply be her inner ramblings, or it could be her secrets laid bare for all to read. Her sister's most intimate thoughts.

The thought of trespassing into Steph's inner psyche didn't sit comfortably with her. She'd respected her privacy; even as a teen when she was curious about Steph's first boyfriends she'd kept away, never wanting to be given the label of the annoying little sister.

She'd never pried into her sister's belongings. It was an unspoken rule she observed.

Why didn't she tell me? Why I am the open book to her and she shut herself off from me? Maybe I was and still am the annoying little sister.

The roads were quiet. It was relatively early for a Saturday morning. No school run, or commuters, just a few cyclists and the odd runner; the virtuous people who had avoided a Friday night out in London.

Jess found herself taking in the details of the road ahead, something tangible to focus on. She found that her speed was naturally dropping as she took in the winter trees, whose branches acquired a silvery-grey hue in the February light. Her slow driving was rewarded. At the side of the road stood a deer. Stock-still, as her car passed by. *Beautiful, but I'm glad it didn't dart out in front of me.*

Her musings ended as she left the forest and the area became more suburban. Jess felt as though she was battling to shut so many things out of her mind. She wanted to return to the forest where her thoughts could meander like the road.

Back in suburbia thoughts of Natalie and Steph could not be pushed away.

As she drove up Bower Hill a car pulled out of The Orchards: Adam's car.

She slowed down a little to avoid being seen. It would be a good time to search for the diaries without his presence lurking in the background. She flicked on the indicator but something pulled her forward and told her not to go to the house. She cancelled the ticking sound.

Sensible Matt had said she was being ridiculous but still, she couldn't shake her unease, and trusting her gut normally led to success. She would listen to her suspicious side, it could be heard and hopefully disproved. *Fuck sensible Matt.*

She held back a little, slowing down. Her hands shook, so she tightened her grip on the steering wheel. Following Adam's car seemed ridiculous but necessary.

Jess slowly drove behind Adam, maintaining a good distance and allowing another motorist to go in front of her. The SUV dwarfed the Mini. She hoped it would hold its position and protect her from being seen in Adam's rear-view mirror.

The route was becoming familiar. It was the same route she'd taken yesterday when she ferried Rachel to Princess Alexandra hospital.

Traffic increased as they approached the hospital. Three cars now separated her from Adam. They approached the roundabout just before the hospital and she expected him to proceed to the hospital, but instead he turned off before entering the queue for the roundabout.

Shit. It's too obvious if I follow him down that road.

With no cars behind her she paused at the roundabout and took an exit which took her into the hospital grounds. She passed the main entrance to A&E and followed the road out again. By following the road she knew she'd meet the same one Adam had taken. *If he wasn't going to the hospital again where was he going? No he has to be.* She turned off down the first street in the hope that he was looking for a place to park.

Her heartbeat quickened as she saw a familiar figure round the corner of the road up ahead. Jess pulled into a space, thankfully on the opposite side of the street to Adam. She couldn't help but slowly sink down in the driver's seat to obscure herself from view.

Closing her eyes, she silently chanted: *don't look over, don't look over, keep walking, keep walking.* Her eyelids flicked open.

He had gone.

She turned her head following the curve of the pavement. Definitely gone.

Her brain provided her with a vision of him reappearing at the passenger window, opening the door and asking her what the hell she was doing?

Her heart felt like it was going to explode out of her ribcage. Her whole body pulsated. This wasn't how she wanted to spend her Saturday morning, stalking her brother-in-law and then searching through her sister's belongings.

She scooped up her hood over her head, hoping it did enough to disguise her and protect her from the rain that had started to fall. The iciness in the air suggested the rain could turn to snow, and the voluminous white clouds up above agreed as the rain turned to sleet, blurring the street ahead.

She had noticed that Adam was wearing a cap with a peak, it looked odd, inappropriate in the cold weather, something he should be wearing in the summer. She winced. He didn't want to be recognised either.

Urged forward by the sleet and fear, she sprinted. She was unsure what she'd do when she rounded the corner. His strides were long, he had a head start, but she caught a glimpse of his back entering the hospital grounds. She sprinted as though she was at the end of a race and followed him into the hospital.

He maintained the same pace. Long strides, confident strides. He knew exactly where he was going. Keeping her distance and crossing her fingers, she hoped he wouldn't turn around. He didn't.

They left the wide open entrance space behind them as the building narrowed to form a corridor. A few patients or visitors shuffled by, but the corridor was relatively empty; if he turned around at any moment he'd see her. Her palms moistened with sweat. *What is he doing here?*

The sign told her he was heading towards the lifts. Jess slowed up, she pondered her next move. If he was to get into a lift, she'd lose him. She hung back as he came to a set of double doors.

Instinct compelled her to bend down to tie her shoelace. She could barely loop the laces over. Her eyes strained looking upwards. He glanced behind him.

Dipping her head down to avoid being seen, she fiddled with her laces. She held her breath and slowly glanced up at the doors. He'd gone.

Jess shot up abruptly and through the glass she saw him move to the side, away from the lift. She walked at speed, remaining near the wall in order to peer through the frames. *Stairs. He's taken the stairs.*

Holding her breath, she entered the stairwell.

Up ahead she could hear footsteps, and by now she'd become accustomed to the rhythm of his walk, she knew they belonged to him. She crept up the stairs, listening intently, making only the softest of sounds as her trainer clad foot pushed down on the step. Pausing before turning to take the next flight, Jess noticed that the footsteps had ceased. A noise which sounded like plastic sticking and then being pulled away reached her ears.

She tiptoed to the doors and peered through the glass. Beyond the door was a corridor and another set of double doors. Tentatively she entered the corridor. Adam passed through the second set of doors and she could see him standing still and staring at a door about halfway down the walkway. He glanced back down the corridor in her direction.

Flattening herself against the wall and clamping her eyes closed she willed him not to see her. She opened her eyes just in time to see him enter a ward. *Who is he visiting?*

Making her way along the length of the corridor to the second set of double doors she pushed the door, but it refused to move. It was sealed shut. To her left she saw a buzzer. *How the hell did he get through?*

A cleaner appeared at the end of the corridor. He was pushing a trolley and slowly shuffled towards her. This was her chance, her only way in. She held her head high, and as the cleaner manoeuvred his way backwards through the door, she held the door open and in her most confident east London accent she cheerily uttered the words, 'Here you go mate.' The cleaner nodded his appreciation and continued on his way.

Muffled voices seeped through the first door. She was tiptoeing again. The act made her feel ridiculous. Sweat trickled down the back of her neck and her pulse thundered in her ears.

At the doorway she bent down again to tie her shoelace and to catch a glimpse of what the first room looked like.

Through the bottom glass panel she could make out three beds on each side of the room. The second ward was where Adam had entered. She felt exposed beyond the double doors. If Adam left the ward he'd walk straight into her.

She darted past the first set of doors and then past the ward that Adam had entered. The third door offered her a lifeline: a hiding place. A unisex toilet. She could wait in the loo until Adam left. Then she'd get a chance to look into the second room which he'd entered.

It was her only option. She wouldn't be able to see him exit, she would have to rely on hearing him leave, recognising his footsteps.

Ducking into the loo she locked the door. She stood as still as humanly possible and strained to hear any noise outside. Her wait was short. About sixty seconds later she heard the swoosh of a door. Again she held her breath.

Her heart was in her throat. She waited. Counting the minutes in her head. For authenticity's sake she flushed the loo and washed her hands.

Silence enveloped the corridor. Her heart rate began to slow a little. She moved towards the second set of doors and peeped in through the glass. From here she couldn't see the whole ward, she could just make out that two of the beds were occupied on the left-hand side.

Voices. Someone in the room was talking. She listened. She could make out snippets of conversation. *Shit. Doctors doing their rounds.*

She edged forwards towards the door and tried to tune in to what the doctor was saying. She didn't catch the first part of the conversation, something about giving him a hundred milligrams of some drug, but the next bit was clear.

She heard a male voice tell his colleague that police were still clueless about what had happened to the patient, he'd received a blow to his face and another blow to the back of head.

The voices grew a little louder as the doctors moved towards the door. She had nowhere to hide.

Again she stood up straight and confidently smiled at the doctors who emerged from the room. She held the door for them. They were still deep in conversation and gave her just a cursory glance, before continuing to talk as they made their way into the first ward and away from Jess.

Without thinking, she threw herself into the room. Six beds. Three occupied, one more than she'd anticipated. Two older men both on ventilators and a younger man, one who she hadn't seen through the glass, who also required a machine to do his breathing for him.

She moved closer to him. It was difficult to make out his features as the tubes, taping and wires obscured his face. Fixed to the wall above his head was a whiteboard which detailed the date of admission, who his consultant was and which nurse was monitoring him. The date struck her first. The day before Steph had disappeared. *Shit! Why doesn't it say his name?*

She scrutinised the bleeping monitor and the rhythm of his heartbeat. And there in the top left-hand corner of the screen was his name. Her fingers shook as she typed his name into Google. The first result revealed his Twitter profile. A reporter at *The Mirror.*

He worked with Steph.

A bead of sweat trickled down her cheek, but the chill which she still couldn't shake, filled every sinew. She had to get out of the ward. Turning on her heels she retreated back to the doorway. She peered through the grey outlined squares in the glass panel. Not a soul occupied the space between her and the double doors.

She left the room. The sound of the ventilators rang in her ears. The steady rhythm of hisses and clicks.

* * *

Having left the hospital building she now felt compelled to run. There was no sign of Adam anywhere. The roads were deserted. Panic flooded her again as she wondered whether he'd noticed the car.

Sitting in the driver's seat Jess pulled out her phone from her pocket and checked the Google search results. Jason Balderson. Journalist at *The Mirror.* Steph's colleague. And wait, an ITV News report.

Scrolling through the article, she absorbed the key pieces of information. Her eyes lingered on the image of his house with police tape cordoning off the drive.

He was attacked in his own home and police were pleading for information. The news report she'd seen came back to her.

The one which resulted in Adam sweating and shaking and then telling her about Steph's suicide bid. *His timing hadn't been off. It had been perfect.*

The phone began to sing. She nearly threw it in the air in surprise and it slipped out of her hands into the footwell. As she drew the phone towards her his name came into focus. It was Adam.

Her hands trembled and her finger hovered over 'answer', but she couldn't. She let it ring through to voicemail. She needed time. She needed to focus and calm every nerve in her body. Her phone vibrated indicating that he'd left her a voicemail. She couldn't even bring herself to listen to it. Not yet. The face of Jason materialised as she closed her eyes. The tubes. The ventilator. The beeping of the monitor.

She gripped the steering wheel, she needed to hold something to centre herself. She turned the key in the ignition and slowly pulled out of the tight space.

As she drove past the hospital a police car turned into the entrance. She squeezed hard on the accelerator. She wanted to get away from what she had just witnessed. Away from the face of a man she didn't know but who would be etched into her brain for ever. The tubes. The ventilator. *Adam. What did you do to him and why?*

His words from yesterday leaked into her thoughts. The innocuous conversation about how Steph never talked about her colleagues, how she didn't really socialise with them. *Was he trying to steer me away from them? He made it clear that he'd talk to her colleagues, he didn't want me to look for Jason.*

When she reached Epping High Street she pulled over and listened to Adam's message. She felt the blood drain away from her face.

Before she pulled away a police car moved level with her: she glanced at the driver. PC Hawthorne. She knew she'd follow the car back to Adam's: her fingers slid over her phone to play Adam's voicemail. He confirmed that PC Hawthorne was on his way. Following a car twice in one day. One legitimately, the other surreptitiously, and neither an experience she wanted to repeat.

The police car parked on the street outside her sister's home. Jess edged the Mini onto the drive. She clambered out of the car, her legs felt unsteady, as though they were going to give way and let her fall to the pavement in front of the officer. Thankfully they did their job and she managed to stay upright as she walked to the door.

'Do you want to knock?' PC Hawthorne asked her.

'Sure.' Her voice was barely audible. It sounded like someone else's voice, a child, or someone on the other side of the street.

'Adam said you were on your way.'

He nodded.

Adam opened the door. Jess noticed his unshaven face, two days' worth of stubble pushed its way out through his skin, his pores looked strained as though the growth was irritating him.

'You better come in.' His words were accompanied by a sigh. His stride was short, head down, as though unsure of himself, a figure at odds with the man she'd been pursuing.

Jess sat herself down at the kitchen table. Adam leaned against the Belfast sink.

'Can I have a glass of water?' Jess asked. Adam tentatively opened the cupboard and took out a glass, filled it and clumsily placed it in front of Jess, nearly spilling the contents on the table.

'Mr Henderson, come and have a seat,' PC Hawthorne urged Adam.

Jess studied PC Hawthorne . He was young, mid-twenties maybe, he'd possibly only been doing the job a couple of years, and he didn't look old enough to be a dad.

He had a nice manner though; she felt safe in his hands. He exuded a confidence beyond his years, perhaps that's what the job does for you, she mused. Adam pulled out a chair for him, but he remained standing.

'We tracked your wife's car to Meadowhall Shopping Centre.'

Adam turned to Jess with a puzzled look on his face.

'It's in Sheffield,' said Jess.

'Oh. That kind of makes sense, I mean there's nothing there for her, but it's where she grew up, so that fits, that's good, right?'

PC Hawthorne remained silent, there was something unnerving about him remaining standing while she and Adam were seated. The balance of power all seemed wrong, unequal.

'CCTV shows her leaving the car park and walking to the train station there. She is carrying your daughter as she leaves the car park, we can see her face on camera. She's wearing the black coat you said was missing and jeans. We are waiting on further CCTV images to confirm her movements between exiting the car park and entering the train station.' He paused, shifted his weight and turned to Jess.

'As you mentioned Ms, an incident occurred at the train station yesterday. A woman, fitting the description of your sister, wearing a black coat and jeans, was seen on the station platform before committing suicide.'

Adam looked at her, again confusion hung on his face.

'Sorry … I saw a news report and called the police. I didn't want to tell you over the phone. I should have got here earlier.'

Jess felt her cheeks flush, she knew she wasn't very good at lying and realised she had a lot to cover up since she left her flat this morning.

PC Hawthorne now sat down next to Jess. She stared intently at him, watching his lips, wondering what he was going to utter next. He faced Adam and clasped his hands together and straightened his back. He didn't require his notebook today.

'CCTV shows a woman in a black coat and jeans standing on the edge of the platform. They look like the clothes that you say are missing. She looks about the same height as your wife and appears to be holding a baby. However, she has her hood up and her head bent down to the child. We can't positively ID this image as your wife. The woman never looks up. Her face isn't caught on camera. We will be able to recover DNA from the scene, but this will take time.'

PC Hawthorne paused and took in a deep slow breath. 'We'll need your wife's hairbrush or toothbrush and if possible a blanket your daughter slept with.'

Time slowed. Everything came to a standstill.

Jess felt the breath stick in her lungs. She spluttered as though she was choking. Blinking rapidly, she turned to Adam.

'Tell him. Tell him what you told me yesterday about Steph.'

Adam stared blankly, his hands were trembling and the angry stubble now appeared to be soothed as there was no colour left in his cheeks.

'She … no … she wouldn't. Not to Nat—'

He buried his head in his hands.

Jess reached across the table and put her hand on top of his while maintaining eye contact with PC Hawthorne.

'Adam told me yesterday that at university she had a traumatic time and attempted suicide.'

A puzzled look spread across the PC's face. He inhaled and his brow relaxed. 'Until we get a positive ID, using DNA, we will continue to treat her as a missing person. I'll raise the level of risk again as you've shared this information with us.' PC Hawthorne grimaced.

The hope she clung on to vanished. It had to be her. She didn't need DNA evidence.

Steph and Natalie on the edge of the platform.

Steph and Natalie under the train. She'd tried to kill herself before, and now she'd succeeded.

'I'm sorry … I wish we could have brought different news.'

Jess let the tears continue to streak down her cheeks. One dripped onto her hand causing her to push it away with the knuckle of her forefinger.

'Sorry, I don't mean to be rude, but can I show you out, unless there's anything else?' Jess hoped she didn't sound as desperate as she felt. She wanted him out of her sister's home. Get the bearer of bad news out.

'Yes, of course. Would you be able to get a hairbrush and a blanket?'

Adam slowly pulled himself up and disappeared to their bedroom. He returned with the hairbrush and a pink sheet. Beads of sweat glistened around Adam's hairline.

Hawthorne delicately placed each item in separate evidence bags. Jess watched him as he wrote on each one.

'If you need to speak to me further, please don't hesitate to call. One of my colleagues will update you and let you know what happens next.'

Hawthorne rose from his seat and retraced his steps back to the front door. Jess followed silently and softly closed the door behind him.

She leaned against it and collapsed to the ground in defeat. *She's wearing the missing clothes. Her car is in the car park. It has to be them.*

Adam

Adam bent down to stroke the dog's chest, his front legs were held up in the air allowing him to gently rub the streak of white fur on his chest.

'Handsome dog.'

He hoped his voice sounded light, he wanted the conversation to stay calm, calm but threatening. Maybe that would work; an unsuspecting menace.

It took him a moment to realise that Jason was expecting him to follow him through to the kitchen. He stopped stroking the dog. It trotted ahead of him but disappeared into the lounge, circling before lying down in its bed. He remembered his childhood best friend's dog performing the same action before he'd settled down to sleep.

The room was dimly lit, unusual for a kitchen. Several empty wine bottles littered the side, pushed against the wall ready to be recycled. Dishes were piled up waiting to be washed, and cooking utensils lay scattered along the counter, all signs that Jason lived alone. Unkempt mess with no one to tell you to clear up after yourself, or to do it for you.

'I'm in the middle of cooking, so I'll carry on if you don't mind. Take a seat at the breakfast bar.'

'Go ahead. I'll stand though. Don't think this will take long.'

Adam shifted his weight, Jason continued to chop some vegetables, he turned on the under cabinet lights and the knife's blade gleamed as he worked quickly to chop a courgette.

'My wife tells me you've been stalking her.'

Jason didn't turn around to look at Adam; he added the courgette to the pan which hissed and the smell of frying onion made Adam's stomach rumble.

'That was ages ago. Why is she bringing this up now?' He jabbed the vegetables with the wooden spoon.

'Ages ago? So you are admitting you hounded her? Followed her home from work, sent her nasty emails.'

Jason turned around to face Adam, wielding a wooden spoon. The action made Adam step back.

'Yes. I did, but I've stopped now.' He waved the spoon around, punctuating his speech with it and ceasing when he uttered the word 'stopped'.

'I've been through a lot over the past year, I wasn't thinking straight.'

'Not thinking straight is an understatement. She should have gone to the police, grassed you up to her boss. She's too nice.' Adam paused, he wanted Jason to think about how lucky he'd been that his wife didn't go to HR. He should have been fired.

'So, at least you are admitting to sending the emails and stalking her in the past.'

Adam felt anger burn in his gut, he swallowed hard, hoping to keep it there. He figured he needed it to help warn him off, but he must appear calm. *Stay in control.* He breathed deeply.

Jason nodded and turned back to the pan, aggressively stirring the sizzling vegetables.

'I get why you wouldn't want to admit you are still stalking her. I mean now she's on maternity leave and has a newborn baby I wouldn't want to admit that I was still hanging around her house, leaving flowers and nasty notes.'

Again Jason didn't turn to face Adam. He slowly poured a jar of passata into the pan, methodically scraping the last streaks of sauce onto the vegetables before stirring the mixture. The sizzling was replaced by a bubbling sound. Jason adjusted the heat a little and continued to stir.

'I'm not stalking her now. I know I was an idiot. I sent emails, followed her home from work the odd time and I know I shouldn't have. My head was all over the place.' His hand paused as he lifted the spoon to his mouth, blowing it gently before sticking his tongue out to taste the mixture.

Returning the wooden spoon to the pan it slid down the side coming to a stop without sinking into the sauce. He reached up to a cupboard and pulled out a salt grinder. Twisting the top with a flick of his wrist, a few flakes dropped into the pot and scattered over the hob. He began stirring again.

He sighed loudly before resuming his speech. 'I brought her some flowers to congratulate her – and you. Honestly, I know I was in the wrong. I was fucked up and there's no way I'd stalk her or send emails again. I'm really not sure what you're going on about mate.'

He spat the last word out, turned down the hob, and moved towards the sink. He filled a glass with water and slowly sipped. Placing the glass back on the counter, barely making a sound.

'As I said I've been through a shit time. My fiancé left me for someone else. I became obsessed with your wife, she looks like her, my ex that is.' He paused and moved back to the pan, placing a lid on it and turning the hob off. He walked by Adam and sat down at the breakfast bar.

'I started taking coke to take the edge of things. Loads of my mates are into it, you know. Just the odd line here and there, but it helped to stop me feeling so depressed about my ex. My mates all seemed to be able to stop, but for me, I wasn't in control and that's when I started to get obsessed with Steph.' He paused and scratched the side of his nose.

'I was fucked up. But now, I'm clean, honestly, I just wanted to give her some flowers, congratulate her on the baby. I didn't write her a nasty note. I wrote her an apology. Sort of part of my treatment plan, to make amends.' Calmness returned to his voice.

'Are you saying my wife is lying?'

'Well she wasn't exactly herself when I came over.'

'Would you be if some fucking stalker came to your home? You scared her shitless.' He felt vehemence surge through his voice. This sad wanker was now telling him that Steph was lying. *His word against hers. Just like before.*

'OK, it might have seemed like an odd move, but I felt like I needed closure.'

'Closure?' Wrinkles formed above Adam's nose.

'Wrong word, I don't mean that. But, honestly she wasn't herself. She tried to kiss me.'

A smile twitched upon Jason's lips, he let it develop. Adam noticed the grin, it reminded him of the expression he'd made when he insinuated that Steph could get up to mischief while he was away on business.

'I'm supposed to believe the words of someone who admitted he was obsessed with my wife and sent her dirty threatening emails while he was on drugs? You're fucking lying. Stay the fuck away from my wife and our home. I'm going to the police. You need help.'

Adam felt a wave of adrenaline wash over him. This was what he'd been working up to. It felt good. It felt like he was reclaiming the power. Reclaiming it for his wife from the lying little prick.

Jason stood up and shoved the stool under the breakfast bar. Scraping the metal on the tiles, he moved towards Adam who stood a few paces away from him. He squared up to him getting in his face.

'You don't fucking deserve her. She was desperate for me. Climbed all over me, pushing her tongue inside my mouth. She tasted so good.'

Adam felt every fibre in his body galvanise. Anger coursed through his arteries. He took a step back and his hand formed a fist.

In an instant the fist connected with Jason's jaw. The surprise blow propelled him backwards. And as he fell, the back of his head hit the corner of the breakfast bar.

His body crumpled heavily to the floor. Blood oozed from the wound, leaching onto the grey tiles.

Adam blinked and stared at his own hand. He began to shake as the effects of cortisol took hold.

He eased himself down to crouch down next to Jason. His eyes were closed and Adam couldn't tell if he was breathing. He stared at the blood seeping towards his feet. It took all the energy he had left to push up through his knees to stand. His hands violently shook and he swallowed down saliva which served to warn him he was about to vomit.

He had to get out of the house now. He ran to the front door and a patter of feet followed him. He turned to see the spaniel at his heels, wagging its tail.

When he reached the door he paused before touching the handle. He pulled out his gloves from his pocket and struggled to pull them on to his trembling hands. He grasped the handle and managed to grip it to open the door a fraction. The stupid dog pushed past him and trotted out into the street.

Glancing around before softly closing the door, he edged his way down the path and firmly planted his feet on the pavement to steady himself. Shoulder-width apart to maintain his balance, his legs felt like they were about to give way at any moment.

Adam scanned the street looking for the dog and taking in the windows of the surrounding houses. He noted no movement from the neighbours. Thankfully the spaniel got distracted by a lamppost and didn't follow Adam as he began to walk away from the property. He exhaled, realising how shallow his breathing had become.

He checked every house for any sign that he could be spotted, but thankfully the occupants of the street had better things to do with their evenings. Not a single blind or curtain twitched as he passed along in the darkness, unnoticed.

When he reached the end of the road and turned the corner he ran. Fear and self-preservation propelled him forward. Wine swirled in his empty stomach and all he wanted to do was get home, hold Steph and tell her everything was going be OK, but as his feet pounded the pavement he wasn't convinced. *What the hell have I done?*

* * *

The spaniel returned to the door. It began to whine and bark to be let in, circling frantically in preparation for the door opening, but an answer didn't come.

Later, as the barking and whimpering didn't cease, an irritated neighbour paused their TV intending to put a stop to the noise that was ruining the tension in *Game of Thrones*.

He banged on the door for some time. He didn't know the man who lived inside, but he knew he lived alone with the soppy dog to keep him company. Something wasn't right. The lights were on and through the window the TV could be seen. Adverts. The Go Compare opera singer filled the screen.

He'd never seen the dog out on its own before. Not like number two's scruffy little mutt who was always wandering in the road getting in the way of everyone's cars. He took out his mobile and called the police.

Missing Day Three

Jess

Jess pulled herself up from the floor. She sluggishly returned to the kitchen, her legs unsteady, causing her to stumble as though she was drunk. She bumped into the doorframe before collapsing into the chair. Adam had remained seated at the kitchen table, staring at the wall.

She was unsure what to say to him. He looked as though he was in a trance. He didn't acknowledge her entrance. Jess rose moving tentatively towards the large store cupboard. She scanned its contents. The bottles of spirits lined the high shelf and she stood on her tiptoes to take out a bottle of Jack Daniel's. She poured a large measure into one of those old-fashioned Waterford crystal glasses. They must have been a wedding present, probably from Adam's parents. She flinched at the choice and almost considered pouring it into something else, but Adam possibly wouldn't notice. She placed it on the table in front of him. He was still shaking.

'It's good for shock, I think.' Her words didn't sound like her own.

He drained the whiskey. Jess automatically refilled it and returned the bottle to the cupboard. She returned the bottle to the cupboard. As she pushed the door shut an icy breeze struck her neck causing her to pause and scan the room for the source of the draft.

'I need some air.' Adam pushed his chair backwards and staggered a little. The alcohol couldn't have taken effect yet. The shock made his legs wobbly too. He put his hand on the table to steady himself. 'I'm going for a walk.'

'I'll come with you.'

'No. I need some time alone.' He pulled on his coat which he had slung on the back of the chair. 'Fuck it's so cold in here.'

'Do you want me to go home?'

'Christ Jess, I don't know. I want my wife back and my baby, my baby girl. How could she do this to us? I mean, I thought she … she was … ah fuck. Fuck! You stay here, I just want to walk to get my head straight.'

Jess nodded and let him go. She wandered into the lounge to watch him through the window as he walked away down the road. She wanted to run after him. Ask him about Jason. Ask him why he was visiting him. But she knew that would be cruel. Not now. Not after what PC Hawthorne had revealed.

How could she do this? After everything she's been through, we've *been through. And the joy of getting pregnant and having Natalie to then end it all? To succeed in what she tried to do years ago. It's too much of a fucking coincidence for it not to be her. I don't need DNA evidence. The CCTV images are enough for me.*

Jess ambled back to the kitchen and pulled out another bottle from the oversized cupboard, gin this time. She searched the fridge for a bottle of tonic, but as her sister hadn't been drinking for over nine months there was none. The thought of neat gin caused a wave of nausea to surge up her throat and propel her to the bathroom.

She gripped the toilet seat to steady herself, waiting until the heaving ceased. Pushing herself up to stand, she felt the same coldness spread across her body. The temperature had definitely dropped by several degrees.

She washed her face and hands and dried them on the towel. The towel rail was hot to touch and the heat startled her. She'd assumed the radiators had gone off some time ago.

There was a strange noise in the room next to the bathroom – Steph and Adam's bedroom. She walked into the room. It was icy cold. She could see her own breath appear as wispy clouds.

She glanced out of the window expecting to see snow falling, but there was none. A cold blue light illuminated the room; a strange light, ethereal. Like the pink light you get before a storm in the summer, maybe a winter storm was on its way. A blue tit darted by the window and landed on a branch; it tentatively pecked for food before flitting away.

Jess remembered that a sound had drawn her into the room. On the floor next to the chest of drawers was a photograph. It must have slipped off, she couldn't understand how it had fallen to the floor at this moment.

The glass had shattered, spider web-like patterns obscured the picture. The photograph showed Steph, herself and Mum in the centre of image. Jess stared at the image.

Mum in the centre. Mum and Steph. Both have their arms around each other, whereas I'm resting my hand on her shoulder. To at least put on a show of affection. Mum and Steph. Confidantes. Fuck her privacy. Let's find out her secrets.

She replaced the frame on the top of the dressing table and began to look through Steph's drawers. Nothing.

She searched the book case, methodically pulling out every book.

She found a few photo albums. Unlike Jess, Steph was meticulous at recording moments and unlike most people she still printed out her photographs rather than keeping them locked in a digital realm.

She flicked through the first album. Wedding photographs, honeymoon and other holidays. *Steph. My beautiful big sister. Look at you. So happy, so gorgeous. How could I not know you'd already tried to kill yourself?* She pushed the album back on to the shelf and reached for the next one. This one showed house renovations, more holidays and walking tours.

There was something tucked away between the last page and the cover. She slid out a slim notebook, not unlike a school exercise book. She turned to the first page. It was full of Steph's spidery handwriting. She traced the imprint of the ink on the page, stroked the words and began to read.

Slowly at first, taking in each sentence, but then she frantically flicked through the pages in disbelief.

What have you done?

She snapped it shut, closed her eyes and crossed her fingers. She clutched the diary tight to her chest. *Adam cannot read this.*

Jess returned to the hallway and grabbed her handbag, slid the diary inside and dug out the car keys for the Mini. Slamming the car door shut she pushed the gear stick backwards, reversed off the drive and flew down the road towards the Wake Arms roundabout and the M25. Northbound, towards the M1.

Part Three

Princess Alexandra Hospital, Harlow

'Time of death, 11.03 a.m.'

The team stood down. The room quietened. One of the nurses took a step back to survey the scene. The body lay at peace after the intense activity of the doctors and nurses who had struggled to keep this patient alive. Someone coughed, breaking the silence.

'Shall I inform the police?'

Dr Woo nodded. 'Yes. Thank you. Can you also contact his brother? I think that's the extent of his family; he's the only one to have visited.'

Dr Woo and Nurse Reiley left the room, in step with one another.

'I thought he'd pull through after the initial surgery.' Dr Woo's phone vibrated, she read the text and excused herself as she dashed away.

Reiley went to the nurses' station and searched the system for Jason Balderson's file. He called his brother but the number must have been entered incorrectly as it wasn't recognised. Reiley had seen him a couple of times at Jason's beside. He never stayed long and didn't talk to his brother, just quizzed the nurses about his progress or lack of. On the surface they didn't seem close.

His fingers pressed the familiar police station number and he asked to speak to PC Hawthorne.

* * *

PC Hawthorne leaned back in his chair. The image of the missing mum stared back at him from his screen. He winced at the thought of the difficulties that the BTP would have in recovering DNA from the scene.

He switched files and glanced over to his boss's office. He was on the phone and could be heard expressing his dislike of the caller as he attempted to bring the conversation to a close. He crashed the receiver down, muttering something under his breath.

Hawthorne made his way to the office and stuck his head around Inspector Merson's door.

'PAH just called. Jason Balderson, the chap who was assaulted in his home, died around 11.00 this morning,' said Hawthorne.

'Best call CID. Odd one this incident, not a whiff of information.' He reached for his phone.

Hawthorne withdrew from the office and returned to his desk. He looked over his notes. They knew one thing: it was likely that the attacker was known to the victim. There was no forced entry, the attacker could have tricked his way into the property, but other than that, information – like his boss's hair – was thin.

His phone began to ring, pulling his attention away from his screen.

'PC Hawthorne?' a northern voice asked.

'Yep.'

'My colleague spoke to you earlier regarding your misper and her probable suicide?'

'Yes, do you have an update?'

'We've started another missing person's investigation here. A local female fitting the same description went missing yesterday and was last seen getting off the tram at Meadowhall. Same build, same height and also wearing a black coat and jeans.'

'Carrying a baby?' Hawthorne felt electricity surge through his body, maybe, just maybe it wasn't his missing mum.

'There's some confusion here regarding the child. Our misper's parents saw the local news and are convinced it's their daughter who jumped in front of the train.'

'Confusion?'

'The parents of the misper had to be sedated before we could ask them any further questions. Once the hospital gives us the all-clear to speak to them again we'll get some answers.'

Hawthorne thanked his colleague and replaced the receiver. How many women are out there wearing nondescript black coats and jeans, carrying a child? He knew the answer.

CCTV showed Mrs Henderson leaving the car park. She put her hood up, probably because of the rain, therefore obscuring her face to CCTV cameras. Next it picked her up, or someone else fitting the same description, standing on the platform. Same build, height and clothes. It was a natural conclusion to believe that this person was Mrs Henderson. But this new info gave him hope.

Missing Day Three

Jess

Snow fell in large heavy flakes which clung briefly to the windscreen wipers before being flung into the next lane. Despite the weather Jess had made good progress as she ventured onwards up the M1. The chill that had taken hold of her body had all but disappeared and outside, despite the wintery showers, the snow lacked the required icy crispness to stick to the road, so instead the surface was covered in a thin layer of brown slush. Conditions weren't ideal and only a few people had ventured out, allowing the Mini to progress quickly towards Jess's childhood home.

Throughout the journey Jess's memories continued to resurface. The face of Jason Balderson kept pushing its way into her mind. She understood now why Adam had hurt him. But there were so many other questions swirling around her head that concentrating on the road was a Herculean effort. *Natalie isn't Adam's? No. I can't believe that. I can't accept that Steph would cheat on Adam and I don't believe a word she's written after reading the details of Mum's visits. Because how can any of it be true as Mum is dead.*

A black Land Rover whizzed past her making her jump as it had been a while since she'd noticed another car on the road. Rag'n'Bone Man's gospel-like tones drifted over the airwaves and Jess began to sing along in order to keep her mind in the present.

The flakes stopped falling once more and the blue mileage sign caught her attention. She was twelve miles away from Nottingham, forty-three miles from Sheffield, and seventy-six miles from Leeds.

Sheffield. A place she never wanted to go back to. Her childhood home was anything but a home. It was a place where she existed. At the first opportunity she'd left. She couldn't bear to live at home with Mum. *With HER. She doesn't deserve to be called Mum.*

The bitterness increased with every passing mile. Her hands gripped the steering wheel forcibly and her eyes narrowed into a concentrated scowl. The DJ talked over the end of 'Human' and Jess phased out his irritating and over-excited voice.

Memories kept flooding back with a vicious intensity as the miles dropped by, and without music to fix her attention on the present, images flashed in her mind's eye. Birthdays where she received little gifts, tokenistic presents, never a bike like Steph, or a guitar, or the longed-for decent stereo, which of course Steph was gifted instead. She'd become adept at hiding her feelings, pushing down the disappointment as Mum would always chime in about how she was lucky compared to the homeless, or starving children in a far-off land.

And then the clothes. Jess remembered slipping on jumpers with frayed cuffs or jeans with holes in them, which she ripped to make it look like they were at least a step away from being cool. Steph was showered with new items continuously while Jess only received hand-me-downs. At first she thought it was because cash was scarce, but she soon realised, especially when they went shopping as teenagers, that Mum did have money. She just refused to spend it on her.

The blame fell at Jess's feet. She knew too much. It was her fault that Dad left. Her fault that her mum couldn't be with her lover. All. Her. Fault. She'd swallowed this truth as a child, but as an adult she no longer accepted the blame. But this blame, the guilt she felt for all those years, couldn't be swept aside; it drove her, coloured her thoughts, feelings and actions. It was as integral to herself as air is to breathing. She couldn't let herself remember any more. It was too painful, she needed to keep a lid on the memories and the pain her mum had caused.

It was becoming too much. The presence of home, Mum, and all her childhood hurts were threatening to overwhelm her. She gripped the steering wheel hard in an attempt to crush the memories. *Stay focused. It's Steph and Natalie I need to think about. Nothing else. I'm coming to find you both.*

The road was free from traffic, causing the miles to diminish. She promised herself that at the first hint of snow she'd find services. As she approached Chesterfield, a place that always signalled to Jess that home was close, the sky abruptly dumped its contents. Huge flakes plunged down in front of her, obscuring her view. She sang the chorus to 'Rockabye'. The deep breathing required to hit the high notes helped ease the tension in her jaw. She belted them out as loud as she could.

The sign for Tibshelf services appeared. *Keep singing. Keep going.* Tiredness was causing her eyes to burn and the poor visibility made her ease her foot off the accelerator. It would probably only take another twenty minutes or so to reach her destination, but the weather and fatigue troubled her.

The exit came into view and she breathed out a long deep breath while slowly decreasing the pressure on the accelerator. Pins and needles prickled her finger tips. She couldn't wait to let go of the steering wheel.

The almost empty car park meant she could find a space near the entrance. Her whole body sagged as she stopped the engine. She jogged into the services and made her way to Costa.

A couple of people formed a queue in front of her. The smell of coffee and cake permeated her nostrils and reminded her that she'd skipped lunch again. She contemplated the sandwiches. A young lad, with acne-inflamed skin, greeted her with a warm, winning smile. She couldn't return the smile, so she rubbed her temple and took in the chocolate brownies and muffins which filled the counter unit, and mumbled her order to him.

Tables were easy to come by in the near-empty café. She sipped her cortado. Bitter but good, she knew it wouldn't take long for the caffeine to buzz through her. She stretched her arms out upwards in a V shape and then quickly covered her mouth to hide a yawn.

Scattered throughout the drab café were a few people seated alone, the odd couple silently enjoying a cup of something hot and one family: a mum, a dad, and a toddler who waddled from one parent to the other, giving them his ball and then taking it back and passing it to the other parent. Their faces lit up every time they received the ball and returned it, thanking their son.

Jess couldn't help but smile at the scene. Its cuteness sent shivers down her spine as she pictured Natalie repeating this game with Steph and Adam. It gave her hope and despair in equal measure.

As she picked up her panini, her eyes settled on a woman who sat alone at a table at the other side of the café. Jess watched her push her spoon around the rim of her large coffee cup. She looked like she was in her mid-sixties and she was wearing a brilliant blue coat. Peacock blue, familiar, but Jess couldn't quite put her finger on why.

The woman glanced up from her coffee. She found herself rising from her seat and moving slowly towards the woman. Her movements were automatic, like she was being pulled forward by an invisible conveyor belt.

When she drew close to the table the woman looked up at her.

Jess stopped in her tracks. She felt heat seep across her cheeks.

'Can I help you, love?' The woman had a soft Sheffield accent. She gave Jess a warm smile.

'I'm sorry. I thought you were someone I used to know. It's the coat, and similar face shape.'

'Ah, the coat, I love it. My daughter bought it for me, never seen another like it.'

'Sorry to disturb you.' She felt her blush deepen.

'No bother, duck.' The woman nodded her head and returned to stirring her cappuccino.

Jess smiled at the Sheffieldism and slowly returned to her seat.

When she'd drawn level with the woman in the familiar coat, she knew it couldn't have been her mum, but she couldn't stop her from intruding on her thoughts because Steph had brought her back to life. Back from the dead; visiting her, counselling her. Once she'd read those words she didn't trust anything that she'd read in those pages. *Why did she write it? What was going on in Steph's head?*

The woman in the blue coat began to gather her things to leave. Jess couldn't stop staring at her. The resemblance was uncanny and of course her rational self knew that there wasn't a chance that it was her mum, but something innate had taken over her and pulled her towards the woman. Memories. Ghosts from the past. It wouldn't be long until she set foot back in her childhood home. She wasn't ready to do this. She wasn't ready to face the inevitable rush of pain as each memory seared her skin, creating scar upon scar. *I never wanted to go home. I can't do this.*

She broke off a piece of panini and the chicken filling dropped onto the table. It hurt to swallow the bread. Every joint ached like a virus was taking hold.

She looked out towards the near empty motorway and tried to picture Steph and Natalie in her old home. *They have to be there. I know it's not them under the train. She's coming to meet Mum. I can't believe she thinks she's still alive.*

She drained the cortado, left the panini half-eaten, and retraced her steps back to the car. The snow ceased again. *Just a few more junctions and then... What then? Steph, what will I find? What does she think is real?*

Jess pulled away and took the exit back onto the motorway. She didn't doubt she was doing the right thing, but she had no idea what she'd find in her old home.

What have you done and what did tell you tell Adam?

That question repeated until Jess wished she could turn off her thoughts. She couldn't get past it. She needed answers.

Too many questions...

The traffic was building now as they neared Sheffield. Stop, start as she approached the exit for the A630. Her mobile began to ring. She gave it a cursory glance. It was Adam. She was surprised it had taken him this long to call as she had left without leaving a note. She was glad she couldn't answer it. She didn't have enough answers for him yet. She needed to see her sister and Natalie before she could tell him they were safe.

Instinct told her they were safe. The diary told her Steph was running away and she knew exactly where she was running to.

The Sheffield Parkway cut through the city; industrialisation fused with the urban. Jess felt a familiarity wash over her. It wasn't comforting, it was contemptuous. Terraced houses, box-like, small, no period features, not grandiose like the Victorian properties Jess had come to love in London but functional homes for workers. She turned down the road of her childhood home and parked across from her old house.

Memories of her and her sister playing with the other kids who lived on her road flashed before her eyes. All on bikes cycling around. Running in and out of each other's gardens. Making a nuisance of themselves, the adults frequently declared.

What were their names? Jess peered at the surrounding houses as though the answer would appear and be written on the walls or doors. *I remember a Millie with long curly hair who never wore a helmet or shoes, and a Nina and her sister Kate. Freckles and always giggling.* Their friends appeared, like apparitions, throwing down their bikes and legging it into her home through the side entrance.

Home. She was transfixed by the sight of her old house. Her body refused to move out of the Mini. She wasn't ready to be catapulted back to being a vulnerable child again.

The for sale board stood at an angle. It had been erected for a while now and as far as Jess knew the flurry of viewings had ceased. The estate agent had encouraged them to take it off the market and let it out, but Steph had said no.

Her mum's house was incongruous in comparison to the red brick buildings of her neighbours on Maltravers Road. There were a few semi-detached properties interspersed throughout the terraced houses. Their 1930s family home had been rendered and painted white. This, and the combination of its position on the curve of the road, made it stick out from the rest of the red-bricked properties. The large gap between the houses enabled passers-by to view the side of the house.

An odd lack of privacy, but as a child Jess enjoyed the additional space to the side of their house. A garden that wrapped itself around the house from front to back yard. It was unusual, or now it was a feature, the estate agent's brochure had declared. But Jess didn't want a feature; she wanted privacy. She didn't want to be seen. She knew curtains would twitch. They always did. But maybe that was a good thing. If Steph was here, maybe one of the neighbours had seen her? Her hand hovered next to the car door handle.

What am I going to find in there? Her palms felt clammy as her hand slipped off the handle. The door swung open as the camber of the road pulled it downwards. *Coming! Ready or not.* She fished out the key that had lived in a succession of purses since she left for university. Its tarnished silver coating was beginning to flake away. Snow began to float towards her as she put the key into the door. It opened with a slow creak revealing a small drab hallway. Empty.

A musty smell hit her immediately. A slight dampness hung in the air causing a tightness to attack her chest and narrow her airways as the heavy oppressive atmosphere slowed her movements as she reached to open the lounge window. The windows were stiff, stuck fast as though they were painted shut. With a strong nudge she broke the seal and hooked open the window. Dust flew up her nose causing her to sneeze.

The room felt huge, every item of furniture was missing, cleared out. The estate agent had said to leave a few things behind to give an impression of size and potential. *If only a developer would come along and snap it up, but those days are over for the moment, nothing was selling.*

She shook herself and moved to the kitchen. Despite the dampness, and the feeling that the last person to sit at the little melamine-topped table did so about a year ago, an upturned mug next to the sink suggested otherwise.

The smell of damp disappeared as the breeze from the lounge circulated throughout the house. A creak struck her ears. Her heart raced. *A footstep on a floorboard?* She tiptoed out of the kitchen back down the short drab hallway with bare floorboards towards the stairs.

Her first step announced her presence. 'Steph?' she called up the stairs.

Her brain replayed games of hide and seek. Counting at the bottom of the stairs. Creeping up, avoiding the second step. Now the first step also creaked. The stairs also lacked carpet; the floral patterned runner had long since been removed. Either side of the missing carpet was painted white and laden with dust which on some steps had been disturbed. It was no longer easy to sneak up the steep staircase. Her trainer-clad foot still rang out in the silence.

There was no answer and no more sounds hit her ear as she reached the top of the stairs. A breeze brushed past her cheek. Ice-cold.

Her chest became tighter and she couldn't hear her own breathing as her heart thundered in her ears. The first bedroom door swung open with a creak. The room was empty.

My old room. No bolt on the door now. She remembered her sparse teen room. The single bed fit snuggly against the wall on the left, and under the window she had a chest of drawers with a small CD player on top. She pictured the chest of drawers covered with make-up, nail varnish, books and CDs. She closed her eyes and she could see her band posters: Arctic Monkeys and the Kaiser Chiefs. But now, nothing, no sign of anyone disturbing the layers upon layers of dust.

Mum's old room. Oddly, curtains hung at the window, rippling slightly as the old windows allowed air to glide through unrestricted. Despite the sheerness of the fabric, the light-blue hue permeated the walls. They weren't the curtains that used to adorn the windows. They didn't match the plum chimney wall, and they struck Jess as being out of place. Outside, snow began to line the panels of the window panes, clinging to the old-fashioned wooden frames. Jess sighed and her breath was visible in the room.

She moved towards the window. The curtains billowed as a breeze seeped through the ill-fitting frames and revealed a teddy bear sitting on the shallow windowsill. The threadbare fabric still felt soft to touch. It wasn't Natalie's teddy. It was her own much-loved Sunny Bear. She picked it up and cuddled it close to her chest, which ached from her thundering heart. Sunny Bear. Sunny because he was golden and a holiday memento. Bought by Dad.

She clenched her jaw to prevent her teeth from chattering. She was sure the bear had been dumped ages ago along with all her mum's old things.

As she moved back to the door, she noticed that the bed had been made. Old sheets and a blanket messily covered the mattress. *Steph, you've been here. Where are you now?*

She looked into the box room. Empty, no sign of anyone. Immediately to the left the bathroom door was wide open. But again. No one was hiding in there. Jess clung to the doorframe and looked at the seventies-style bathroom suite. *Avocado. Who ever thought that was a good look?*

The bath had been her favourite place to hide as a kid. She remembered lying flat on her back holding her breath and stifling laughter in the hope it would take the other kids from the street an age to find her. Whenever they found her there they'd be in fits of giggles and always attempt to turn the taps on to give her a good soaking before she scrambled out. *That's one happy memory. Me, my sister and our friends.*

She jogged down the stairs and returned to the kitchen and stared at the mug. Someone has been here. *Where are you now Steph?*

In her peripheral vision, a movement made her shift her attention from the cup. Something fell off the kitchen counter.

A soft thud hit the old-fashioned, garishly patterned, lino. A ring bounced as it hit the floor, the metal blurred creating several rings before it came to rest to form one circle. She edged towards it and tentatively reached out to pick it up. The solitary diamond sparkled under the harsh kitchen light.

Mum's engagement ring.

Her breathing accelerated. She had no idea how the ring simply fell off the counter by itself. Again she could see her breathe escape from her mouth. The plunge in temperature made her teeth chatter. The ice-cold metal of the ring made her fingers tingle, as though she'd picked up an ice cube. Transfixed by the diamond she held the ring up to window of the back door. Snowflakes had begun to descend, they sparkled more than the diamond. The cool metal began to numb her fingers.

She flung the ring across the kitchen and turned her attention once again to the snowflakes which wafted down and were in no hurry to settle. Flitting upwards and floating groundwards before disappearing into nothingness. As a child she'd stood at the kitchen door and watched the flakes float gently to the ground hoping that they'd settle. Back then they usually did. Now, staring through the same pane of glass, another memory demanded to be replayed. She remembered watching her mum and Steph build a snowman. Her mother told Steph that Jess had a cold and was too ill to play outside with them, but before she joined Steph in the snow she bent down low, eye to eye with Jess, and whispered. Not a gentle whisper, but filled with menace. *You don't get to play in the snow. You don't get to have fun. Ever.*

Memories, once buried, seemed to seep through into all her thoughts. Bursting forth, like water breaking down a dam. Returning home broke down the barriers for Jess. She couldn't stop the flood of memories. She couldn't stop the anger percolating through her bloodstream. Mesmerised by the flakes, a noise at the front door broke her daydream. A key biting the lock. Her muscles tensed. She moved tentatively to the entrance of the kitchen and peered down the short hallway. The door swung open revealing Steph, with Natalie strapped to her chest in a sling, holding two over-stuffed shopping bags.

Missing Day Three

Adam

Adam found himself in their bedroom staring at the Moses basket. Walking hadn't achieved the desired effect. He had hoped it would clear his head, give him a clarity he had lost when his fist connected with Jason's jaw. In that instance, everything fell apart and led him to this moment. He knew a positive ID was needed, but it was too much of a coincidence. His wife was dead, his daughter too.

The what ifs swirled around his mind. What if she and Jason *had* kissed, or something *had* happened between them? What if Jason was telling the truth? Again Adam concluded no.

Steph would never cheat. There had never been any signs of infidelity. None that he had noticed and, despite the difficulties they'd had over the past year, they were happy. Natalie had cemented their marriage, they were a family now. No. This what if he couldn't subscribe to, nor did he want to.

But the version where she kills herself, he couldn't push that out of his head. Since her disappearance his brain kept replaying the defining moment in their friendship, that moment that eventually led to their friendship becoming a relationship.

They'd lived in the same halls of residence at uni and her room was a few doors down from his. He realised he'd not seen her emerge for a few days and when he asked her friend Anna if she'd seen her she told him she'd been unwell and had skipped lectures.

Anna had spoken to her that morning after breakfast and brought her a packet of paracetamol. He recalled the horror-stricken look on Anna's face when she realised what Steph had done.

She said Steph had opened the door to her briefly, told her she was fine and not to worry. She wasn't fine. She'd been amassing several packets of paracetamol over the past few days.

Hammering on her door resulted in a low groan. Adam raised the alarm and the warden unlocked the door to find her laid out on the floor. Vomit covered her shoulder and matted her hair.

Unlike some of her so-called friends, he stuck by her, and slowly they fell in love. She got better, after lots of therapy sessions. The Steph of the first year had disappeared, until now.

He crouched in the corner of their bedroom. Cramp spasms caused him to move and realise where he was. He'd zoned out. Drifted back into the past.

He needed to be in the present. Were there signs he'd missed?

The sleeplessness, mood swings and tearfulness, they all pointed towards post-natal depression, didn't they? *For fuck's sake, she's my wife who I helped rescue from the brink before and I didn't think to take more fucking care of her.*

Pins and needles attacked his feet. He needed to stand, get another drink to numb the pain that throbbed in his brain and silence the voice that screamed at him, *It's your fault, you selfish bastard, it's your fault they are both dead.*

Stumbling to his feet, he lurched into the kitchen. The empty glass reminded him that Jess had poured him a drink earlier. Digging his hands into his pocket he pulled out his mobile. It rang repeatedly until he reached her voicemail. Her soft voice advised him to leave a message. He shoved his mobile back into his jeans.

The glug of liquid splashed around the glass and Adam winced as the alcohol hit his soft palate. It had a burnt taste to it; Jack Daniel's wasn't something he'd normally drink, but there wasn't anything else in the cupboard except gin.

He dragged his feet as he made his way to the lounge. He touched the switch on the TV. BBC News filled the screen. He searched through the digital channels in an attempt to find a version of the BBC which covered Sheffield. His search resulted in frustration only. BBC News would have to do.

After a while, Jason's face loomed large, filling the TV screen. He was laughing at the camera and had a pint in his hand. His eyes were wide and red as the flash illuminated the dark pub. He looked relaxed, nothing like the Jason he'd encountered a few days ago or the man laid prostrate in a hospital bed.

The news presenter told him what he already knew, that he had been attacked in his own home, and then the sound seemed to grow louder as though he'd accidentally sat on the remote and turned the volume up full blast.

Jason had died this morning and police were now conducting a murder enquiry.

Adam ran to the kitchen, he stumbled forwards, and threw himself towards the sink. He couldn't swallow down the burning liquid and he just managed to vomit into the basin. Grasping for the kitchen roll he wiped his mouth. Sweat dribbled down his hairline as his whole body convulsed.

Trembling hands made it difficult for him to grab his mobile from his back pocket. Jess didn't answer again. He listened to her voice: flat northern vowels with a London twang.

'Jess, please call me. I need to talk. I need you to help me. I've done something terrible and I don't know what to do.'

Missing Day Three

Jess

Jess stood stock still, mouth open wide. The perfectly normal scene in front of her was not what she had anticipated.

I was right. She is alive.

It took all her energy not to run and fling her arms around her big sister. Since entering the house she'd been wondering how Steph would behave. How she'd react to being found. The diaries told Jess that Steph needed to escape. Paranoia and fear were etched into each page and she still wasn't clear what was real or imagined. For now, her instinct told her to play along with Steph's last entry. *She's running away to escape two men. She thinks they will take Natalie away from her.*

Steph straightened up awkwardly and patted Natalie's back. She turned to softly close the door and then pick up the shopping bags. Before she began moving towards the kitchen their eyes met.

'Oh my god, you scared the life out of me just standing there. Come and help me, these bags are well heavy.'

Steph picked one up and moved it towards Jess. Jess did as she was asked.

'Where's your car?'

'I left it at Meadowhall. I couldn't drive any more, the motorway was getting too much and I had such an awful headache. I worried I'd end up having an accident, so I got the tram here.'

'Thank god Steph. Thank god you're here.' *Thank god you're both alive.*

'Where else would I be?' Steph tilted her head and frowned at her sister.

Jess scooped up the shopping bags and returned to the kitchen. Steph followed her but stopped in the doorway.

'Why are you here? Because I don't remember calling you.' Her voice sounded different. Cold, untrusting.

Steph clapped her hand to her mouth and her eyes widened. She fled the kitchen. A creak and a slam signalled that the window was now shut and the curtain rings clunked heavily across the metal pole. She returned to the street door and locked it, then pushed past Jess to the kitchen door. Again checking if it was locked.

'Oh my god, if you've worked out that I'm here then he'll be coming for us too, I know he will, he's going to take Natalie from me, don't let him, don't let him take her.'

'Steph, sit down.' Jess kept her voice calm but assertive. 'It's OK. Adam doesn't know where you are.'

Jess wasn't sure if they were the right words to say. It seemed natural to follow on from what she had read in the diary. *But what is natural? What is normal to her? She thinks mum is still alive. What else does she think is real?*

Steph lowered herself awkwardly into the seat as Natalie remained in the sling. She wriggled with the change of position, but remained deep in slumber. Jess longed to stroke the jet black wisps of baby hair which poked out of the sling.

'No Jess, not Adam, I've done something terrible.' Steph began rocking, gently soothing Natalie who wasn't making a sound. Patting her back as though she had wind.

'I should have told you ages ago, but I had an affair.' Steph stood up abruptly, swaying from side to side. She reminded Jess of Rachel rubbing her bump and rocking her baby, and she hoped her labour was speedy and her first days as a mum were calm and filled with joy. *A million miles away from feeling anything like my sister.*

'I ended it but I know Natalie isn't Adam's baby. She isn't Adam's.' Steph stared at her sister. Her eyes bored deep into Jess's. Jess bit her lip and swivelled the ball of her foot on the floor. She swallowed hard and opened her mouth to speak, but Steph held up her palm. Jess nodded and leaned back against the kitchen units. Her fingers traced the twisted metal drawer handles.

'Don't. Let me finish. We were taking for ever to conceive and me and Jason had an accident and she's the result. Jason's gone crazy, he's threatening to take her from me and to tell Adam. He's trying to force me to leave Adam.'

Jess listened to Steph retell what she'd read in the diary. She dug her nails into her own arm and watched the crescent moon marks dent her skin. *I'm not imagining this. She's here. Standing before me. The CCTV must show someone else. They are both alive.*

'Can you help me Jess? We can't be found. I can't let them take Natalie away from me. They're out to get me. Please help me.'

Covering her face with her hands, Jess couldn't watch Steph pace around the kitchen any more. Her movements were making her feel dizzy. She'd never seen Steph behave like this before. Her speech was so quick and rambling that it was difficult for her to keep up. She folded her arms.

'Gosh, Steph, that's … a lot to take in.' Jess paused, unsure how Steph would react to any of her words. 'I'll do whatever you want. I'll help you.'

Steph sat back down in the seat, patting Natalie's back. It wasn't soothing, it was aggressive, too firm. Natalie began to wriggle in the sling, she let out a sharp cry. Steph stopped the patting. Both sisters froze, waiting to see if the cries would signal her waking up. Silence wrapped itself around them. *I just need some space to talk to Steph. Stay asleep baby girl, stay asleep.*

Jess crouched down so she was slightly smaller than Steph. She didn't want to intimidate her or panic her. And she didn't want to betray her own fear.

'Only I know where you are. I didn't tell Adam, and Jason won't be going anywhere at the moment.' She flinched, she wasn't sure if they were the right words. 'It's going to be all right Steph. We can fix all this. We can go home, Adam is worried sick, he loves you, honestly, it is going to be fine.' She stood up and kissed Steph on the forehead. *Am I convincing enough? Is this the right thing to do? To play along with what my sister thinks is happening?*

'How did you know where to find me?'

'I read your diary. I had to.'

Steph covered her mouth with both hands.

'I'm sorry about intruding on your thoughts but I was desperate. I had to find you. I was so worried about you both. Disappearing like that, running away. You scared the hell out of us. I thought the worst and when we heard that a woman, who looked like you, had jumped in front of a train, I had to do everything possible to find you.'

'No, no, no, no. You didn't let Adam read them did you? I thought I'd packed them, along with my phone, but I ... I panicked Jess, I had to run. I can't think straight.'

'Steph, I wouldn't do that, you know that, don't you? I brought your diary with me to make sure he couldn't read it. As soon as I read about Mum I knew where you'd be.'

At the mention of their mother, Steph's face changed. The panic evaporated and instead of dread exasperation moved across her face.

'Are you going to manage to be civil to her when she gets here?' She began rubbing Natalie's back again.

'When she gets here? Where do you think she is?' A twitch of a smile rippled across Jess's lips, but she stopped it and reminded herself of the role she was playing. In Steph's world Mum was very much alive. She'd visited her. Advised her and now she's coming back to the house to meet her. *She genuinely thinks she's still alive. She has to be having some sort of breakdown.*

'She said she'd meet me here.'

Jess sighed and sat in the chair opposite her sister. She reached forward to hold her hand, she wasn't sure what to say next or what to do.

'Yes, I read about her visits.'

'That's why I've got all this food. We can hide here from Jason, and hopefully Adam will forgive me.' She began pacing the room. 'I'm sure Jason told him everything. Surely he would have? I was an idiot to think that Adam would be able to warn him off. Threaten to expose him, how could I have been so stupid, so naïve, to think Jason would keep quiet.'

Her words flowed too quickly; Jess found herself inhaling deeply in order to focus on her sister's words and prevent the panic spreading throughout her body.

'And I'm sure Adam believes him, he was so distant. I could see it in his eyes. He knows and he's going to take Natalie from me. Everyone is out to get her Jess. They are going to take her away from me. I can't let that happen. You have to believe me. Help me protect her.'

Terror flashed across Steph's face as she returned to the chair. She reached for her sister's hand again and began stroking her knuckles, before moving to trace the shape of her wedding ring.

A story began to form in her mind. She needed to reassure Steph, play along with her. Like the pretend play of their childhood. Pretend Steph had an affair. Pretend Adam will be OK. *Play along and get back home to get her the help she needs.*

'Jason hasn't said anything to Adam. Adam has no idea about the affair. Honestly, he doesn't. He is worried sick about you. He just wants you both back. And, don't panic, but I think Adam and Jason had a bit of a fight and Jason is in hospital. He is fine, he'll be out in a few days, but I'm sure he won't be bothering you or Natalie again. I promise. I think we need to get home. The police are looking for you.'

'Why? Why? Oh god they think I'm an unfit mother, don't they? They'd be right of course. How could I ruin everything?'

Steph stood up and wriggled her shoulders to keep rocking Natalie. She heaved the bags up onto the counter and began to rifle through the items she'd bought. Jess noted the baby stuff, at least she'd remembered the important things like nappies and baby wipes. *She's still in there, the real Steph. She's still doing the things she needs to do for Natalie.*

The movement propelled Natalie from her sleep and her cries began to fill the kitchen. For the first time, Jess welcomed the noise. She longed to take her niece in her arms and hold her, hug her, breathe in that smell that everyone always talks about because, just a few hours ago, she'd thought she'd never hold her niece in her arms again.

Steph's movements were rapid. Item after item was being pushed into the empty cupboard. She knew she couldn't yet ask her to let her hold Natalie, she wasn't sure how she'd react. She'd probably panic and think that she was trying to take her away, too.

'Steph, stop it, come and sit back down.'

'No. We've got to get ready for Mum.'

Jess got up and helped her sister unpack the bags. Placing kitchen roll and Dettol into the unit under the sink. The movement soothed her, but Steph began to rapidly rifle through the bag. Shoving salt, pepper and a jar of pasta sauce into the cupboard.

She needed some kind of distraction to calm Steph down.

'When did you say Mum was going to get here?'

'Not sure. Soon though. Why?'

'How about you have rest. Be good to get some sleep and I'll start cooking something for all of us. As Natalie's awake now, maybe you could feed her and then I can have a play with my niece.'

Steph looked down at Natalie. She smiled at her and began to unwrap her from the sling.

'Yes. That's a good idea. I am exhausted. Thank you.' A glazed look washed over Steph's face as though the exhaustion had suddenly hit her.

She settled down at the table and began to feed Natalie. Jess had thought she'd never see her do this again. Her niece's little hand rested on Steph's breast. It was the first time since walking through the door that she looked at ease. *She looks normal. They both look like nothing has happened.*

She turned away. She couldn't cry again. Opening up the cupboard she pulled a few things out on to the counter and hoped it would convince Steph that she was preparing enough food for three adults. Potatoes, baked beans, and laying at the bottom of one of the shopping bags, a bag of grated cheese. Jess rolled her eyes. *Mum's favourite meal.*

Mum was an awful cook. Everything had come out of tins, or was frozen, or from the chippy. This was probably the most nutritious meal she'd prepared for them when they were kids. It struck her how both of them had managed to learn how to cook without her guidance. Another thing they were adept at, in spite of her neglect. She slammed the cupboard door closed and resisted the urge to scoop up the ingredients and throw them in the bin.

Missing Day Three

Steph

Steph lifted up the throw and wriggled into a comfortable position on the double bed in her mum's old room. The blanket smelt musty and hadn't protected her from the cold which kept her awake in between the times she was feeding or soothing Natalie. On arrival she'd searched the cupboards. There was one single sheet and a plum-coloured throw. It had to do.

She'd intended to wash away the smell. Lying here reminded her that she was going to, but she'd realised the washing machine was gone. *What have you done with everything Mum?*

She pulled the blanket up to her chin and took in the cobwebs which clung to the light pendant highlighted by layers of dust. Her eyes refused to close. *So much to do. So much to sort out. So much to hide.*

Sleep wasn't going to come. Thoughts of Adam buzzed around her brain. And Jason. *Jess said he was in hospital. That was good. That meant he couldn't talk to Adam. He couldn't tell him everything. Although he probably had. Of course he had. All the details. Everything.*

She rolled onto her side and stared at the Victorian fireplace. She loved the sumptuous plum colour of the chimney.

It made the fireplace look regal. A light dusty film covered the blackness.

Feet arrived first. Red rubber wellies with a hint of glitter. Knees bent and then, leaning forward, ducking out of the hood of the fireplace a toddler emerged. Red wellies, black tights and a pillar box red duffle coat.

The toddler's face was obscured by the red hood of the coat. Its head dipped downwards as though it was watching its step on the floorboards, steadying itself. It began to run around the room.

Another emerged from the fireplace. A replica toddler joined the other. And then another, and another slipped from the chimney, until six identical figures waddled around the room.

All wearing wellies. All hoods up.

All running around the bed.

Steph sat up and pulled the cover up around her. She wanted to cover her eyes to make the children go away but she couldn't. She had to watch them. Mesmerised.

'We're only three foot tall. We're only three foot tall,' they chanted as they continued to dance and skip around the room.

'We're only three foot tall. We're only three foot tall.'

Steph clasped her hands over her ears to shut out the helium high-pitched voices.

She peered closely at them. Simultaneously they all stopped, like clock-work dolls whose wind-up mechanisms ceased at once.

They looked at her. Silence fizzed in her ears. She dropped her hands to the bed. She could now see their faces.

They weren't childlike at all.

Wizened brown faces, deep wrinkles and beady black eyes. Beady black rat-like eyes.

She flung the throw at them and lurched out of the door.

Missing Day Three

Jess

'Steph? Are you OK?' Jess bellowed from the kitchen.

Her sister's scream had made her jump, her heart beat rapidly. She had the phone pressed to her ear but PC Hawthorne failed to pick up.

Steph's footsteps flew down the stairs. She rushed into the kitchen and scooped up Natalie out of Jess's arms.

She was trembling. Jess moved to embrace them both.

'It's OK. It's going to be OK,' she whispered in Steph's ear.

'We have to get out of the house. I don't know where to go. I can't sleep here. I can't there's...'

'There's what?'

Steph stepped back out of the embrace. Natalie was crying, she'd picked up on her mum's distress. The cries took up all of Steph's attention and she began to rock Natalie, but this time in a gentle boat-like motion. The movement seemed to calm them both. She kissed her head, nuzzling her hair. Natalie's crying ceased and Steph seated herself at the kitchen table, gently stroking her daughter's wispy hair.

Jess sat next to her. She wanted to capitalise on the brief moment of calm. She hoped the manic activity prior to Steph's brief attempt to nap wasn't about to resume. She put her hand on Steph's knee and stroked it gently as though soothing a bruise.

'Listen, don't take this the wrong way, but you've been wearing that outfit for a few days, right?'

Steph nodded.

'Let's pop to Meadowhall, get you some clothes. Mum won't be here for another hour or so.'

'Yes, I am starting to feel a little grubby. I didn't have time to pack!'

Jess heaved a sigh out of her lungs and crossed her fingers.

One step at a time. Out of this house, find the car, get her home. Sounds easy, but it won't be if she disagrees. And everything seems to panic her.

Jess held her arm out motioning to Steph to move towards the door. For a moment she stared at Jess, holding her gaze.

'Yes, be good to get out of here and do a little shopping.' She kissed Natalie's head and smoothed down her baby-fine wisps of black hair.

Jess pushed all the air out of her lungs. *One step. One compliance.*

She opened the door to the Mini for her sister who precariously manoeuvred herself into the back seat. Jess half expected her to comment that she was driving her car, but she didn't appear to notice, or be aware of her surroundings. She was humming a lullaby to Natalie.

'Shit. You're going to have try and strap yourself in with the seatbelt over Natalie.'

Steph awkwardly thrust her hips forward as she attempted to get something out of her coat pocket. She pulled out a little blue rabbit and placed it on the seat next to her. It was an old toy, not a new one, and it was blue unlike every pink present that Natalie had received. The seat-belt clunked into place.

'Where's the rabbit come from?' Jess asked.

'A woman gave it to me in the train station. Strange lady. She said my baby needed a new toy and pressed it into my hand. She held my hand when she passed me the toy and wouldn't let go. She scared me a little. I tried to refuse it and told her I thought her baby still needed it, but she began to cry. When she showed me the baby she was carrying I knew why she no longer needed the rabbit. She was clinging on to a doll, not a baby. As soon as she showed me she ran.'

Jess's mobile rang causing her to jump. Adam's name flashed up again, she cancelled the call immediately. It wasn't the right time to talk to him. She was overcome with a myriad of emotions: relief, sadness and confusion. She needed time to think how she was going to explain this to him; to tell him over the phone how ill Steph really was seemed inappropriate. Dealing with words, that was her job, but what do you say to a husband whose wife needs hospitalising?

He'd have to wait. As much as she wanted to share the news with him that they were both safe, she also wasn't sure what Steph would do on hearing her speak to him. She glanced at her in the back seat via the rear-view mirror. A faraway look fell across her sister's face. She was stroking Natalie's hat-clad head with one hand and holding the odd blue rabbit in the other.

* * *

Jess drove around Meadowhall car park, she daren't ask her sister where her car was, she didn't want to panic her, or give her a clue to her intentions. Thankfully, she located the car with ease.

'Steph, your car is over there. Let's get Natalie's pram from the boot, it will be comfier for her and you.' Steph nodded, her face was expressionless; her movements had slowed down now, less manic.

Jess clung to her sister at all times, she didn't want to let her out of her sight. She felt the need to grip her to show her that she was real and not something that her imagination had conjured up. She knew Steph was unstable, but she was unsure as to how it really affected her behaviour other than propelling her to flee her home.

At the moment Steph appeared to be in a dreamlike state, not really taking things in, or engaging with her; she was focused solely on Natalie.

Jess steered her sister, who was pushing the pram but not looking up to see where she was going, past the shoppers. Her face seemed vacant, unreadable. She wished she had another pair of hands. *If only Matt was here. He could have whizzed in and grabbed her some clothes, or stayed in the car to look after her.*

The Oasis food court was crowded. Steph's eyes were wide, like a fox caught in headlights, she seemed to be scanning the room, looking for someone.

Beads of sweat gathered around the nape of Jess's neck. *Perhaps this wasn't the best idea. The crowds. People everywhere.*

'Let's go get some food together.' The words escaped from her voice box, squeezed tight by the anxiety that was again flooding her body.

Steph blinked and then squinted at her sister as though she was trying to focus after removing strong glasses. She shook her head, causing her waves of hair to ripple off her shoulders and fall down her back.

'Yes. I'm hungry. Starving actually.'

Jess wanted to grab something quick.

'Hey, last time we came here together was when you were, what, sixteen?'

Steph stared blankly back.

'Cinema, or shopping and grabbing a Maccie D's. Queue's short in there, shall I grab one for old times' sake?' Jess wondered whether anybody had ever eaten a Big Mac to recall time spent together; fast food wasn't normally associated with nostalgia in her book.

'Yes, go on, as we seem to be on a trip down memory lane being back here. Feels so strange being home.'

Here feels so far away from home for me, almost like being on another planet.

She steered the pram and her sister into McDonald's and ordered two sweet chilli chicken wraps. She really couldn't bring herself to order the teen food of cheeseburger and fries.

They sought out a table at the edge of the circular space away from the crowds and hidden slightly by potted palms.

Steph began to eat the soft tortilla wrap and Jess finally managed to eat. McDonald's sweet chilli chicken had never tasted so good. Steph removed the lid of her diet coke and swirled the ice around with her straw. She seemed calmer and it pleased Jess to see her finish her meal.

Perhaps it was time to call the police and let them know they were safe; maybe Jess could broach the subject again. She drained her drink and reached across the table to hold Steph's hand. These tender touches were not what she wanted to be doing. She wanted to hold her tightly and revel in the fact that she was alive, they were both alive and not scattered across the train tracks. A worst-case scenario that she'd tried to supress when she first read the local paper's insubstantial article.

'Steph, I have to phone the police to let them know that I've found you.'

Steph stared at her sister.

'Do you understand?'

She nodded.

'They need to know that you are safe.' Jess swallowed.

Steph began to jiggle the pram. She looked around the food hall. Scanning the tables. Refusing to look at Jess. Jess moved to sit next to her. Steph stiffened.

'It's OK.'

'No. It's not OK. He wants to take Natalie away from me, I had to run away here, we can't go home, we can't go home.' Her voice sunk to a whisper and her eyes darted around the crowded food court as though she was searching for a glimpse of Jason and Adam.

Jess kept her voice even, despite the panic rising inside her.

'I promise you that I will keep you and Natalie safe. Jason can't hurt you. Adam loves you. I need to take you home.'

Steph violently shook her head. 'How can you keep me safe?'

'I promise you. I've never let you down have I? And—'

Steph grabbed her arm. 'Get her out of there, get her out of the fucking pram Jess.'

'Steph, she's fine—'

Steph jumped up and scooped up Natalie. She began to rapidly stroke Natalie's skin as though she was attempting to brush something off her.

'Help her Jess, get someone, she's covered in ants, they're everywhere, all in her hair and face and—'

Jess took Natalie from her arms. She remained calm, not wanting to draw attention as she was aware of several pairs of eyes trained on them.

She turned her back to Steph, now gently stroking Natalie and soothing her, and then she turned to face her sister.

'Look, they've all gone, nothing there, she's fine. You hold her. I'll shake the blanket.'

Steph complied, she held Natalie up on her shoulder and patted her back.

Jess continued the pretence of shaking the blankets, Natalie's hat, the blue rabbit, and she began to brush down the outside of the pram. Flicking imaginary ants off the sides and hood of the pram.

'All gone now darling, put her in again, all gone, we'll go back to the car.'

She could feel the eyes of onlookers follow them as they left the food court.

As they walked back through the shopping centre Steph was loudly humming 'Twinkle Twinkle Little Star' as she pushed the pram. She gripped the handle tightly. Her knuckles were white. The humming grew louder.

Steph shuffled forwards, her head dipped low as she sung to Natalie. The same lullaby over and over. Jess took a step away from her sister, to the side, and continued to monitor the singing. While Steph was preoccupied it would give her a chance to call PC Hawthorne. A brief moment to reach out and get help. She redialled Epping Police and this time Hawthorne was quick to answer.

'I've found her. I'm with her now and we are in Sheffield. I can't speak for long, I'm bringing her home. She needs urgent psychiatric care.' She lowered her voice to a whisper as she delivered the last sentence.

Steph was still humming and seemed totally unware that her sister was talking to someone. Jess took a few more steps away from Steph who was totally oblivious, consumed by the lullaby and her slow plod onwards. Aware only of her own voice and the movement of the buggy, keeping her eyes fixed on her baby.

Jess kept her voice low despite being convinced Steph could not hear her. For further protection she cupped the phone to her face, covering her mouth. She hoped PC Hawthorne could hear her.

'I found her diary, it detailed meetings with Mum, but she has to be hallucinating because Mum's dead. She's a danger to herself and to Natalie. I don't know what she's going to do next. She's paranoid about everything and I just witnessed her have a hallucination.'

She glanced at Steph, who continued to sing to Natalie.

'Help her, please. I need her to be kept safe.'

She listened intently to his response. He explained that he'd speak to his contacts in the NHS, but the police had the power under section 136 of the Mental Health Act to detain her. His words began to swim in around her ears at the mention of detaining Steph. *Detained under the Mental Health Act.* Jess shook herself and refocused as he explained to her how the street triage team would meet them back at Steph's home.

Jess swallowed. She was about to lie and she knew she wasn't good at it; even over the phone she felt like she was so transparent, and she needed to be convincing.

'I can't get hold of Adam. He doesn't know they're alive and he left me an odd voicemail. I'm worried about him, he was convinced that the woman at the station was Steph. I'm scared he might do something rash. Can you go and check on him and explain everything?' She refrained from saying 'silly'; it was the word he'd used yesterday to describe the possibility that Steph could do something rash. The word irritated her. It trivialised such a decisive act.

PC Hawthorne agreed to her request.

'Thank you. Thank you for everything'.

She ended the call and moved closer to Steph and Natalie. The humming continued, but the tune was now unrecognisable. Steph's eyes remained fixed on her daughter, even Jess's hand closing over hers didn't prompt her to look up.

Jess replayed the conversation in her mind. *She'll be detained under the Mental Health Act.* PC Hawthorne's words reverberated around her brain. *Detained.* Gripping the handle of the pram to stop her from fainting, she felt the blood drain from her head as the floor tilted and began to spin. *Shit. What have I done?*

Jess pushed aside her fear and focused on Adam instead. She was worried about him, but not because she thought he would attempt suicide; it would be better for him to confess.

He is a good man. A good husband. Perhaps the police calling would prompt him to explain what happened. He has to get his side of the story out.

Jess guided her sister to the car. Together they struggled with the travel system and eventually secured a sleeping Natalie into the back seat. Steph folded down the frame and placed it back in the boot.

She realised that she'd not got her sister any more clothes; after the incident in the food court she'd just wanted to get her safely back to the car. An uneasiness rippled through her body. She worried about her looking exactly like the woman who had killed herself, she wasn't sure why, but it freaked her out, more so than her sister's hallucinatory episode. Ever since Steph had walked through her mum's front door she'd tapped into an inner reserve of patience and calmness, despite outwardly feeling anything but.

She held onto the car door to steady herself and the clunk of a seatbelt told her Steph was ready. Steph's Ford Focus was more comfortable than the Mini, the seat enveloped her as she sunk into it. She peeped around the driver's seat.

'I want to go home Jess. You and Adam will protect us. And the police, are you sure they aren't going to take Natalie away?' She was shaking.

'Honestly, I promise, they are going to help you.'

'Can you call Mum? I don't know where my mobile is. Where did the ants come from?'

'When we get to a service station I'll call Mum. I don't know where the ants came from darling, but I got rid of them, I protected you. See, I can look after you despite you being my big sister.'

Jess reached behind her and squeezed Steph's knee. 'Let's get you home, we can work all this out together.'

Exiting the car park, she followed the signs for the M1. She had no intention of stopping. She would drive back to London without a break and hopefully exhaustion would take over and Steph would sleep. The speedometer crept beyond seventy. PC Hawthorn's words replayed in her mind.

'The street triage team will see your sister. Let me know your eta and I'll have one waiting outside her house. Please be aware, following an assessment she may be detained under section 136 of the Mental Health Act.'

I'm having my sister committed.

Day Three

Adam

The words of the news report looped again and again in Adam's mind. He surveyed his right hand, the one that dealt the punch. It hadn't felt like it belonged to him since he struck Jason. Everything since that moment felt like an out-of-body experience. Clenching his fist and then unfurling his fingers he dug his stubby nails into the kitchen table.

He'd killed him, left him for dead. His hospital visits – pretending to be Jason's brother – he knew how close to death Jason was, but there had been hope. Hope he'd pull through after the surgery to stop the bleeding in his brain, and then what? Adam rubbed his temples and slammed his fists down on the table.

He had willed Jason to wake up, wake up and together they'd explain what happened and perhaps it would have all been sorted out, smoothed over. Everything could return to normal. Jason would not tell the police who did this. Steph would return home. The stalking, the punch, could all be left in the past and they could move on. They could have figured it out together, made up a convincing story to explain how he hit his head.

Done. No need for charges of assault or harassment.

Adam stood up. The smell of vomit and stale whiskey forced him out of the kitchen. His legs felt disconnected from his body as he stumbled towards the bedroom. The empty Moses basket caused his stomach to lurch, but he managed to swallow down the acrid saliva. He picked up the remaining sheet and inhaled Natalie's fading milky scent.

The hairs on the back of his neck began to tingle as a shiver rippled across his back and a coldness infused his bones. Again his legs gave way and he found himself sinking down to the bed as he screamed Natalie's name. Within a few days the landscape of his life had become unrecognisable. His right hand throbbed, the one that dealt the killer blow.

Scooping up his mobile that had slipped out of his back pocket, he gingerly stood up. He noticed the shattered photo frame and shook off the broken glass. Steph beamed back at him. He stroked her face and slipped the photograph out of the frame as he made his way to the door. Wriggling his coat on, he slid the picture into his inside pocket.

The car lights flickered as he squeezed the key. He slid into the driver's seat and gripped the steering wheel.

I can drive. I'm fine.

He swallowed down the stale taste of whiskey and vomit and erratically pulled away from his home. The houses blurred into each other. Adam's eyes burned as the road ahead seemed to pulsate. Houses were replaced by trees and the road became eerily quiet, not a single car in front of him. He wanted some tail lights to follow to help him moderate his speed.

Driving wasn't helping. Getting out the house, away from everything, all he wanted was to push it all aside and think of nothing. A velvety black nothingness. But, as he drove through the forest, memories clouded his consciousness.

All Steph. The first time he saw her: dancing on a table in the union bar. Her warm smile, her flowing curls bouncing around as she moved to the music. She beckoned him over.

Sweat dripping off her brow as she jumped off the table into his arms.

Her body. The first time they had sex; greedily consuming each other. His hands on her breasts. His arms wrapped around her. The smell of vodka and a scented candle she'd lit in her small halls of residence room. The Degas prints on her wall. A ballerina? The room faded away, out of reach and then another memory filled its place.

The last time they'd made love, how gentle he felt he needed to be as her belly was swollen, tightly swaddling the new life they'd created. The first time he saw her holding Natalie.

He could barely see the road in front of him through his tears as image upon image flashed before him like a surreal montage.

He took his foot off the accelerator as he realised the trees were whizzing by too fast. The light faded as the branches reached skyward, welcoming nightfall. His eyes struggled to focus on the road ahead as it plunged its way through the winter trees.

The roundabout loomed up ahead and he attempted to slow up on the approach. Without thinking he took the road towards Loughton. *Shit. Wrong road. This isn't going to take me to Jess.* It was a detour, but there was no turning round now. He found himself automatically slowing down as the road twisted through the forest.

A fog began to form. The wispy clouds appeared in pockets swirling across the road. He drove cautiously through it, unsure what he would meet within the cloud. Deer were notorious for darting out in front of cars on this stretch of road.

The fog pockets melded together. Enveloping the road ahead, clouding out everything in his path. Adam's head continued to pound. He was losing the ability to focus through the fug of whiskey.

There's a right turn ahead. I need to stop. Get some fresh air. He broke sharply as he swung into the road; he could just about make out the houses ahead now on the left as the fog continued to thicken. To his right the green and the trees were barely visible.

He ventured halfway along and slowed the car to a halt. Stumbling out of the vehicle he vomited on the grass. His hands rested on his thighs, head throbbing from throwing up. He took a deep breath before rising to stand up straight.

In front of him the fog clung to the bare trees and behind him it shrouded the houses. He'd arrived at a place which he, Steph and Jess had visited a few times: Baldwins Hill Pond.

Summer walks in the forest, picnics by the pond. And the time when he and Steph were daring, they couldn't keep their hands off each other, they just had to have sex against a tree. He pushed the memory away. He wanted his brain to stop torturing him.

He felt compelled to walk towards the trees. Maybe he could find the pond in the faded light, sit there, absorb the cold night air, take in the smells and remember a time before everything had spiralled out of control. A last moment of freedom, before the inevitable. He knew he couldn't hide from what he'd done, and now he didn't want to.

He needed some space where he could find peace. Where his thoughts could slow down. The thought of watching the ripples on the pond pushed him onto the green. *I need to get my story ready. Tell Jess everything. She's good with stories. She'll help me with the police. I can't do this on my own.*

He edged forward through the grass, and his feet found a natural worn path. In front of him, illuminating the fog, a flash of blue streaked through the trees. Someone was out there.

Running into the gloom. He peered into the darkness. *No. There's nothing there.*

It was impossible to see anything. He unzipped his coat and took out the now crumpled photograph. He kissed his wife's image as he edged towards the wood. The carpet of spongey grass slowed down his feet. He stepped between two trees. Darkness enclosed him.

It's hopeless. What the hell am I doing? I'll never find the pond.

He tried to turn around to go back to the car, but his feet seemed to refuse his brain, and he swayed on the spot, peering out into the gloom. Again, further into the wood, a flash of blue streaked through the trees.

Edging forwards he was unsure why he was being pulled towards the trees, to the darkness of the woodland, but he continued to stagger through the first line of trees. The blue light vanished. Adam swayed, feeling the effect of shock and alcohol rinse through his body.

'Mr Henderson?'

A voice boomed from behind him. He spun around and a torch was being shone in his direction.

'Mr Henderson? Adam? It's PC Hawthorne. Are you OK?'

The torch bobbed up and down as it moved towards him. Adam shook himself and ran to meet the officer.

'Are you OK? What are you doing out here in this weather?'

'I ... was going to see Jess and then I took a wrong turn and I felt, I had to go to the pond, one more time, a final time.'

Adam's trembling hand rose to shield his eyes from the intense torch light.

'The pond? At this time of night?' PC Hawthorne dipped the torch and shone it to the left of Adam.

'Yes, ridiculous I know. I'll never find it in the dark.'

What am I doing? I can't control any of this. That control, I lost it when my fist flew towards Jason's face. Did I think that taking a moment to think through my story would help? My head hurts. Nothing makes any sense any more. I just need to tell the truth. No more hiding or lies.

'I wouldn't like to be wandering the forest at night, especially around that pond.'

Adam felt his brow pinch. 'You're right. Sorry.'

'No problem. That pond has a reputation. Some call it ...' Hawthorne shifted his weight and shone the torch towards the trees. He coughed and shook his head. 'Anyway, sorry, never mind what the locals call it. Mr Henderson, I was on my way to your house when I saw your car heading away. I've been trying to get hold of you. It's good news. The woman at the train station isn't your wife. Jess has found your wife and your baby. She's bringing them home.'

'But the CCTV image?'

'Not her. A young woman, same height and build, and dressed just like your wife, took her own life.'

Adam threw himself at the policeman. He held him tightly, as though he knew this man well, as though he could have been the younger brother he never had. As the relief flooded through his body, he released him from the embrace. He took a step back, keeping his eyes firmly closed.

She's alive. They are both alive.

But, I can't live with myself.

He opened his eyes and looked over the officer's shoulder towards the houses. The fog smothered the rooftops and swirled around the street lights. He simultaneously lifted his hands and placed his wrists together.

'Cuff me.' Adam's voice was small.

'Sorry, what did you say?'

'I've hurt someone, I hit him, I didn't mean for him to die. Cuff me.' Adam pleaded.

PC Hawthorne stared at him. A look of puzzlement scrawled across his brow.

'Hurt someone?'

Adam nodded and put his wrists forward. 'I hit Jason Balderson.'

'You hit Mr Balderson?'

'Yes. I hit him, he'd been harassing Steph, threatening her, stalking her, emailing her nasty stuff. I've been visiting him in hospital, calling the nurses at least twice a day to check on his progress, I saw him this morning. I thought he'd pull through, I didn't think he was going to die.'

PC Hawthorne placed the handcuffs around Adam's wrists.

'Mr Henderson, I am arresting you on suspicion of murder. You do not have to say anything, but it may harm your defence if you do not mention, when questioned, something which you later rely on in court. Anything you do say may be given in evidence.'

PC Hawthorne moved him into the police car, gently shielding his head to prevent him from bumping it on the car roof. All he could hear as he slid into the back seat were the words that his wife and daughter were alive. A smile spread across his face as PC Hawthorne swung the car around in a slick three-point turn.

They are alive. Alive.

Day Three

Jess

Jess pulled onto Steph's drive, the engine whirred to a halt. Where was Adam's car? There were no lights on, the house looked like it was holding its breath, frozen in darkness with the curtains wide open.

Surely he'd be waiting up for us? He must know she's safe now. Where the hell is he?

She felt her heckles rise and her heart begin to thump loudly in her chest. A police car and another car was parked outside the house, a white Ford Fiesta, with two occupants.

She inhaled deeply.

It's nearly over.

Steph's childlike snoring made her crumple. She stared at her through the rear-view mirror.

What have I done? Perhaps all she needs is my support and some sleep? They are going to take her away, maybe even take Natalie away from her. This isn't what I should be doing. It's my turn to take care of her.

She squeezed the steering wheel; the diary entries swam around her brain, particularly the conversations with their dead mum. The affair that she was ninety-nine per cent sure didn't happen. *Surely Steph wouldn't repeat what Mum did?*

She turned to look at the baby seat. She couldn't see Natalie's face as the seat faced away from her but she tuned into her snuffles. *What if they separate them? How would I live with myself? Steph would never forgive me.* But the image of Steph frantically brushing invisible ants from her niece's body told her that, despite her fears, this was the right thing to do.

She carefully eased the car door closed and crept towards the Fiesta. Two women occupied the front seats. The one on the passenger side began to get out of the car as Jess approached.

'Hi I'm Jess – Steph, my sister is still asleep.'

The woman pulled her lanyard forward showing Jess her ID.

'I'm Dr Sloane, but please call me Mary. How are you doing?' Her warm Irish accent made Jess smile, it sounded comforting. The doctor had wide hips and her folded arms seemed to be holding up her ample chest. She was matronly, rather than doctorly, if that was even a thing. Her whole demeanour was comforting.

'Me? I'm fine. Exhausted but fine.'

Mary's colleague stepped out of the car and joined her on the pavement. She too was a stout woman with her hair unsympathetically scraped back into a ponytail. She smiled and introduced herself as Catherine, a social worker. She had an overly firm handshake, which was both reassuring and frightening in equal measure. Her briefcase accentuated her business-like manner.

'Right, before you wake her, how do you think she's going to react? How was she when you talked about the police?' asked Catherine.

Jess glanced towards the police car. The officers remained seated in the vehicle, presumably on hand if Steph was going to put up a fight.

'She was freaked out at first, she doesn't know everything that I told them, but I managed to go along with the delusion and she seems to think they'll help protect her.' Her bottom lip began to tremble.

'Good thinking, well done, that will help us. You did the right thing there, she probably thinks the delusion is totally real now. For her there's no difference between reality and the hallucinations. Now, hopefully she'll be fine, but the officers will restrain her if needs be. Sometimes it's the uniform that hits home that something is terribly wrong,' said Dr Sloane.

Jess felt her brow furrow and her legs begin to shake. She breathed in deeply. *I'm having my sister committed.*

'I told PC Hawthorne as much as I could. She thinks her daughter is a result of an affair. I can't, at this point, completely dismiss that, but I'm pretty sure she'd never have an affair; it's just not in her make-up, you know?'

Jess glanced back to the car. Both occupants were still, wrapped up in a much-needed deep sleep. The rest of the street was just as silent. No blinds moved, not even the bark of a dog broke the peace. She hoped that the quiet would last and the neighbours wouldn't witness a scene on their doorstep.

'He told us about her hallucinations. She thinks your mother is still alive?'

'Yes. She wrote about her visiting, giving her advice, she's very much alive in my sister's head despite dying a year ago.' Jess paused and pictured the woman at the service station. The woman who reminded her of Mum. *She's very much dead in my head. She's been dead to me for a long time.*

'Then at the shopping centre, she thought that Natalie was covered in ants. She was frantic. Brushing them off her. They were real to her, totally.'

The two professionals exchanged a knowing glance. It was not news to their ears, they'd had cases like this before. Steph was about to become a statistic.

'Now, unfortunately for your sister there are no beds available in the mother and baby unit at Chelmsford, but one becomes vacant on Monday. We've put wheels in motion to secure that bed. She will have to be admitted to the psychiatric ward first, which means you'll have to look after your niece until Monday. We've managed to get some breast milk from the milk bank, so that should help you with feeding her; sometimes babies won't take a bottle, sometimes they won't accept formula.'

Jess hadn't thought about being literally left holding the baby.

'Shit. I assumed she'd go with Steph?'

'Yes, ideally we wouldn't separate them, but she's lucky to get a bed in a dedicated unit at all, so a couple of nights apart should be manageable for all,' replied Dr Sloane. She shifted her weight from one foot to another and hitched up her bag a little, as the strap was threatening to slip off her shoulder.

Jess became aware of movement behind her. She turned to see Steph unstrapping herself from the passenger seat. Opening the door Steph stepped onto the pavement and ran her fingers through her curls and smiled awkwardly at Jess. Jess moved towards her. She wanted to scoop up her big sister in her arms and tell her that everything was going to be fine. But at this time, Jess still wasn't sure she could guarantee that anything would be. Nothing was going to be completely fine again.

'Go and get Natalie.'

Steph walked around the back of the car and opened the door. Her movements were slow and precise as she carefully lifted Natalie out of her car seat and held her to her chest. Jess bit her lip at the tender sight, so precious, so beautiful.

She exhaled, pushing the thoughts away which had been creeping around her consciousness all throughout the drive. Jack Nicholson's face kept pushing its way into her mind and then being substituted by Nurse Ratched. She kept reminding herself that this wasn't *One Flew Over the Cuckoo's Nest*.

She glanced back at the two women, neither had victory rolls or a prim white uniform. They looked like your average social worker or GP, because that's exactly what they were.

It is the right thing to do.

Jess put her arm around Steph and steered her towards the two women.

'Hi, I'm Mary, and this is my colleague Catherine.'

Catherine stretched her hand out for Steph to shake. Jess held her breath. *Take her hand. Please take her hand.* Steph turned to her, the puzzled look in her eyes softened, and she slowly reached out for Catherine's hand.

Jess slowly released the air from her lungs.

'Steph, I told you someone from the hospital would come and help us.' Steph looked around.

'Why are the police here?'

Mary smiled, 'They are here to protect you both, they'll escort us to the hospital to protect you. Is that OK?'

'Yes, good, good, he can't get her, he can't take her away.' Steph began to look around the darkened street. The same way she had scanned the Oasis food court earlier. She was looking for both of them again.

'You're both safe with us. We need Natalie to stay with Jess tonight while you are in the hospital. We've got her all the things she needs, like milk and bottles, and Jess can call you if she needs your help, but she needs to stay with Jess tonight.'

Steph stepped back. Her grip on Natalie tightened and she began to violently shake her head.

'No. No! I don't need to go to the hospital. It's a trick. And you're in on it, Jess. It's not Jason I need to worry about is it? It's Adam. He's going to take her away. He's going to punish me and you're helping him.'

At the sound of raised voices, the officers, who had silently exited the car, began to hold Steph.

'Get off me. Take your hands off me.' Natalie let out a shrill cry.

Jess stepped towards her. Darkness seemed to swallow them both as everyone around Jess faded into the background while she concentrated solely on her sister and niece.

'Steph, you've got it wrong. I love you. Adam loves you. No one is going to hurt you or take Natalie away. Remember how you've always looked after me? Always. Now it's my turn.' She searched Steph's face for a glimmer of recognition.

'If you go to the hospital they'll protect you there and I'm sure one of the police officers will stay here with me and protect us. You need to go to the hospital. You need help. Remember the ants? They weren't real.' Jess had spent the whole day avoiding telling Steph that everything she was going through was all in her mind. Something had broken and needed to be fixed. It was the last thing she wanted to say now, but perhaps it was the only thing that could bring her round? It was a gamble, she knew it, she hoped it would pay off. The last thing she wanted to witness was the police officers forcibly placing her in the car. She couldn't let that happen to Steph.

One of the officers released his grip and spoke to her softly.

'I'll stay here with your sister. What do you think? I can make sure no one takes Natalie away. We are here to protect you, all of you. It's our job to keep you safe.'

Jess nodded in agreement with the quick-thinking officer and searched Steph's face for a response. She hoped her best pleading eyes were going to work.

'Can I look after Natalie for you? And the officer can protect both of us?'

Steph bent her head down, she nuzzled into Natalie's short black wispy hair and kissed her. She looked up abruptly at Jess and stared into her eyes.

She was reminded of all those nights when Steph held her in bed and told her over and over that it wasn't her fault that Dad had left, always looking her in the eye, always, so she knew it wasn't yet another lie. She knew that there was probably one last thing to say to convince her.

'I called Mum while we were driving and while you were asleep. She'll be here soon to help me. It's all going to be all right. She always knows what to do.' The words in Steph's diary had imprinted themselves in Jess's consciousness.

Steph peered over Jess's shoulder and a smile spread across her face. Her eyes brightened with genuine love.

'She's here now, she's come to help you. Thank you Jess. I know it must have been so hard speaking to her after all this time.' She paused and took a step towards Jess. 'What you said about the ants, they weren't real?'

'That's right. You need help. You need to sleep. I think the lack of sleep has made you see things like the ants. The nurses will give you something to help you sleep. I think the car journey was the first time you'd got some proper rest?' Every muscle in Jess's body was wound so tightly that she worried about controlling her own limbs as they were frozen in position. Her arms raised stiffly in an offer to hold her niece.

'Yes. You're right. I am exhausted.' Her voice was a flat whisper, as though all the air in her lungs had been sucked out.

She slowly wriggled Natalie into Jess's arms.

Jess stroked her niece's cheek. Her still sleepy body radiated warmth and Jess felt an unfamiliar swell of contentment swirl around her chest.

Her niece's eyebrow twitched but her breathing remained in a steady rhythm as sleep held fast. She looked at Steph, who turned her head, so her gaze no longer fixed on Natalie. She was looking over Jess's shoulder. Steph lifted her hand gradually and waved at an empty space behind Jess.

'Be kind to Mum, Jess.'

'I will.' Her voice caught in her larynx.

Jess wrapped her arms tighter around Natalie, just in case Steph had a final change of mind.

The officer stepped back from Steph as the doctor and social worker moved towards her; they shepherded her into their car, gently helping her into the back seat. She looked diminutive sitting in the back seat despite the small size of the vehicle. She raised her hand to the window, placing her fingers to the glass.

Droplets of water dripped on to Natalie's head. Jess realised she was crying. She felt like she was watching a scene unfold in a play, she was acting a part, a part which Steph had cast.

Images of people in straitjackets wailing and screaming jumped into her mind. She dipped her head and inhaled the baby powder smell of her niece.

A hand on her upper arm made her jump.

'Sorry to startle you, we are heading back now, you did a good job there.' The officer nodded, his mouth set in a grimace. 'Before we go, Sergeant Browne wants you to give her a call. She needs to have a chat about your brother-in-law.

Get yourself and the little mite indoors and give her a ring.' He nodded again and returned to the police car.

Jess looked at her niece.

'What the hell am I going to do with you?' Natalie settled into her arms, rooting towards her breast, but remaining in a light sleep.

'Not going to find anything there sweet girl.' She murmured as she walked to door and forced the key into the lock. She carried her into the silent house. Jess wanted to lay down on her sister's bed and cuddle her niece and revel in her safety. But that would have to wait.

She closed the curtains before carefully laying Natalie in the Moses basket. She wriggled and then settled into the cute baby breathing pattern which Jess had heard only a few times before. A sheet lay on the floor at the foot of the wooden stand. She gently placed it over Natalie.

Plugging her phone in to charge she hugged her knees to her chest and snuggled into the sofa. She redialled the now familiar Epping Police number.

'Sergeant Browne?'

'Speaking. What can I— '

'It's Jessica Morley here, one of the police officers who accompanied the street triage team told me to call you about Adam – Adam Henderson? Where is he?'

'Sorry about that. Thought it better if I talked you through a few things. Firstly, how is your sister? Did she comply with the team?'

'Yes, all fine, thankfully. Please can you thank PC Hawthorne for sorting this out and getting her the help she needs.'

'Of course, will do.' Sergeant Browne paused and sucked the air through her teeth. 'Right. Mr Henderson is helping us with our enquiries regarding the murder of Mr Jason Balderson.'

The mobile slipped from her hand and bounced off the sofa on to the carpet. It took every ounce of depleted energy to haul herself up to retrieve the phone.

'He's what? I mean, he can't be dead, he was … can I speak to Adam?'

'I'm afraid not. He's currently being interviewed.'

'Interviewed? Does he have a solicitor? Do I need to get him one?'

'His solicitor is present. There's not much else I can tell you at the moment.'

Jess nodded and stared at the blank TV screen. She imagined Jason's face appearing on screen, complete with oxygen mask and the hissing sound of the ventilator. She said goodbye to Sergeant Brown, before rushing out to the car to retrieve her handbag.

She slid out the thin notebook and flicked through the pages. *Lies. All delusions. All of it?* She re-read the pages which detailed her confession to Adam. *The stalking, the emails, the letterbox. Is there some truth amongst the lies? Or is it all a product of a diseased brain?*

She touched the chrome icon on the screen of her mobile. Google appeared and she typed in 'assault, epping, jason balderson'. The most recent article, a news report, detailed that he died from his injuries sustained in the attack. She closed her eyes, lay the phone on the table and put her head in her hands.

She could see him clearly. Lying in the bed, hooked up to the ventilator, eyes closed, nothing stirring. The hushing noise of the ventilator filled her ears.

Oh Adam, what have you done?

Before hauling herself off to bed she texted Matt. A numbness took over her, she didn't want to speak to him, she just wanted to do the right thing and let him know her sister and niece were no longer missing. Now wasn't the time to tell him everything that had played out. All emotion had drained from her body, she couldn't go through any more. Now all she needed was sleep.

I found Steph and Natalie. I can't believe I'm texting this. Steph is mentally ill, I've had her committed. I can't talk now I need sleep. I just wanted you to know they're safe. I'll call you when I'm ready to talk. Love you. XXXX

Day Seven

Jess

Jess approached the one storey newly built hospital unit. It didn't look like she'd envisaged. There was a homeliness and smallness to the façade. Ingrained into her subconscious was the image of a large Victorian asylum, with a grandiose arched entrance and clock tower.

She knew where the image came from. Middlewood Hospital in Sheffield. Many locals still recognised it as the hospital, despite it being redeveloped into flats and houses. It remained listed and therefore the three stone arches and clock were preserved in the local's minds for ever.

As she made her way through the small entrance she was greeted by a nurse who wore a warm smile. She pushed back a strand of russet brown hair, looping it behind her ear, taking care not to catch her finger on her hoop earrings.

'You must be Steph's sister. You look very much alike. I'm Caroline, one of Steph's support workers.' She proffered her hand.

'She and Natalie are settling in well.' She swept her arm towards a doorway and ushered Jess through it. 'Shall we have lunch together and then we can talk about her treatment. Her room's this way.' The nurse beamed at Jess. The smile was genuine.

Jess hardly had a chance to get her bearings. Perhaps the nurse was worried about lingering in the entrance, or seeming too nurse-like, or more likely she was pushed for time. Through the light and airy corridor Jess followed Caroline. Her lithe frame sashayed in front of her and her wedge-heeled boots caused her to sway rhythmically. Jess was struck with how the hospital smelt of crisp fresh laundry and not the usual cabbage and bleach. The only hint of the clinical about Caroline was her lanyard which swung in time with her footsteps.

'Steph's room is down the corridor at the end. I need to speak to a patient in the room next door, so pop down and say hi and I'll be with you in a moment.'

Jess paused, frozen in the corridor, wondering what she'd find in the room.

Caroline put her hand on Jess's elbow. 'It's OK. Your sister's doing well. We've reduced her level of risk. Go ahead.' She nodded towards the end of the corridor before knocking on the door to her right; a voice immediately asked her to come in.

Jess moved towards the end of the dimly lit corridor. A mixture of tiredness and relief enveloped her again. It kept coming in waves after she'd handed Natalie over to the nurses. One minute she was feeling good, getting on with her usual routine, and then the next she wanted to collapse in bed. It reminded her of the waves of revulsion that would hit her unexpectedly after Mum died.

Her sister's door was wedged ajar and she could hear her speaking in a gentle high-toned voice to Natalie. She paused before moving towards the door. Steph's soothing voice wafted through the doorway. Jess couldn't help smile at the motherly language and the comforting sing-song voice which signified to her that Steph would beat this. *She will get better and get out of here.*

A breeze caressed her face and sent a ripple down her spine. She pulled her navy blue-bird print scarf tighter around her neck.

Jess gently pushed the door open. She was surprised to see someone sat on the end of the bed. The body shape was familiar, ramrod straight back, slight frame and she was wearing a peacock blue coat.

The woman had her back to Jess. Jess couldn't see Steph, but she could still hear her talking to Natalie. She took in the shape. Maybe it was a trick of the light?

Jess couldn't move, her feet felt like they were nailed to the spot and her gut reaction was telling her to run, but she couldn't lift her feet, they were dead weights.

The woman turned her neck awkwardly to look at Jess. Jess's hands automatically covered her gaping mouth. Her eyes were showing her the impossible. She tightly clamped them shut and when she opened them there was no one there. The bedspread moved, a gentle ripple.

She felt a light touch to her shoulder, as though someone had put a hand to it; her whole body stiffened. The pressure on her shoulder lifted. A breeze rushed past her. She looked back towards the entrance of the long thin corridor. Caroline was still in the other patient's room. A stillness prevailed.

Steph appeared at the door, Natalie in her arms. She blinked again. *Just the two of them. No one else.*

'Jess! Are you OK honey? You look very pale?'

'I'm fine, still tired, you know, from everything that's happened.' She loosened the scarf. 'You are looking better already,' she said as she moved to embrace them.

'Thank you. Things are a little clearer and having Natalie here is helping.'

And she did look better. Jess knew she had a long way to go, but there was a hint of colour in her cheeks.

'Can I ask you, when you saw Mum in your hallucinations, did you ever feel her or touch her?'

'We talked. She'd appear and I never really wondered why she'd simply appear and disappear, because so much was happening to me. I was seeing so many things, like those ants in the shopping centre, spiders, Jason.'

'I didn't know what was real. There's so many things going round and round in my head.' Her voice changed, it became flat and she dipped her chin to kiss Natalie's hair.

'Sorry, probably too soon to talk about it all. I shouldn't have mentioned it.' Jess sighed, she felt like she needed to explain herself, but wished she hadn't asked.

'I guess with all this talk of Mum, I'm wishing I could see her, too.'

Caroline stepped out of the neighbouring room and the sisters ended their conversation. Jess felt prickles of heat spread across her cheeks.

Did that just happen? Is my mind playing tricks on me? The image of her mum twisting her head awkwardly around to look at her bubbled up in front of her. She winced and hoped the image wouldn't replay like all the other traumatic moments of her past did.

They walked back down the corridor in silence and entered a small kitchen. Caroline opened the fridge, pulled out some peppers, courgette and onion. She began to chop the vegetables.

'Veggie stir-fry and noodles OK?' The sisters nodded.

They sat at the table in silence as Caroline cooked for them. Jess didn't know what to say. Words swam around her brain but refused to exit her mouth. She wished she'd not mentioned Mum. Steph had regained the colour that she had when Jess first saw her, but she was quiet and looked like she didn't want to speak to Jess or even want her there.

Jess played with her necklace. She twisted the white gold ball that hung above her chest. It made a soft clicking sound as she rotated it. The large kitchen opened out into a dining room, with just a handful of tables and chairs. The dining room gave way to carpet to create a lounge space. A sofa, TV and some play-pens stood awkwardly attempting to create a small relaxing space. The window was obscured by a venetian blind. A patch of grass was just about visible and she could make out a few trees some yards away. *I wonder if the mums are allowed outside in the garden alone? I was expecting bars on the window too.*

Another nurse joined them, distracting Jess from her thoughts. She held Natalie while Steph ate. The new nurse, Lindsay, chatted about Natalie. Telling Jess how much weight she'd gained over the past few days, how well she was feeding and how her sleeping pattern was settling nicely.

Jess knew it wasn't really for her benefit, more to fill the silence that enveloped them during the meal. Jess smiled and nodded as Lindsay kept talking. She watched Steph eat. It was good to see all the food disappear from her plate.

She thought Steph seemed a little vacant, she wasn't present in the room, her mind was somewhere else. A mask of exhaustion covered her face and once she'd finished her meal she asked to go for a nap.

'Will you still be here when I wake?' Her words were slow, but there was a familiar warmth to her voice.

'Yes. Of course.'

She rose from her seat and left the little dining area. Lindsay accompanied her; she still held Natalie in her arms and Jess wondered how much care Steph was able to provide her daughter. A rush of anger – no, not anger – thought Jess, a sort of fierce protectiveness, fizzed through her body. She wanted to be the one caring for Natalie, supporting Steph, not a stranger.

The scraping of plates broke her thoughts. Caroline jammed the plates into the dishwasher and straightened up, putting her hands on the small of her back and thrusting her hips forward.

'Struggling with hideous back pain today. God knows why. Wondering whether I've done too much heavy lifting recently? Must reduce my weights at the gym I guess.' Caroline smiled and waved her hand in a sweeping motion towards the door. Jess noticed that she did this a lot.

'So, as I said, Steph is doing well, we've reduced her risk level as she's able to care for Natalie with some support. We currently check on her every fifteen minutes.' Caroline paused as she held the door open to the reception area. 'But we are impressed with how well she's doing, so it won't be long until we increase this time.' They reached a room tucked a way from the reception entrance and Caroline opened the door, and motioned for Jess to take a seat.

'We can discuss her treatment and you can tell me a little more about her husband.'

Jess followed her into a small box-like room and sat down on a typical office chair. The desk was a picture of organisation. She always admired people who were able to have such a clear desk. Her own was always overflowing with paper. The thought of work made her want to crawl under a duvet and hide, she didn't want to return tomorrow. Maybe her boss would give her another day or two. *Perhaps I could get signed off sick? Perhaps I should quit? Once Steph and Natalie are out of here won't they need me even more?*

Caroline explained the treatment plan and that Steph would remain as an inpatient, pending her progress and how she responded to medication. The words anti-psychotics made her shudder.

'As you probably noticed the meds make her tired. It will take her a little while to adjust to them, but they are working well. They've stopped the psychosis, she'll no longer hallucinate or suffer with delusions.' Caroline paused and slid open the desk drawer and pulled out a notepad. She flicked through the pages and removed the lid from a pen. 'So, her husband has been arrested?'

'Yes. Here's the difficult bit. Steph told him she was being stalked. She believed that her colleague, Jason, was Natalie's father – the delusional affair which you've now read about in her diary. Adam went to his house and hit him. He left him, didn't call for an ambulance, and despite surgery, Jason died. Adam's now facing a murder charge, but I spoke with his solicitor this morning and he hopes to reduce the charge to manslaughter. Her diaries again have proved useful.'

Caroline sighed heavily. 'That's a lot of information for anyone to take in. Obviously we won't be informing your sister yet.'

Jess winced at the thought of lying to her. She'd have to trot out the line that he'd gone away on business.

'Do you have any more questions?'

Jess stared at the nurse. She had so many questions. The first thing that came into her head was whether she was going crazy too, was she hallucinating?

'When are your visiting hours?'

'Four to eight p.m. So you can visit after work?'

'Yes, I guess so.'

'She'll need to see someone as she can't see her husband.'

Jess winced at her clumsy delivery. She didn't mean it to sound like she didn't want to visit her sister. She did; it was work and the thought of leaving early each day and the impact it would have which made her sound reluctant. So far her boss had been understanding, but she knew his tolerance of her absence would decrease as time passed.

'Yes. Of course I'll visit, as much as I can. Thank you again. I know she's got a long way to go but she's looking a little better already.'

Caroline nodded tentatively and smiled. 'Yes, she is making good progress, we sort of expect a setback or two, as this is often the way with postnatal psychosis, but she's doing well and more importantly she's looking after her baby with minimal support. She was lucky. Really lucky to have a sister who didn't give up on her. It was a brave thing to do and pretty quick thinking in the way you played along with the delusion. Dr Sloane was impressed.' Caroline pushed herself up to stand. 'As I said, please do visit as much as you are able, and I don't say this lightly – take care of yourself too. Do you have someone you can lean on for support?'

'I do – he's away travelling but ... I'm pretty sure I can get him to cut his trip short and come home and support me,' Jess crossed her fingers, she hoped that her needs and wants could be met. If she could convince him that she'd open up – and get help like her sister – then perhaps he'd come home. 'Are there any other support services available to family? Like counselling or, something along those lines?'

'Yes, there is. We run support groups to help family members cope with looking after their loved ones once they come home. We prepare you for their release. As for counselling, well, you'll have to see your GP.'

Jess nodded. 'Can I go and say goodbye?'

'Of course. Pop along to her room, then return to reception. I'll swipe you out. Maybe bring a few more home comforts for Steph and Natalie. Can you label the items? That should also help her settle in to her routine here.'

Jess nodded. She made her way out of the office and retraced her steps down the corridor. The door silently eased open to reveal Steph sound asleep.

Natalie too lay peacefully still in her cot. Lindsay was sat in a wicker woven chair scribbling notes in a folder. She looked up and smiled at Jess.

Thankfully Mum isn't perching on the end of the bed. I can't be seeing things too. I can't be getting visits from my dead mother.

Jess mouthed goodbye and closed the door silently. She made her way out of the unit, thanking Caroline again for her help. She refused to look back as she power-walked away. Not looking back, just in case Mum was standing in the doorway waving her off. She wanted to run, to hide from what she'd seen earlier, but she knew that running away would make no difference. She couldn't escape her mind and her memories.

* * *

The quietness of the flat wrapped itself around Jess like an old acquaintance. Peacefulness was much needed.

Jess smiled at the familiar sight of her neighbour, wrapped up in a large purple puffer jacket, assuming her usual position at the top of the fire escape, inhaling and exhaling swirls of smoke. Jess almost waved to her, she was a constant in her ever-changing landscape.

She made herself a coffee and searched through the cupboards for emergency chocolate. The idea of emergency chocolate made her smile: it was an addiction she'd managed to curb, an addiction, unlike her neighbour's, which wouldn't result in cancer.

Cancer. A word she'd avoided saying or thinking about for some time. But after what she believed she'd seen today she couldn't stop thinking of Mum. Steph's words rang in her ears.

Ovarian cancer, stage four. She's going to rent a flat close by so we can see her as much as possible before the end.

After years of ostracising her mum the illness thrust her back into her life. She couldn't shy away from visiting her, she'd be the one who looked cruel and vindictive, and Jess never wanted her mum to assume the victim role. Ever. *Vindictive. Now there's an adjective that summed her up. Even at the end, she spilled her poisonous words into my ears.*

Anger pulsated through her limbs. She slammed the coffee down and moved away from watching 'fag lady', away from the cancer sticks and into the lounge. The low winter sun shone through the window and bathed the lounge in a blue haze. The light bounced around the room, scattered by the large mirror which hung above the faux Victorian fireplace and the mirrored candle holders she bought on her first trip to Camden market. Matt hated them. *Matt. Maybe it's time he knew the truth.*

She slumped into the dining chair and opened up her laptop. Firing up Facebook in the hope that Matt had sent her a message or posted some pictures. Nothing. She fished out her phone from the bottom of her handbag. Her staccato tapping fingers hammered out a text to Matt. Telling him to call her now.

She held the phone in her hand and stared at the screen but it refused to ping in reply. She wanted to fling it across the room, but instead she placed it down on the table and petulantly pushed it away. It skidded to a halt where the table butted up against the wall.

Scrolling through the Facebook status updates on the laptop, her eyes came to rest on a post from a friend from home. A link to a story about a young woman who had committed suicide. Comments littered the space below the story, all expressing sadness in varying degrees of eloquence. She *had* to click and read.

Police release details of woman hit by train

British Transport Police were called to Meadowhall Interchange after 4pm on Friday 3rd February after a woman was seen jumping from the platform as a high speed train approached.

Today, the force confirmed the death of a woman, aged 29, from Sheffield. She has been named as Keeley Hareton of Wadsley.

Miss Hareton had been struggling to come to terms with the sudden death of her three-month-old son. Speaking to The Star, *Keeley's father said: 'Keeley was unable to cope with her grief. Our grandson died last year and over the past few months she has become very distressed. She started to take a baby doll everywhere with her.'*

Mr Hareton explained that his daughter had refused to seek help despite repeated pleas from both him and his wife.

Over the past twelve months there have been three fatalities at the station. Network rail have been asked to comment on the layout of the station.

Jess re-read the words. It wasn't the outcome she'd envisaged. It felt wrong to feel relief, but she did, and she felt joy. Joy that her niece wasn't under a train. Her sister was getting the help she needed. They'd all been given a second chance, a reprieve.

But this family, already ripped apart by grief, now had to deal with a new hurt and had lots of loose ends and chaos to sift through as they went through the inevitable search for who is to blame, how they could have prevented this, and the whys and what ifs.

Jess felt her jaw drop. *She gave Steph the little blue rabbit, she must have. A woman with a doll, it had to be her.* She shivered at the strange turn of fate.

Tears dropped onto her keyboard as she stared blankly at the news article. She wiped them away with the back of her hand. It felt wrong. The tears weren't for her, or the woman's family. It embarrassed her that those tears were selfish ones.

A strange bubbly sound erupted from the computer. She frantically pushed the tears from her cheeks and sniffed before clicking to answer the Skype call.

'Broadsword calling Danny boy!'

'Michael Caine?'

'Richard Burton actually. No it's me, Matt.' The familiar chortle filled her ears.

'Don't think there's a call for a Richard Burton sound-a-like. You and your obscure old films.'

'Obscure? *Where Eagles Dare* is a classic. I'm not going to give you the satisfaction of telling me not to give up the day job.' She almost heard the smirk spread across his face.

'No need. You already have.'

'Ouch. Just removing the knife from my back.' And he mimed the removal of a dagger from his shoulders.

'Sorry, couldn't resist the dig. Thanks for calling me.'

Her voice was flat. She'd put off calling him but sent lots of texts explaining everything that had happened to Steph and Adam. She felt so exhausted, every fibre of muscle ached, and today was the first time the ache had eased. Today was the first time she felt like she could deal with him. Deal with all the emotions that resurfaced whenever she thought of him. *You abandoned me. Gave up on me when things got tough.*

'Did you see Steph today?'

'Yes. She looks a little better. The meds have taken the edge off her paranoia and the nurses are pleased with her progress.' She sighed as her mind replayed the apparition, the way her mum slowly turned her head to look at her. She felt the familiar coldness, which had wrapped itself around her over the last few days, creep over her skin again.

'Matt, I ... I, know she was hallucinating, I know that, but I saw Mum, too. I saw her sat on Steph's bed in the hospital today. I closed my eyes and when I opened them, she'd gone. I feel like I'm losing it. Just before I found her diary a photograph of the three of us fell off and smashed. Nothing made it fall off, no lorry trundled by or anything. I'm being ridiculous, aren't I? It wasn't Mum trying to tell me something, was it?'

'You're not being ridiculous, you've been under a hell of a lot of stress. The photo frame was probably on the edge and fell off. You read about your mum, about Steph seeing her, and what with all the stress you've been under and all that driving too you must be exhausted. You probably wanted to see her, didn't you?'

Jess nodded and swallowed down the lump that had formed in her throat.

'It's just your brain playing tricks on you. You're not going mad and you're not seeing her ghost either.'

Jess felt the lump disappear and be replaced by an acrid taste. She felt a rush of blood as Matt smiled back at her.

'What would you know? You're not here. You're not here to see me, to know exactly how I am. I could be going mad too. It's hereditary isn't it? You don't know what it's been like here. Alone. Left behind.' She pushed her chair away from the table and resisted the urge to snap the laptop shut.

'Babe, I'm sorry, I'm sorry I'm not with you, holding your hand, but honestly, look what you have done. *You* found your sister. You did that. I don't think you are going mad, you're stressed out. There's a difference.'

'Is there?' She honestly didn't know if there was. Reality, sanity, the line which marked the boundary could so easily become blurred.

'Yes there is and you know that. And it's OK for you to be angry with me.'

'For fuck's sake, you are always so fucking reasonable.' She spat the words out, she wanted to hurt him, but arguing with Matt was like attempting to wind up a broken clockwork toy.

She drew breath, ready to speak, but the words refused to roll off her tongue. She sighed noisily and wiped away a stray tear which hung on her chiselled cheek bone.

'One of us has to be.'

Her shoulders softened and the scowl she'd been wearing disappeared.

'Come home. Come back. There's so much I need to sort out and I can't do that alone. I need to visit Steph and Adam and fit work in and then, when eventually Steph and Natalie come home, I want to look after them. I need to look after them and I can't do that all by myself.'

Her whole body quaked as the tide of emotion over took her. She couldn't speak, the only thing she could do was lay her head on the table. Conflicting emotions rushed over her. Anger, hurt, love. She couldn't settle on which feeling was most prominent or powerful. She rested her chin on her hand and stared at him on screen. 'Cut your trip short and come home. If you want to make us work, then do that for me. Don't fucking abandon me again. I've seen enough over the past week now to know I can't keep secrets any more. Come home and I'll tell you why I lost it when Mum got ill and why I accused you of having a fling.'

A rueful smile took hold of his mouth.

'I'll look into flights home.'

Nine months later

Steph

All the visitors were seated first. Steph glanced around the hall. She wondered whether any of the other visitors were first timers. Were they as anxious as she was? She watched a woman seated alone fiddle with a ring, possibly her wedding ring, she twisted it around her finger rapidly. Everyone seemed to be holding their breath as they waited for the prisoners to file in and take their seats.

Nine months had passed. Time had slipped by in an institutional drug-induced haze. She gave a wry smile at the thought of being institutionalised; she wasn't encouraged to think of her hospital stay in that way. It was a hospital stay, not a detention, not like her husband was experiencing.

Remand. Sentencing. Four years in prison.

She blinked back a tear which attempted to spring from her left tear duct.

No. I will not cry. He will not see me crying here, not this time.

Time. Four weeks in the unit.

A week of being released daily. And then, it has taken me all this time to get here, to be able to see my husband. To come to terms with the fact that I caused this. My broken mind put him in here.

No. He will not see me cry.

The door opened to allow the prisoners to file in. She inhaled deeply, further lengthening her spine, her eyes widening as Adam entered the room. She took in his features. He looked older, so much older. Grey hair sprung up around his ears and now sprinkled across the top of his head too. His jaw seemed to jut out more due to weight loss, but she took in the shape of his arms and chest and could see muscle definition which was absent before. *Before all this.*

Adam sunk into the seat opposite her, and he reached out to take her hands. He squeezed them tightly and stroked the backs of her hands before furtively looking around the room. He removed them as a guard began to walk down the aisle towards their table, before taking a seat to watch the prisoners and visitors. Steph mirrored him and for a while they remained still.

'How are you?' Steph broke the silence.

'A little better for seeing you. And you?'

'I'm doing OK. It's good to be home. Shit, sorry, I shouldn't have said that.'

'Don't be silly, it is good that you are home. Do they keep an eye on you? I don't like the idea of you being home all by yourself.'

He stroked her hand again. She longed for his arms to encircle her and not let go. Her eyes settled on the cuffs of his grey sweatshirt. Prison-issue clothing. Frayed at the end and too short as the sleeves rode up his arms. She could make out his hairs resting on the flash of skin the sleeves exposed.

'I'm not alone. Jess is always there.'

He raised his eyes to look at her again, his chin still dipped down.

'Jess.' He exhaled her name.

The familiar warm smile appeared on his lips. It was infectious.

'She's been amazing. I don't know what I'd have done without her when they first took me into custody.'

Steph nodded. Her little sister was amazing. She'd surprised her, how she was able to take control of so many things. It was the first time that she'd really seen her, recognised that she wasn't simply her little sister who needed her. The tables had switched. Jess was the one who was taking charge, and the role suited her.

'I'm so sorry Steph. I'm sorry you've had to go through all of this. I just keep thinking how I could have done something, been quicker off the mark recognising the signs.'

'The signs?'

'That you were depressed, that you were—'

'Losing my marbles?' The corners of her mouth lifted a little. 'I don't think you could have done anything different. It's not like I told you about seeing Mum. She was all wrapped up in the delusion. My reality was to keep the imaginary affair from you. I did everything I could to convince you to believe that Jason was still stalking me. I was genuinely terrified.'

She tucked her quivering fingers underneath her thighs. It steadied her a little, like an anchor securing her to the shifting sands. His face looked grave. A permanent scowl etched on his forehead, more wrinkles and evidence of stress. She blinked back the tears and wriggled her fingers free to rest her hands on the table top.

'It all made sense to me at the time – I thought he'd confessed to the affair and that you believed him. After you'd visited him you seemed so cold and distant. It confirmed my fears, you didn't believe me, so I ran.'

Blood rushed from her face, she gripped the seat of the chair as she felt she would faint. Closing her eyes she inhaled deeply. The room settled, the dizziness subsided. She put her hand to her brow and stroked her left eyelid; wrinkles appeared in her forehead.

'You don't have to tell me again, Jess explained everything. The diaries explained everything. You don't have to put yourself through it again.' He shifted his weight in the chair and tilted his head to the right.

'I should have looked after you more after the birth.' His brow furrowed and he looked down at the floor again. 'Like I looked after you before.'

'But you picked up the pieces *after* I attempted suicide. You didn't see me before, you didn't know the signs and—'

'No, that's not the point, I should have realised that you were vulnerable. You deserved better.'

She felt the tears attempt to form, she looked to the ceiling and the neon strip light flickered hypnotically.

'No. You deserve better,' she whispered.

He squeezed her hand again.

'I … I did kiss him though.' Steph wanted to look away from him, but she knew how important it was to maintain eye contact.

'When he came to give me the flowers – he was there then, that was real not like when I imagined him shouting through the letterbox. And what he said, what I thought he had written on the card, all of that was a hallucination. But the kiss. I wish I hadn't pounced on him. He recoiled and pushed me away. The kiss was real, but the affair, the rest of it, all my deranged mind.'

I remember his tongue exploring my mouth and then he pushed me away and left. Like he'd thought better of it. Something he'd wanted to do all that time and when he did, he knew how wrong it was.

Adam now had no colour left in his cheeks. His eyes glazed over. She wasn't sure why she needed to tell him this, but she felt she had to. She wanted to take the blame. *It is my fault. I caused this.* After all, it was the kiss that drove him to hit Jason. Jess told her what Jason had said to Adam about how she tasted. That was the trigger for the red mist.

He put his head in his hands and it felt like hours had passed before he sat up straight again.

'No. You aren't taking the blame for my actions. And look, he shouldn't have started harassing you in the first place. If anything like the stalking or emailing, or anything ever happens to you again, don't hide it from me.' He leaned back in the chair and sighed.

'They read out some of the emails in court. They were hideous, you shouldn't have kept them a secret.'

For the first time in months a crawling sensation spread across her arms – paresthesia – she knew the medical word for it now. *Breathe.* She doubled-checked her arms. The creeping feeling wasn't accompanied by a hallucination. She folded her arms across her chest as though she was hugging herself.

'I know,' her voice fell to a low whisper, 'I felt sorry for him. I know this is all my fault.'

Adam clenched his fists and sat bolt upright.

'No. Don't ever say that. Me being in here, it's not your fault. I lost it. A moment of madness, the red mist descending, but ultimately I hit him. My fist. My loss of control. You can't be blamed for that.'

As he looked up at the ceiling his cheeks filled with air. He noisily exhaled. Steph longed to touch his face, stroke his cheekbones, kiss his lips and do all the things that were now forbidden. Every fibre of being ached for him.

He sunk further into the chair and looked back down at the floor. His voice became small.

'I thought you wouldn't come and visit. I thought after what I'd done, you'd stop loving me.' He wiped his nose on the back of his hand. 'I mean,' he caught her gaze now, but his voice remained small, 'I killed someone. And at the time, in that moment, when I hit him and saw the blood, I was glad, and then afterwards I was a fucking coward.'

Steph longed to reach over, pass him a tissue and hold him and do all the normal things that she had taken for granted. And tell him it was all going to be fine. But she wasn't convinced. She'd barely managed to put herself back together, never mind rebuild and create any semblance of their former lives or selves. *Everything feels hopeless.*

'Never. I'll never stop loving you. You must know that?'

She searched his face. He looked uncertain and ashamed.

'You will get out of here and we'll start again. Somewhere fresh. Away from everything, all of this.' She felt fierce, she wanted to protect him, take him out of here and get away now.

He nodded, but she recognised the look, the one that told her that he wasn't convinced.

She wanted to change the subject.

'Are they treating you OK? Is it scary? I can't imagine what it's like in there.'

'It's fine. Not as bad as I imagined.'

His words fell out of his mouth too quickly. Steph recognised his irritation.

He sat up straight in his chair. 'I don't want to talk about being in here, ever. I only want to hear about you and Natalie. I'm going to ask if you can bring her next time, I'd love to see her. The photos you've been sending are keeping me going.'

He looked down at the floor again and Steph watched as he linked his fingers together and dug them into the backs of his hands. She noticed that his wedding ring was missing.

'The thought of you and her, that's what's keeping me going. I need to know what she's doing. I'm going to miss out on all of the milestones.'

He leaned forward and Steph mirrored him.

'I love you. Let's not talk about the past next time, only talk of today and tomorrow. When I'm with you, I don't want to look behind me, or think of what I've done.'

'I think I can do that. I love you, too. I always will.'

They continued to look into each other's eyes as though they were seeing each other for the first time. A solitary tear escaped and trickled down her cheek.

A buzzer sounded. Adam glanced around the room. Everyone was rapidly talking.

'That's it. Where did the time go? You're booked in to visit again, right?'

'Yes. Of course I am.'

Adam stood up and Steph waved, he nodded in acknowledgement and mouthed to her again that he loved her. He shuffled out of the room with the other prisoners. The hall fell silent.

It took all her energy to haul herself out of the chair and follow the officer out of the room. When the door clicked behind her she let her tears flow freely.

Her feet trudged along the pavement away from the prison. A racing-green Mini came into view and pulled into a perfect space a few cars away. Steph raised her hand in acknowledgement and despite the drizzle her feet refused to jog to the car. She slipped into the back seat and sat next to a wide-awake Natalie. Her smile illuminated her baby's face but Steph couldn't return it despite it melting away the emptiness. Jess passed her a box of tissues.

'How was he?'

'He was, sort of better than I expected and, well, exactly as I expected. It was so hard. There's so much I want to say and I tried to talk more about everything that happened but … well it's not easy. None of it is easy.'

She loudly blew her nose. 'He looks like he's aged, but then there's the newly developed muscle tone.' Steph felt her cheeks heat as a blush raced across them.

'I didn't notice that.' Jess smirked.

'Yes, well, he's still my husband and I do miss him. All I wanted to do was to hold him.'

She stroked Natalie's hand and in response her fingers curled around Steph's index finger.

Jess looked over her shoulder, carefully reversing out of the space.

'How did you feel seeing him?'

'I felt like there was so much that I needed to say but couldn't, and I wanted to explain everything to him, everything that I can explain, everything that was imagined, everything that was real. I told him about the kiss. I felt like I had to Jess. You said that's what triggered his anger, but I don't know, I don't know what I should say to him. Sorry, I'm rambling, my thoughts don't seem to come out right these days.'

Jess nodded, she concentrated on the junction ahead as she drove away from Chelmsford Prison.

'It's OK, it's understandable to be overcome by it all. Just take each visit one at a time.' Jess swallowed and waited for Steph to stop sobbing. 'When I've visited him he's been low, but seeing you must have given him a boost?'

'I think so. He said me and Natalie are the only things that are keeping him going. He won't tell me what it's like in there.'

Jess bit her lip and kept her eyes on the road.

'No, he wouldn't tell me either.'

* * *

Back home Steph found comfort in the ordinariness and domesticity of caring for Natalie. At home she could focus on one task at a time. Teaching her brain not to jump from one thing to the next. To take her time and use the dull domestic chores as time for mindfulness. Well, her own brand of mindfulness. It worked. It soothed her and kept her focused. Her alarm sounded on her phone and she dutifully took her medication.

Natalie was napping, she could hear Jess's fingers attacking a keyboard in the dining room – the sound stopped abruptly – but the tapping began again. Her glass of water created a perfect circle on the worktop. She resumed her chores and the heat from the tumble drier gently warmed her fingers as she pulled the endless supply of babygros, dresses and tiny trousers into the laundry basket.

The striking of the keyboard ceased and Jess's footsteps moved towards the kitchen. She knew that her sister would be checking that she'd taken her medication. *Bound to the pills for now, or for ever, who knows?*

She put the last of Natalie's clothes in the basket and lifted it onto the table. Steph picked up the glass of water and finished it. It was a gesture to suggest that she'd been a good girl and taken her pills. Jess acknowledged it with a smile and then flicked the switch on the kettle. A silent dance.

'How's work going? I'm not sure I could ever set up a business with Adam.'

'And you thought I was hanging out here to keep an eye on you?' Jess pursed her lips and arched an eyebrow. 'It's all good. Well great, actually. We won another new client this morning. I keep thinking something is going to go wrong. We can't have all the luck come our way at once, can we? I still can't believe he actually agreed to my plan to set up a digital marketing agency. Who knew I'd manage to throw caution to the wind or even write and execute a business plan? I'm enjoying being my own boss. And Matt's boss.'

'Yes. I can't believe it either, but I reckon it suits you both brilliantly.'

She felt a sadness creep over her, another loss. Loss of her husband, loss of her mind and a loss of her sense of self. She couldn't see herself ever being able to work again.

The woman who got her colleague killed. The woman who had a baby and went mad. The woman who can only retain information for a nanosecond. It's unlikely I'll be able to string a sentence together or manage to explain how Brexit may or may not affect consumer rights. Ridiculous. Unhelpful labels. Unhelpful critical voice.

'Steph, I said would you like a peppermint tea?'

Steph blinked and picked up a vest out of the basket. The soft fabric still retained the heat from the drier. She rubbed it between her fingers and a watery smile spread across her lips.

'Sorry I zoned out there.'

'What were you thinking?'

Now everyone seems to want to get into my head. Jess should come with me to my therapy sessions.

'I was thinking about never being able to work again.'

'Of course you'll work again, but right now, your job is to look after Natalie and yourself. You're doing really well.'

'Am I?'

'Yes. No hallucinations, no voices, right?'

'Right.' Steph wound a curl around her finger and then flicked it away.

'And Natalie is doing brilliantly, isn't she?'

'I guess.'

'She's a happy, beautiful baby, content, healthy. It's a hard job and you should be proud of yourself.' Jess placed the tea on the table and slid into a chair.

Steph nodded and suppressed the urge to cry.

'I miss the warm days,' she murmured.

Jess meant well; she wanted to fix her, put her back together as she was before. The little sister who could look after her big sister. *If only it was that easy.*

She stopped folding the laundry and sat down; she tentatively sipped the tea and turned to look at the familiar view of the garden. A handful of leaves clung to the trees, but the glorious colours of autumn were fading fast. The barren gloom was beginning to take hold.

'Yes, I've loved taking breaks and walking in the forest here. Which reminds me, did Adam talk about when he was arrested? He had a funny episode. I don't mean funny ha ha either.'

Steph shook her head. There was so much she wanted to know. She'd got all the info from Jess about his court appearance, but she wanted to know what it felt like for Adam to hear the sentencing, to know that he was going to be locked up. At least it was swift. No drawn-out trial due to pleading guilty. *Guilty. Who is really guilty? My warped mind.*

'The police came to check on him. The officer saw his car leaving the house and he followed him. He said he was going to mine as I hadn't told him I'd gone to find you. He took a wrong turn and found himself near the forest, at the entrance to Baldwins Hill pond.'

Steph closed her eyes at the mention of Baldwins Hill pond.

'He went to the pond?' She felt her brow crease.

'It was foggy, he walked towards the trees but the police officer called him back. Didn't we go there when you and Adam first started seeing each other? I think we came down together and you stayed with him and his parents in Ongar? I stayed with – oh arse, what's her name? Oh, yes, Lilly who was on my course. Fuck knows what happened to her.'

Steph felt a prickle of heat erupt on her cheeks. 'Yes, we had a picnic there and then a drink or two in the pub, what's it called? Ah, the Forrester Arms. Nice place.' A smile spread across her face and she couldn't help giggling.

'What are you sniggering at?'

'Me and Adam, we had sex near the pond. Up against a tree. Probably the most thrilling thing we've done together. It's not exactly private if you recall.'

'Get you going all al fresco.'

It had been a long time since their laughter had rang out together. Steph enjoyed the sound and the feeling of closeness to her sibling.

She began folding the clothes again, but paused to hold a babygro close to her chest.

'Baldwins Hill pond? Funny place for him to end up though.'

She put the babygro down and began smoothing down a pretty little red dress, one of the many presents from Jess. Cute little white floral print. She blinked and refocused her thoughts.

'You know there's a folktale about a pond in the forest. No one knows which pond it is, but there's one they call the "suicide pool". A father murdered his daughter, possibly by accident, possibly in a fit of rage because she refused to leave her lover who he disapproved of. The lover witnessed the murder and he drowned himself. Subsequently a couple of women were drawn to the pool and committed suicide, too... I remember writing a freelance piece about the "folk Olympics", another tenuous link to the actual Olympics, and there was a poet who had written a song about the pond. '

'You've written some weird stuff,' Jess said.

'Ha, and you're not just referring to my journalism are you?'

They both smirked and simultaneously took a sip from their respective drinks. Jess pushed her cup to the side and tilted her head to the left.

'That's your pretend therapist face.' Steph let a wry smile play across her lips.

'God I'm so obvious, aren't I?'

Steph nodded and picked up another baby item and folded it neatly, pressing it down on top of the rest of the pretty little outfits forming a small pile on the table top.

'You can tell me to back off if you don't want to talk about your hallucinations, but Adam said it was all a bit odd in the forest. He didn't know why, but he felt compelled to go the pond. He said he saw a flash of blue run into the trees. Now he thinks it was the police lights and a trick of the light in the fog. But at the time he said he was about to follow it into the night.' Jess paused for a moment.

Steph raised her eyebrows.

'When you saw Mum, what was she wearing? I know they were hallucinations, but… I saw her too. She was sat on your bed in the hospital.'

'Perhaps you need to take some of my pills?' Steph paused midfold of the last item, a cute pair of jeans with red flowers embroidered on the back pockets.

She sighed and the image of her mum sat at the kitchen table began to form.

'When I saw her she always had that blue coat on, the brilliant peacock blue coat. I always picture her in blue, she wore that colour a lot. I think it's natural for your subconscious to use that memory of her.'

She could almost hear the conversation they'd had. Her confessing the affair. Mum telling her what to do. *As always telling me what to do, at least my hallucination was consistent with my memory of her. The advice giver, the one in control.*

Steph blinked away the image.

'She was there, sat on your bed in the unit and she turned to see me in the doorway', Jess added. 'I closed my eyes and she vanished and then she touched my shoulder. I'm sure of it. I've been wanting to talk to you about this, but was worried it would upset you. I probably need meds, too…'

Steph's lips began to tremble.

'I think you need therapy, not pills. Have you seen her again since?'

'No nothing. Which is a fucking relief.'

'Well, you were very stressed at the time and I think you could do with some help with the way you dealt with her illness and death. It was your overactive imagination. You didn't see a ghost and you weren't hallucinating. I promise. You're not a few sandwiches short of a buffet.'

Jess folded her arms. Her cheeks filled before she puffed the air out of them.

'I'm sorry if it upsets you Jess, but you shut her out of your life for such a long time. Don't let resentment eat away at you.'

A noise at the window drew the sisters' attention away from each other. A blue tit had landed on the window ledge and was tentatively hopping and bobbing and pecking for bugs.

She wished her sister would open up, she used to confide all her teenage woes, then her job worries, spats with friends, and arguments with Matt, but when it came to Mum she was a closed book. She'd always kept quiet even when she was small.

'I'd prefer it if I was the only crazy one in this family. Talk to someone. It's time, and honestly, it's not that bad.'

She wanted to free her sister from the pain she'd carried for years. She had an inkling what it could be, but she never wanted to push her, silence had always been her default mechanism.

'Why are you always right?' Jess unfolded her arms and ran her fingers through her hair.

'I'm not always right.'

'You are when it comes to me.'

'See, I'm not completely broken, I am still your bossy big sister.' Steph smiled at Jess but it was not returned. There was a glimmer of anger in her little sister's eyes. The same look she'd seen as a child when they'd have a fight, or she couldn't get her own way.

Steph enfolded Jess in a hug; she would have held her longer but Natalie's cry heralded the end of nap time.

Jess

Jess no longer stayed the night at Steph's. It had been agreed that it wasn't necessary. Those first few weeks when she had returned from the unit seemed a distant haze. Being hyper-alert to everything. Worrying whether she'd stick to the treatment plan, making sure she'd take her medication: the little pills that chased away the physical manifestations of her demons.

Working at Steph's gave her a break from being in the flat with Matt. Its limited space made her feel claustrophobic. She didn't want to admit to Matt that working at home with him was distracting and oppressive. Maybe once they'd become more established they could find an office somewhere. Shoreditch possibly – actually, probably too expensive – or one of those shared, rent-a-desk type places. Somewhere more business-like. But for now, working at Steph's and returning home fixed the problem.

She gripped the steering wheel. Mum was an ever-growing presence. Before all this she'd been packed away into the depths of memory. All her thoughts had revolved around Matt's absence and the arrival of her niece. But Sheffield, her old house, and Steph's diaries opened her personal Pandora's Box. Agonising memories continued to plague her. Like a playlist that looped and relentlessly selected full technicolour films from her past.

She wondered whether she too should start journaling, get the thoughts out, stop the playlist. A wry smile took hold of her mouth. She tugged the stiff handbrake upwards as she miraculously found a space near their flat.

She was getting used to returning to a home full of noise. Matt always had music on, it helped him work, and sometimes he'd be chatting away on the phone to a client, but tonight the sound of oil crackling in a pan could be heard filtering through the music's bass. *Always drum and bass. Bet the neighbours are fed up of the tinny snare.*

His sandy hair fell forward as he looked down into the pan. He was in full flow: bobbing his head to the chords of the synth that kicked in as the track mellowed, less bass, more snappy-snare, beating time with the wooden spoon he was pushing around the pan. She closed the door and the click of the lock alerted him to her entrance.

'Hello gorgeous! I'm still basking in the glory of winning that account! Thought I'd cook us something I learnt to make in Thailand – don't think I've made this one before? And then we could head out, maybe O'Neills?' His voice shouted over the track in competition with a high pitched chipmunk-like voice. Jess reached for the little remote to turn the volume down. *If only we could turn down our emotions at a flick of switch, too.*

She put her keys down on the kitchen counter and moved towards him to give him a kiss. Spring onion, garlic, chilli and ginger thrust themselves up her nostrils. He enfolded her in his arms and moved his hips to the music.

'O'Neills? I'm not in the mood for Indie cheese tonight. Food smells amazeballs. Will it be as delicious as that ginger thing you made the other week? That was gorgeous and pretty much knocked that cold I had on the head.'

'But you love Indie cheese. Come on. It's been ages since we went out.'

She stepped aside and he shook the wok, flipping the contents and wafting the smell around the kitchen.

Hanging her laptop bag up in the cupboard, she opened the fridge to check for wine. One bottle of her favourite white wine, a Sauvignon Blanc, and Peroni for Matt. She smiled; the fridge had been empty this morning. She opened the beer and passed it to him.

'Cheers darling, go and put your feet up.'

Swirling the wine around her glass she told herself to drink slowly. Steph's words had lodged themselves into the forefront of her mind.

Get therapy. Tackle the rage.

Since his return she'd made a promise to Matt that she would get help, and she'd agreed to tell him about her past, but the timing never seemed right. She'd been so focused on Adam and Steph, sorting them both out had been her main priority, and then there was setting up the business together and looking after Steph and Natalie once they'd returned home. Matt had been patient with her so far, but she knew she wasn't fulfilling her side of the deal. She took a sip of wine, the lemony tones refreshed her senses. *Tell him tonight.*

Matt emerged with some kind of prawn noodle dish. During his stay in Thailand he'd worked in a restaurant, or noodle hut as he called it, and had learned to cook. It amazed Jess that before his trip abroad he'd never made anything other than pasta, fish fingers and chips, and beans on toast. Now he would often be throwing a meal together for them. He'd taken over the kitchen. It was a welcome relief from boring salads or the odd piece of pan-fried salmon she'd managed to rustle up for herself. Cooking for one had emphasised his absence.

'This looks amazing, as always. Thank you.'

'No problem. How's Steph today?'

'She was fine, saw Adam, that went well and—'

'Oh shit, yes, I'd forgotten she had her first visit.'

'Yes, it was fine, she found it hard not being able to hold him or kiss him, but apart from that...' She scooped up some of the noodles. Chilli hit her palate. She enjoyed the heat. 'She seemed to handle it well under the circumstances – I mean, the last time she saw him was on the morning she ran off. That seems like a lifetime ago.'

Jess began to push her food around her plate; she couldn't help but think about the discussion they'd had about Mum. The hallucinations. Her hallucination. She sighed and shifted her eyes to meet Matt's.

'What is it?'

'Ah, nothing, just stuff me and Steph talked about.'

She put a few noodles into her mouth. Fresh coriander and a hint of something she wasn't sure of. This was the only good thing about his absence. His newfound cooking ability.

'God this is good.'

'I know. Noodle master I am now.' He attempted a Yoda-like laugh and did some sort of kung fu move with his hands, which made Jess giggle.

'So, I'm guessing you talked about your mum today?'

Jess reached for her wine glass and drained the last quarter. She folded her arms.

'You always do that' he said. 'I mention your mum, you fold your arms. You're telling me not to ask about it, not talk about her, but I think we have to. It nearly broke us. You barely spoke to me when she was dying, and the anger you carry around with you ... it's not healthy.'

Jess got up abruptly. Clutching her wine glass she walked through to the kitchen, refilled it and brought Matt another beer. Placing it in front of him she sunk down in her chair. The moulded plastic seat was anything but comfortable. She literally was perched on the edge of her seat. It contributed to the wave of anxiety that gripped her body, causing her to take another slug of wine before continuing.

'You're the second person to tell me that today. I've kept this to myself for a long time. None of it's easy for me to talk about.' *And from you, there's a secret I will always keep buried.*

She circled her finger around the stand of the glass and inhaled deeply. The deep breath gave her a temporary release from the fear. *You can have my childhood memories. You can't ever know what I did.*

'When we were kids we used to spend a lot of time at my aunt's house. We'd play with our cousins and normally Mum and her sister would chat, or clean together, the kind of thing I do with Steph now. They seemed close.'

She took another sip of wine, just a sip this time, she needed a clear head for the moment.

'One time we went over and my aunt was out. She'd taken my cousin, Jacob, to a hospital appointment. Steph and Martha were hiding, my turn to seek. Their house was much bigger than ours, a sprawling Victorian property. It had a cellar and an attic, it was brilliant to play hide and seek in and the garden was huge too. I envied them. Their house made our home seem even smaller.'

She took another sip of wine and swirled it around in her glass before continuing.

'I'd looked everywhere for them. The one room we never hid in was my aunt and uncle's bedroom. The door was closed.

I thought they'd broken the rule and shut themselves in there as I could hear noises, so I silently pushed down on the handle and opened the door.'

She traced her finger around the rim of her wine glass and it began to sing a note; she liked the sound and let her finger create the noise for a little longer.

'It wasn't my sister, or my cousin in there. I saw Mum. Her bare back faced me. My uncle was too busy enjoying himself to notice me in the doorway. I closed the door and ran from the house. I found Steph and my cousin in the garden shed.'

Jess drained her wine, she needed it now; fuck being in control, that didn't matter, nothing had really mattered since that moment.

'I didn't really understand what I saw. I was five. But I knew it was wrong. When it was bedtime I couldn't stop thinking about it. Dad read me a story and every time I closed my eyes I could see Mum rocking backwards and forwards and the odd look on my uncle's face, so I told Dad. I told him what I saw. I needed him to take the image away from me. He told me I'd done the right thing telling him about it and that no matter what happened he'd always love me.'

Matt reached for her hand and squeezed it.

'Fuck Jess, I'm so sorry you had to see that.'

She moved her hand away from his.

'Dad left that night. I knew it was my fault, I shouldn't have told him. I've carried this around with me. The image burns my eyes. Why does your memory do that to you? Why can't I remember other things in such illuminating detail?' She searched his face for an answer but Matt's lips remained closed.

'I didn't trust grown-ups from then on and I certainly didn't trust Mum.'

Jess rose from her seat. In a few strides she'd reached the kitchen. She returned with the wine bottle and refilled her glass.

'He said he'd love me no matter what. First lie. He disappeared. That was the last time someone other than Steph told me that they loved me.' She paused, looked away from Matt and rested her chin on the heel of her hand. 'At least I had Steph. She enjoyed playing the role of the big sister who could sort out her moody little sister, cheer me up, and make me feel better.' She got up and walked to the window to stare out at the road. Cars still whizzed past and voices of those out for the evening rang out above the traffic.

'Mum laid the blame at my tiny five-year-old feet. For a while I believed her when she said I was ill, too weak to eat properly. She'd feed me, but I'd get a tiny portion and never any dessert. We'd get back from school and she'd give Steph sweets and tell me I didn't deserve any because I'd wet the bed. Which I did frequently. And she'd leave the sheets, so sometimes they would be still damp, other times stiff and the smell. Ugh.'

Matt remained statue-like, his beer untouched. Jess swirled the pale yellow liquid around the glass, the alcohol clung to the sides before seeping slowly down the glass. Jess returned to sit at the table opposite him.

'I wasn't allowed to go and play at friend's houses, Steph was. I couldn't go to dance class, but Steph could. I was never bought new clothes, always Steph's hand-me-downs, regardless of fit or whether they were full of holes. If I was rude or said anything out of line I'd be shut in the cupboard under the stairs. When I got too big for the cupboard, she put a lock on my bedroom from the outside. She never hit me or anything physical, anything that could be seen or detected; instead she piled on the emotional exclusion and neglect.'

'Did you tell anyone?'

'I tried, a couple of times, but no one believed me. To everyone else who met her there was nothing out of the ordinary. She helped out loads at school and was popular with the teachers and other parents.'

'And Steph, didn't she see what was going on?'

'The more I was hurt, the worse my behaviour got. I started to get into trouble at school so it just confirmed what Mum told her: I was naughty, bad, and a liar. Plus she pretended I was ill and that's why I didn't get to go places or do anything like Steph. Fuck, she did so many awful things ... I can't tell you all of it in one go.' Jess drank a slug of wine, she'd need a whole bottle to help her detail the litany of hurts.

'And your dad? He just left you all?'

'Yes. Mum always went on about how he was no good, never paid any child support and how everything was down to her. He was the bad guy. She was the good guy. And as there were quite a few kids in my class who didn't have any contact with their dads I began to believe this story. Yes he left because of what I said, because of what Mum did, but why did he have to leave us? *His* daughters.'

Jess paused to give her self some space before she delivered the truth that shook her world.

'So, I got out of home as quick as I could and kept my distance. And then she got ill. A tiny part of me hoped she'd acknowledge what she did to me, not that she could ever make amends, but I wanted her to at least admit her cruelty.' Her hands began to shake as she lifted the glass to her lips.

'She told me she wanted to die to be with him, to be with my uncle. And she saved the best bit of her story for the end. Her last goodbye, her parting shot. Have you guessed yet?'

Matt stared blankly at her, the corners of his mouth sagged a little and his deep brown eyes widened.

'Why did Dad not bother to stay in contact? Because he was firing blanks. Him and Mum had tried for years to have kids. After a couple of "encounters" with my "uncle", Steph was conceived. They continued their affair and along came me.'

Matt stared at her open-mouthed.

'So, Mum dies, I grieve for a mother I never had and for the dad who died years before. The dad I never really knew. So that's why I'm often a huge ball of rage.'

She half smiled, but it faded quickly. She downed the rest of her wine and stared blankly into Matt's face.

'Jess I'm stunned. I don't know what to say.' He rubbed his temple and sighed.

'You just thought it was some mother-daughter thing didn't you? Steph thinks that. When I was little, I thought about telling her that I wasn't really ill and that Mum did things to me, but every time I remembered the look on Dad's face. Secrets make people disappear and as much as I hated Mum, she was still my mum. I didn't want her to disappear. As a teen I channelled my anger into rebellion and all my energy went into getting out. Steph thought I never got over my adolescent angst and that me and Mum were too alike to get on. Too alike. Poles from one end of the globe to the other.' Her staccato speech fired around the room.

Matt knelt on his knees in front of her. He placed his hands on her lap and as he opened his mouth to speak, Jess shook her head. She lowered herself to the floor and their bodies shook as they sobbed.

Once their cries ceased, Matt stroked her hair and smoothed away a few strands from her forehead, before cupping her face and kissing her, tenderly, as though he could take her pain away from her with his touch.

'I'll never hurt you. I'll make sure no one hurts you like that again. Ever.'

'I know. I'm sorry, I'm sorry I accused you of having a fling. Once she came back into my life all the things she said to me kept flooding back. I still believed I didn't deserve to be loved so I pushed you away. I'm sorry.'

They sat on the floor holding each other for some time.

The last image of her mum appeared as she buried her head into his chest. Diminutive, sunken grey cheeks. Her face had aged rapidly. Skin sagged around her neck as though she was melting into the bed beneath her. And then the shaking began, at first a few twitches, then a violent shaking that gripped her entire body. Jess sat bolt upright. The movement was enough to stop the memory playing out in full horror.

Steph

The therapist's room always looked the same. Bright, airy, fresh yellow chrysanthemums in a small vase sat on a low table under the window. Another low table straight out of Ikea sat in the middle of the room. It can't be called a coffee table figured Steph, she was never offered coffee. There was always a jug of water and a glass, and the obligatory box of tissues.

The message here was simple. Drink lots of water because you will cry. However, there was something different in the room today. Her usual therapist had left and been replaced. Steph found herself bouncing Natalie on her knee, not because Natalie needed the distraction, but because she did. She felt a little nervous, she'd have to begin this therapist-patient relationship again.

The therapist began by introducing herself, apologising for the loss of her colleague and then deftly recapped Steph's treatment; her eyes glazed over. The details weren't important, she knew them well. Nodding and smiling in the right places gave the impression that the therapist had her full attention, but she was waiting. *Skip to the real meat of the session.*

'So, how are you doing at the moment?'

'I'm tired. I mean, I'm sleeping fine, but it takes me so long to do everything. Everything is exhausting. Sometimes I miss the manic phase of the illness. Clean the house, look after Natalie, and write the diary – all at top speed. If only I could harness that energy now.' Steph manged a smile. Most of the time when she thought about that phase of the illness – the manic phase of her psychosis – she was afraid of herself, afraid to remember that time, but now and again she could allow herself to look back on the experience with kinder eyes. *I was ill. My mind was ill. And I am beating this illness. I will beat it.*

'Are you still journaling?'

'Yes.' The question threw her a little, she kept her answer clipped.

'When did you start?'

Fuck. No one has asked this question yet. And do I want to share this with Little Miss Bob straight out of university?

She looked at Natalie. She'd made a promise to her when she first held her, before the hallucinations and delusions, the first moments they'd spent together, which were pure, untainted by her mind's breakdown.

I will never betray you.

Steph felt her jaw gape. She stared at her therapist.

'Oh my god. I've realised where it all began. I don't mean the journaling, I mean my thoughts, my delusions, where they sprang from.'

The therapist tilted her head slightly, a silent gesture to indicate to continue.

'When I was fourteen I overheard something I wasn't supposed to.'

Steph felt the room shift. Her mind transported in time and back to her childhood home.

She was supposed to be asleep, but she was gripped by yet another Agatha Christie novel which she couldn't put down. She heard the familiar shrill ring of the doorbell and she tentatively placed the book down on the bedside cabinet and swung her feet out from under the covers onto the floor.

Her toes wriggled into the carpet as she tiptoed towards her bedroom door. She paused at the door. Two voices. Shrill. Mum and... Aunty Betts? Yes.

She pushed the door open a fraction. And then a little more so she could slide her slim frame through the gap. She was glad that Jess wasn't home. She wouldn't waste any time in rushing downstairs to see what was going on.

Steph crept forward and sat motionless at the top of the stairs, holding the wooden balustrade, which offered her a slight obscurity if either her aunt or mum were to glance up the staircase into the darkness. She could see her mum standing next to the door with her back against the wall. Aunty Betts was screaming in her face.

She was a fraction taller than Mum. Her voice dropped low as she jabbed her fingers into Mum's chest.

Tears trickled down her neck, the droplet of water startled her; she hadn't realised that she was crying. The sensation brought her back to the present. She wiped away her tears and took another sip of water. The therapist tilted her head a little. A non-verbal cue to encourage Steph.

'My aunt and my mum had a huge argument. She told Mum that she knew everything and that finally she'd managed to get him to tell her the truth, to tell her what had been eating away at my uncle for years.' She paused, her aunt's strong Yorkshire accent rang in her ears again, her usually soft clipped voice screeched through the hallway. Steph felt her whole body tense.

'My uncle became an alcoholic. He must have started drinking to blot it out.'

Steph paused and reached for the glass of water.

'My aunt told Mum that she knew about the affair and that my uncle was the father of her nieces – that my uncle was in fact my dad.' The therapist wasn't writing anything down. She listened intently.

'Things became a little muffled then. I was sat at the top of the stairs. I remember I felt like I couldn't breathe, or shouldn't in case someone heard me. My aunt started shouting again, but I couldn't make out what she said as her words blurred into each other. She stormed towards the door. I remember trying to make myself small. I was terrified that they'd see me, but I couldn't move now and I didn't want to.'

She closed her eyes for a moment. Her aunt was stood in the open door, her whole body shaking with rage.

'She told Mum she could never have him. He was hers and she'd make sure their dirty little secret remained buried.'

She could see her mum move towards Betts. She put her arm out but Betts pushed her away. Mum stumbled to the floor and was crying in a heap.

'It's OK. Take your time.' The therapist's silky tones interrupted the memory.

Steph looked down at Natalie and was so pleased that her daughter would have no memory of the first month of her life.

'My aunt shouted that she was going to take her husband for a little drive now.'

Steph remembered hearing her mum sobbing for over an hour, sitting in the doorway, glued to the spot. Staring out into the street, into the blackness. Steph reached for a tissue and blew her nose.

'The next day the police came. My aunt and uncle had been involved in a car crash. They said the car had hit a tree at high speed. They were pronounced dead at the scene.'

My mother's affair. My paternity. I've woven all these details into the diary, as though my ill mind had dug up the past and sprinkled it over the pages. Woven together with the real events of Jason's stalking to create a new story, a web of lies.

The therapist's pen began to scribble across her clinical notes. Steph refilled her glass. Her hand was trembling and water splashed onto the white table top. She was cradling Natalie who had gradually drifted off to sleep. She was now adept at carrying out small tasks with one hand.

She concentrated on Natalie's peaceful face and tuned into her soft breathing, which was slightly disturbed by the movement of her body as she finished pouring the water.

Nearly ten months old now, she mused. She was enjoying this phase. The smiles, the laughter, the simple rhythms of their unvocalised communications. The mother-daughter bond.

'So, that's why you began to journal?' Her therapist interrupted her musings.

'I was struggling at school to concentrate. I told one of my teachers what I heard. She suggested I wrote my thoughts down and how I felt about things, and I did, it became a habit.'

'I want you to break that habit. We are going to try a more focused approach to journaling, to diarise your moods and your triggers to help prevent a relapse.'

Steph stared at her. Her whole body began to shake.

'I need to give it up. I do. I've lived in my head too much and became a passive observer of what was happening to me. I found comfort, but I should have been getting real help. The rape, the stalking, the emails; it's like if I write about it, I can somehow distance myself from it like it's not happening to me.'

'Very insightful.'

They smiled together in recognition of the lightbulb moment, the leap forward. The therapist got up and walked over to the filing cabinet, the only piece of furniture in the room that suggested something clinical could be taking place.

She pulled out a thin burgundy book and placed it on the table next to Steph's glass of water.

'Your mood journal. Have a look and follow the instructions. We start off on paper and then we'll move online.'

She smiled again, a warm, yet business-like smile, signalling that the session was over. Steph slowly hauled herself out of the low faux-leather chair; Natalie was like a dead weight in her arms when a deep sleep engulfed her.

The therapist passed her the mood journal. Closing her fingers around it felt like she was holding onto something special. The burgundy cover reminded her of the soon-to-be phased-out British passport. This was her passport to a new self.

'Thank you for today. We've got a lot of ground to cover, you did really well making those connections and that's a step forward. I know how hard all that must have been. You'll probably feel very drained, so make extra time for mindfulness and the other self-care tools I know you've been using.'

'Yes, I will and thank you. It was good to meet you. See you same time next week.'

She closed the door softly and leaned against the dull white wall. She cradled Natalie and kissed her on the head.

'I will never do anything to hurt you or Daddy.' Natalie wriggled in her arms and her mouth twitched a little, as though she'd heard and understood.

The cold November air hit her as she made her way back to her car. It was the first time this autumn she'd noticed a chill. It seeped into her pores and made her feel wide awake, brushing away the sense that she wasn't talking about herself or being herself when she entered that room. Therapy sessions often left her feeling like this. Dislocated. An out-of-body experience.

Strapping Natalie into the car seat woke her up. Her eyes had a twinkle in the corner as she beamed up at Steph. She made some noises, sounds formed, vowel-like. The thought of her first word punched Steph in the gut. *Adam will miss all of this*. She stroked her cheek and Natalie smiled broadly.

'Here's Sophie giraffe.' She gave her the rubber teething toy before settling herself in the driver's seat and pulling away out of the car park.

Adam. How can we make up the time that we'll lose?

A tingling sensation rippled across her arms, like tiny feet marching towards her fingertips. She bit her lip and resisted shaking her hands. It would be the first thing she needed to write in her mood journal. *The thought of Adam gave rise to the physical symptom of formication.*

As she pulled up at the traffic lights next to Wood Street Library she glanced at the mood diary which sat next to her on the passenger seat. Jess would have gone home, the house would be quiet. She figured that once Natalie was asleep for the evening she'd seek out every journal she had. She'd have a bonfire, purge her words from the pages and free herself from a narrative that had made her become a passive observer to the events of her life.

* * *

Steph found every diary she had written. They would make quite a pyre. She refused to read any of them, except her last one. The one that was mainly fiction.

Her words seemed so alien. She stroked the ink. It was real but her memory couldn't recall writing them. Every word greatly removed from the reality of those early days with her daughter; a surreal nightmare.

Jason. Poor, poor, Jason.

She consumed the sections where she worried about Natalie's paternity. It echoed her own paternity.

Her uncle was not her uncle. The knowledge she sought to bury had resurfaced in her delusions, transferred to herself and her daughter. Untrue, but rooted in her real-life story.

She read on. The panic, the fear had all been so real, so immediate. And that's where her narrative had ended. Part of her had wished she'd taken the journal with her to Sheffield. Would she have recorded the new hallucinations? The one where her whole body was covered in spiders?

Even now she could still feel the thousands of legs creep over her torso and then swarm over her face. Covering her mouth, nose and eyes. Drowning in a sea of millions of spiders. She remembered that her attempts to brush them off her body had failed. They kept on coming. Crawling out from under the bed, like an uncontrollable oil slick. She shuddered at the thought of herself fleeing from her mother's bedroom and plunging herself into the shower.

How can your mind create such things that are so real? So alive and oh so utterly terrifying.

She closed her eyes and the wellies emerged again from the fireplace, but this time she pushed the frightful wizened face out of her mind. It was too much to remember again. Never again.

She placed the journal on top of the pile.

It slipped off and fell open.

She glanced at the handwriting. It slanted in the opposite direction to her own. She flicked back to her pages, several pages separated her entries from this one. Yes, the writing was different. Definitely not hers.

Dear Sister,

For years I have kept my memories locked inside. But everything you've been through tells me I need to get them out. I need to release my mind from the grip of rage, the anger that burns my insides like lava waiting to spring up from a volcano.

What I'm writing here isn't meant to hurt you. I have no idea what you know and what you don't. We've never talked about it. Always keeping our childhoods locked away.

You had a solid relationship with Mum. You shared your secrets with her. You always looked after her, not just towards the end of her illness, but when we were teenagers.

I knew it was you who organised the house. Made sure we both were fed and had clean clothes. That I went to school with a packed lunch or enough dinner money. You were looking after her, looking after me and no one looked out for you. It made you so independent, fearless, but vulnerable too?

I've spent huge swathes of my adulthood pushing down the pain and the memories, but they leak out don't they? Just like yours leaked into your delusion. Look what she's done to us Steph. A web of scar tissue that works its way over your skin. Constantly marking us, distorting our thoughts.

Over the past year I've not done a very good job of pushing down the pain. I've let things slip. I was good at keeping quiet, pushing it all away. But you were right. The bubbling rage needs to be released.

When I was five I saw Mum naked, riding our uncle. There I've said it. It's out there.

Aunty Betts was at a hospital appointment with Jacob. We were all playing hide and seek. Turns out so was our uncle.

I couldn't get them out of my head. I didn't understand it at the time, but once I found out about the birds and the bees, can you imagine what it did to me? How sick it made me. Literally. I vomited during our sex education class.

And I needed to get it out of my head. I had to tell Dad. He could help me.

Please forgive me.

I was five, I just needed him to tell me it was all going to be OK and I didn't need to worry about Mummy being naked and my uncle with the strange look on his face.

When Dad left I knew it was my fault.

My fault for telling him. And what should our mother have done? What would you say to Natalie? Would you explain to her that grown-ups sometimes make mistakes and it wasn't my fault that Daddy left us? Because, if it was me, that's what I'd say. I wouldn't transfer that blame like she did.

All the toys, the kisses, the cuddles, the time she spent with you.

Did you ever notice that I never received any of this?

Whenever you were out of the house she'd lock me away. Or when she just wanted to be with you I'd have to go to Mrs Locke's on the pretext that our neighbour needed some company. And not forgetting how often I was too ill to eat, too ill to play at friends' houses and too ill to go do anything fun. Bullshit. All of it.

And then there was the constant poison she'd spew in my ear. Nobody loved me. It was my fault. Daddy ran off because of my lies. My imagination. He wanted to get away from us because I made things up.

That I was worthless – that's why I couldn't play with other children, because they didn't want me, she said. Not because she wouldn't let me! Who would ever want to be friends with a little girl who told lies all the time.

Every day she told me that no one would ever love me. Ever. That I was useless. How I wouldn't achieve anything, or make anything of myself. Stupid Jess. Ugly Jess. Jess the liar. Jess the monster.

Was I jealous of you?

Yes, of course I was, but I accepted all she threw at me as my punishment for talking. And I swallowed her words, because what child wouldn't? Every word she said felt right; I believed I was a monster. And she told me never to tell anyone anything that happened in our house, because no one would believe me. And I knew what happened when I told the truth before: Dad left. I thought you'd leave me and I couldn't bear that.

She was a bitter, twisted mad cow. Your madness may have been temporary, but you accepted help. You're being treated. She didn't notice what she'd become. There's only room for one crazy woman in this family and my darling Stephanie that isn't you. It was her. It's always been her and thank fuck she's dead.

There. I've said it.

When she was dying I hoped that she'd finally acknowledge what she'd become, but no. Instead, after all these years it was time for the truth. She told me that her and Dad had been trying for a baby for years. A couple of shags with Uncle David and bang. Jackpot. You were conceived. Whenever they could, they continued their affair. And yes. Here I am. At least you are my full sister, my blood.

Dad. Poor pathetic unsuspecting Brian never had a clue, so she told me.

Everything spilled out of her evil mouth on her death bed. Finally, out of the mouth of a habitual liar sprung the truth. And here's my truth. I wasn't in the ladies when the fit took hold of her. I didn't just arrive in the room and press the buzzer for help.

I sat and watched her as the twitches became violent spasms and her whole body shook with tremors so fierce it looked like she was about to fly out of the bed. I closed the door to her private room. I watched as the fit subsided. I didn't press the call button. I didn't shout for help. I waited until her limbs grew still, until the monitor bleeped to tell me her heart had stopped. I watched her die.

You know the rest. Staff shortages, it's quiet there at night on the cancer ward. It took a while for someone to come when I eventually pressed the button and shouted for help. Too late. Gone. No more lies. No more pain. No more.

Nine months later

Steph

She read the pages over and over again.

How could she write this? How could she do this now? But the stress, holding all the abuse in for years and years. I don't blame her for finally letting go, for finally cracking under pressure. She needs to release herself from the bitterness before it controls her like it did Mum.

Steph traced her finger over the writing.

She sent her a text.

Bonfire tomorrow. Come alone. We've got fuel for a huge pyre. Xx

She flung the diary across the room and reached for her medication, swallowing the pills with a wash of cool water. Creeping into her bedroom she peered over the cot under the window. Trance-like, she stared at Natalie. Sleep enveloped her daughter's body. She lay on her back. One arm was hidden beneath her blankets and the other lay level with her ear as though she had been performing a wave as she drifted off to sleep.

'My angel. My darling. I will never let anyone hurt you. I will never hurt you.'

Slipping off her navy blue cigarette trousers she rummaged under the bedclothes for her pyjamas. She missed fishing out Adam's t-shirt and shorts. The bed was huge without him. She slid under the covers and closed her eyes but they refused to stay closed. Reaching for her headphones, she plugged them into her iPhone and selected her favourite relaxation track. Sleep would come. It had to come.

She didn't want to see her mum lifeless in her hospital bed. Small, shrunken and greying as the cancer sucked the life out of her. And the last thing she wanted to see was an image of her sister at her bedside watching her die.

She cranked up the volume and buried her face into her pillow.

* * *

Natalie's cries woke her. The clock showed 5.05 a.m. Steph brought her into her bed, stroking her hair, taking in everything; her features, her size. She'd forgotten so much of those first months and now she wanted to absorb every moment, keep it all in her memory and lock it close to her heart. These were the memories she wanted to form and never fade. These memories were welcome to leap forth whenever they chose.

They lay in the bed together. She longed for that feeling again when Natalie was at her breast. Feeding her was so amazing, but her illness took that away from her. Steph squinted at the picture of her and Adam and Natalie, by her mirror on the dressing table. She couldn't make it out in the dim light but she knew the photograph off by heart. Jess had taken it on her first visit to the hospital after Natalie was born. Steph was propped up in bed by several pillows. Adam had snuggled into her side and draped his arm around her shoulders while Natalie was feeding.

Adam was staring at the camera beaming the biggest grin Steph had ever seen. Although the image was tinged with melancholy, it was beautiful, perfect. One that she treasured, despite the grief it was soaked in.

She glanced at the clock, which displayed the date too. Saturday, officially bonfire night tomorrow, but tonight they'd have a huge fire.

'I love fireworks. There are loads of displays tonight honey-bun and, if you are up I'll show you. Aunty Jess is coming over and we'll have a little party, just the three of us. No, party isn't quite the right word Nat, but I'm not sure how to describe it. Said your mother who used to be a journalist.'

She raised her eyebrows at the thought of how inappropriate the word was and how useless her brain had become. *What would suffice to describe our burning of secrets?*

It was another early start to a day, but Steph didn't mind. It meant she had longer to spend with Natalie. Time was important. Adam didn't get this time. She was spending it on his behalf.

Stepping out of bed she scooped up Natalie and placed her in the bouncy chair so she could watch her get ready. She attached the bar across the chair, complete with toys that dangled in front of Natalie. She reached to play with the dancing teddies and set off one which played a twinkly lullaby.

Steph picked out an outfit for Natalie and slipped on her pre-pregnancy jeans. Levi's. She adored them and despite the medication she had managed to keep the weight off. She pulled out her favourite cashmere sweater, midnight blue, off the hanger and slipped it over her head. It was tight-fitting and it flattered her figure. She was beginning to feel a little bit more like her former self again, just a little, the clothes she used to wear to work were hidden in her wardrobe. *Maybe they should go on the fire, too?*

She shook her head. 'No. That's not a helpful thought is it?' she said to her reflection. 'Speaking like a typical mad person now. Talking to myself in the mirror.' She laughed at herself and when she turned around, Natalie was giggling, too.

She moved towards her and she continued to giggle to see if Natalie would laugh, too. She did. A proper baby chortle. The laughter kept on coming as Steph pulled faces, made silly noises and pinged the teddies and toy ducks backwards and forwards.

Natalie's laughter eventually subsided. Sitting in the bouncy chair she kicked her legs with vigour. Steph removed the bar again and hauled her out. She lay her on the bed and fought with the kicking legs to get her dressed. 'Getting big now! Look at you! Beautiful baby, beautiful girl.'

The words stuck in her throat as she realised that nine months would soon be ten and Adam had missed most of her first year, and was set to miss the next four.

'Daddy misses you soooo much.' She scooped her up into her arms and held her up high. 'You look so much like him. I hope they'll let him see you soon.' She lowered her down and placed her on her shoulder.

Opening the curtains revealed the November gloom. The day would stretch out ahead of them. The past would come back into focus, hopefully for the final time.

Drizzle moistened the window pane. A wet November day, not dissimilar to the murky February day when she fled her home. The day that set her little sister on a pathway to face her demons too. And like that day when she escaped her imaginary pursuer, time ran away from her and sped her to a destination she never thought she'd see again. The family home, where they grew up, where they were moulded. A home she'd told the solicitor to rent out. A home that she vowed never to go back to. If she could, she'd burn it down too. It represented too much heartbreak.

* * *

At dusk she assembled the bonfire. Book after book piled up. She created a tepee of branches, other garden debris and anything else flammable. Her breath rose and faded into the night air. There was the first nip of winter in the air, but Steph felt warm despite the crispness. She returned to the house. Perfect timing, as the doorbell rang.

Jess looked pale, like she hadn't slept, blue shadows smudged beneath her lower eyelids. Steph kissed her on the cheek. It was how she always greeted her. This wasn't going to stop. Things were not going to change.

Jess followed her through to the kitchen.

'You cooked?'

'Of course. I assumed you haven't eaten? It's just jackets and chilli. I haven't gone to any trouble.'

'I thought we'd just talk.'

Steph took the food from the oven and began to arrange it on the plates. She placed it in front of her sister.

'Wine?'

'I drove here.'

'Of course you have. I keep forgetting about your acquired wheels. You could stay over if you like?' Her words seemed to trip over themselves.

Jess shook her head and yawned, covering her face with her hands before swallowing loudly. Steph felt ill at ease in her sister's company for the first time in her adulthood. They pushed the food around the plate. Every so often a sound emitted from the baby monitor. Natalie moving, snuffly noises, the odd cry which put Steph on alert, but didn't require any action.

'So, out there are my diaries. My therapist told me to stop the habit.'

'Really, I thought it was the done thing?' Jess pushed the food away from her.

'Not the way I do it.'

'And my entry, did it fit in well? Was it what you were expecting? I assume you've read it?'

'Yes I've read it. Some of it fits well. Other parts, no.'

The plate scraped on the table as Steph pushed it away from her. Her fingers shook as she attempted to separate her curls. A chill ran down her spine. The kitchen window showed that the once clear evening sky was now cloaked in cloud. A blue hue dripped across the skyline, like a painter's wash of watercolour. Perhaps rain would put out the fire, the forecast had said clear skies. As usual it was wrong.

'I don't know why I did it. I read all your entries before I passed it to the police. When they gave it back to me, I felt compelled to write to tell you that I could have got help, but instead I let her die.'

Steph's forehead creased and she blinked rapidly. She shook her head vigorously.

'She died because of a seizure. You didn't cause the fit and even if a nurse had got there in time, you know she didn't have long left to live. You didn't kill her.'

Steph's body stiffened, she just wanted to reassure her that her confession wouldn't go beyond these walls and that it was time to release her from the past. She gradually expelled the air out through her teeth.

'I knew about the affair and who our father really was.'

She raised her eyes to meet Jess'.

'But the other stuff, you're right I didn't fully appreciate what was going on. What she did to you. I always felt that she showed a favouritism towards me, especially as a teenager, but I genuinely thought it was because you were such a difficult teen and because I was holding everything together for all of us. I was too busy to fully appreciate the extent of her neglect.'

'I don't blame you, Steph. I could never blame you.'

Jess reached over and held Steph's hand.

'There've been so many times over the years that I wanted to tell you. But while she was alive, I couldn't bring myself to. I was trapped. Trapped thinking about what my words would do to everyone.'

Steph edged around the table and bent at the waist to embrace her. She'd always listened to Jess, the usual teenage angst, the games she'd play with Mum, the boyfriends. Her problems were always age typical and nothing out of the ordinary, or too serious.

'How did you find out about Mum?'

Steph picked up the baby monitor. She listened for a moment before returning to her seat to sit opposite Jess. Out of the window a firework streaked upwards, screeching as it climbed higher before exploding, causing Jess to jump and for the monitor to crackle as it picked up the sound.

'Aunty Betts. The night of the accident she came to our house. I listened to her at the top of the stairs. I heard her tell Mum what she knew, the affair, us. And then she told Mum she was taking our uncle for a drive.'

She looked at Jess, checking to see if the penny had dropped.

'She told Mum that no one could have him. She was driving, Jess. She drove into the tree. Aunty Betts killed herself and our biological father.'

Jess traced her finger along her hairline and drew little circles with her nail.

'That's the thing about an affair. Two people. A web of deceit, a domino effect. What they did killed our Aunt. Robbed us, and our cousins of parents.'

Steph sighed and clasped her hands together, resting her elbows on the table and her chin on her interlinked fingers. 'And the lies Jess. The lies she spun and told herself, and others. I feel like my whole childhood was built on untruths, shifting sands, nothing was real.'

Jess sat up straight in her chair. 'I'm real,' she smirked. 'I know what you mean. Everything you did for me, how you looked after me, that was real. I don't want to erase those memories. My memories of you. Our sisterhood, that's not broken, is it?'

Jess looked like she did when she was five years old and she'd asked Steph if she was going to run away from her, too.

'Of course it's not broken. I wish I'd seen through her. I mean, her mood swings, her tantrums, I just accepted that was who she was. Why didn't I know what she did? She locked you in the cupboard on several occasions?' She reached across the table and squeezed her hand. Jess stroked Steph's knuckles before squeezing it back.

'Yes. Thank goodness we didn't have a cellar.' Jess swallowed, her mouth felt arid. 'Actually, I will stay over, I'd love a glass of wine or two.'

Steph nodded and pulled out a bottle of Pinot from the fridge. She'd permit herself a small glass, she didn't like how alcohol made her feel now, the medication and the booze didn't mix well in her bloodstream.

'I believed her Steph. I believed every word she said about me. I believed I deserved to be locked in the cupboard. Do you know where I was that night Aunty Betts came round?'

'At a friend's on a sleepover?'

'No. That's what she told you. Our neighbour Mrs Locke often needed help, so Mum made me stay there. It looked like she was being a good Samaritan, helping out an old lady in need with no family of her own. But Mum told me I had to go and help look after her as punishment. Help wipe her arse and nose as a reminder that I'd be just like Mrs Locke when I grew up. A lonely old woman who no one loves; no husband because no man would ever look at me. No family. Nothing. I managed to put a stop to the visits. I called Social Services myself; a real Samaritan told them how she was struggling to cope alone.'

Popping noises filled the kitchen as more fireworks crackled into life. A green shower of sparks illuminated the top left-hand corner of the patch of sky they could see through the window.

'Gosh Jess. How could I have been so blind?'

'Because she was an amazing actress. Nothing was real with her, she had a sparkling veneer and the shit just never stuck. And she did such a good job of keeping us apart, too. You know, when we no longer shared a bedroom she managed to make sure we had very little time together so we could never discuss what was happening. She was frightened I'd tell you and she knew you'd believe me. She'd lock me in my room at night and unbolt the door before you woke up and every day she'd remind me what would happen if I told anyone my lies. She said they'd split us up, we'd both go into care and live apart. And that's what made me keep my mouth shut.'

'And you never tried to tell anyone?'

'I did. Sometimes the rage would build up inside me and I couldn't help it. I'd crack under the weight of it, but she was right, no one believed me.' Jess drained the wine. 'I'm going to have some counselling. I know I need to get the rage out. I keep thinking about Adam and how the rage built up inside him – it wasn't really just what Jason said about the kiss that made him lash out, it was his anger about the rape. He knew him, whoever it was, didn't he? And he must have beaten himself up about not doing anything to make sure he never came near you again.'

Steph swirled the wine around the glass before taking a small sip. 'Maybe. It's possible that he'd let his anger build up. He did try to encourage me to go to the police, but I wasn't strong enough. I wasn't able to go through it all again, having to explain myself, and I knew the evidence was non-existent by the time I told him what happened. I'm not sure he carried the anger with him, but I guess that what I told him about the threats that Jason made, perhaps that brought back his anger.' The feeling of ants running up her legs stopped her words. A manifestation of her guilt. 'You're doing the right thing, getting help. We both need a shit load of therapy to sort out our screwed-up heads. Let's start our own therapy session tonight. Let's burn away the words.'

'Are you sure you want to burn them all?'

'Yes. Absolutely.'

'I should have told the hospital what I did.' Jess withdrew her hand from Steph.

Steph rapidly shook her head.

'Silence, Jess. For the last time in our lives, we'll stay silent.'

'I thought you'd hate me?'

Jess's expression reminded Steph of Adam, the way he looked defeated and sheepish when he asked the same question. It quickly changed as her bottom lip began to wobble. Now she looked like she did when she was five again. The big eyes, the mouth, twitching at the corner, ready to cry at any moment.

Every night after Dad left, Jess would wake up asking for him. She'd hold her until she fell asleep again. Night after night she shushed her back to sleep. Two years her senior, it wasn't her place to be her surrogate mother.

'I don't hate you. She was dying. You didn't kill her, the cancer had spread to her brain; the tumour caused the fit. You doing nothing didn't kill her.'

'I watched her die and I was glad! That's not a normal human being's reaction to watching their mum die, is it? And I wish I'd killed her years ago. When you told me she had stage four cancer I was actually pleased. When you explained she'd decided to rent a flat near us I was angry that she was forcing her way back into our lives. I've wanted her dead for years. And the shame of those thoughts, the shame of wanting her to die fills me with horror because it means I'm exactly what she said I was.'

'Jess, she abused you—'

Jess held up her hand. 'She said that I was evil. That I was horrible little monster who broke up her home. She's made me into a monster.'

Steph held up her hand now. 'My turn. She abused you. Wanting her out of your life, even wanting her dead, yes it's an extreme thought, but it's an understandable one. You aren't the monster. You aren't evil. She was.'

Steph got up, a few distant fireworks could be heard, probably a couple of streets away, but the monitor flashed, still registering the distant rockets.

Walking over to the cutlery drawer Steph took out a box of matches and shook them at Jess as she walked to the other side of the kitchen to the large store cupboard and dug out a box of firelighters from the back.

'Come on. Let's burn the past.'

The wintery coolness made them both shudder simultaneously as they walked out into the darkness holding hands, like children. Together they edged towards the heap of books and garden debris.

Several fireworks streaked the sky. They exploded with a shower of sparks, and again more filled the sky and lit up the garden, bathing the sisters in a pink light as they created flower-like patterns in the sky which glowed fiercely before fading to a smoky shadow.

'Shall I light the fire?'

Jess nodded and finally let go of her sister's hand. Steph crouched to the ground. There was a dampness underfoot. She wasn't sure if the fire would work. She'd never lit one before. They'd had a bonfire last year when Adam finally got around to clearing the garden and there was so much rubbish, he thought the best thing to do was to burn it all. He built it. He lit it and he cleared it away. Steph pondered whether she could manage this task, but only for a nanosecond. She managed so much now her husband was locked away from her.

She lit the pages first. They began to burn, curling and disintegrating in the heat. She lit a few more firelighters and the fire rapidly took hold.

Stepping backwards, she kept her eyes fixed on the diaries. The pages withered and collapsed in the heat. She squeezed Jess's hand and they took another few steps away from the licking flames. Placing her arm around her shoulder she pulled her close.

Inside the tepee the flames ravished the wood. She could make out some more pages succumbing to the heat and more already reduced to ash. She was satisfied that the diaries would not survive the fire as the heat intensified.

Flames lapped the top of the tepee pyre. Reaching the height of their powers they destroyed everything with a touch of their smouldering fingers. Blackened scraps of paper flitted skywards, scooped up in the air on currents. Dipping into invisible pockets they lost their power and plunged back to the earth to join the ash. Cleansing the spirit and setting the ghosts free. Words once etched on a page became no more.

The sisters stepped back a little more as the flames raged, eating up the words, the lies, and the past. They stood apart now as the heat intensified. No longer needing to lean on each other. Steph turned to Jess. Her face glowed orange and her eyes were fixed on the fire; she could see the flames reflected in her pupils.

Despite the heat both sisters shuddered. An iciness began to spread throughout their bones and a shiver rippled down their backs all the way to their ankles. Behind them a light breeze played with the decaying autumn leaves and flattened some blades of grass into the shape of two feet.

The sisters stiffened. Simultaneously they felt an icy hand touch their shoulders.

Something in the fire popped, causing them to jump.

A flame shot up towering higher than all the others. The sisters cowered but the pressure of an invisible hand remained on their shoulders. The flame surged higher, until it peaked, glowing white hot before dying down.

The touch of the ghostly hands lifted from their shoulders. The chill dissipated as the heat of the fire warmed them gently and breathed life into their blood which had run boreal cold.

Tonight they finished what their mother started. Putting an end to her lies, neglect and emotional abuse. And finally, like all ghosts, she was laid to rest.

Ashes to ashes, dust to dust. In fire we trust.

Acknowledgements

For as long as I can remember I've wanted to see my book sitting on the shelf in a book store. The fabulous team at RedDoor Publishing have made this dream become a reality. Thank you to everyone at RedDoor for your passion and enthusiasm. Special thanks to Heather Boisseau for spotting the potential and for holding my hand throughout the whole process.

A huge thank you goes to Laura Gerrard for her editorship and steering me in the right direction. Your insight and interrogation of the text whipped my manuscript into shape and taught me my weaknesses and my strengths.

I will always be grateful to my fellow Faber Academy students. Thank you to my tutor, Shelley Weiner, for giving me the confidence and self-belief required to write to the end. Huge thanks to Midge Blake for being my first 'real' reader. Thank you for your enthusiasm and perceptive comments. I am indebted to Karen Richardson for her multiple readings of various drafts, the long phone calls and endless messages. Your support has carried me through this emotional rollercoaster.

Many thanks to Fiona Cummins. Her encouragement pushed me to apply for the Faber course in the first place, and her words of advice have kept me going even when things got tough and I felt like giving-up on getting the words on the page.

Thank you to Rosie Fiore for her generosity, support, wise words and enthusiasm.

Researching this book has created a suspicious internet history and I must thank Joss Hawthorn for his knowledge of police procedure and his stories about his time in the Metropolitan Police. Esther Fine, thanks for sending me copious photographs of hospital equipment and for discussing scenarios to make sure I avoided any plot holes. Massive thanks to Emma Fields for sharing her specialist mental health knowledge. Any misrepresentations are mine. You all have been incredibly generous with your time.

My love of stories is down to my parents who filled our home with books. Thank you to my mum for taking me to the library nearly every weekend and shaping my reading list as a teen.

Massive hugs and kisses to my children who have cheered me on, suggested titles, and agreed to watch a film or two to give me a chance to finish another draft. Love you both always and forever and I'm sorry it couldn't be called *Secrets Within* or one of their more imaginative proposals: *Nuggets on fire*.

And finally, thank you to my husband. He believed I could write even when I didn't. His encouragement, support and confidence has kept me going through all stages of the writing journey. He pushed me to be braver in my writing and his belief has never faltered. Thank you for your plot suggestions and listening to me talk endlessly about these imaginary people and the things they do.

About the Author

Julia Barrett began her working life as a primary school teacher. She has worked in Public Relations for the NHS and as an in-house journalist for Queen Mary, University of London. She is a Faber Academy alumna and is currently working towards the completion of an MA in Creative Writing at Royal Holloway, University of London. She is currently working on her second crime thriller.

juliabarrett.co.uk

Visit reddoorpublishing.com/mysisterismissing to download Book Club questions

Author's Note

Although this book is a work of fiction, the germination of the story sprung from my own experience after the birth of my daughter. Unable to sleep in the hours after her birth, lying wide awake in my hospital bed, I watched several wellie clad toddlers run around my bed chanting 'we're only three foot tall' over and over again. I hid under the covers, and when I looked again, thankfully the scary figures had disappeared. I decided to keep quiet about this; my rational mind told me it was probably post-traumatic stress induced by the rapid labour.

I did have a few more hallucinations due to sleep deprivation, but thankfully, unlike my main character I was not suffering with post-partum psychosis. Post-partum psychosis occurs in around 1 in 1,000 women each year in the UK. When I discussed my work with the lovely Emma Fields who helped me in my research, she was pleased to hear that I was writing about this condition and hoped that it keeps the conversation about post-natal mental health at the forefront of a reader's consciousness.

The illness shares some symptoms with post-natal depression, but if you, or a loved one experiences hallucinations, delusions, manic moods post-birth please seek help immediately as post-partum psychosis is classed as a medical emergency. For further help and support see:

app-network.org/what-is-pp/getting-help/

nhs.uk/conditions/post-partum-psychosis/

rcpsych.ac.uk/expertadvice/problemsdisorders/postpartumpsychosis.aspx